Early Prais

"My favorite crazy family is back! And nuttier than ever. Love every second of this book!" —*Becky Monson, bestselling author of Just a Name*

"If Fannie Flagg wrote chick lit, it would read like **Relatively Sane**. I absolutely adored this book!" —*USA Today Bestselling Author, Diana Orgain*

"The Masterson clan is back and funnier than ever in this delightful tale. Dineen's comedic timing is pure gold!" —*Jennifer Peel, bestselling author of My Not So Wicked Stepbrother*

"The Masterson's are back in a hilarious new romcom by the irrepressible Whitney Dineen!" —*USA Today Bestselling Author, S.E. Babin*

"Relatively Sane is laugh out loud, pee in your pants funny! I stayed up way too late reading it because I couldn't manage to put it down!" —*Annabelle Costa, author of My Perfect Ex-Boyfriend*

"The Masterton clan is at it again. Small-town with laugh out loud escapades. You'll wish you were born Scottish if only to be a part of this crew! Let go of all the stress in your life and laugh the day away with Relatively Same." —*Kathryn Biel, author of Made for Me*

"While Whitney continues with all the fantastic one-liners, you will have a wee bit of craic while reading this delightful novel. Just remember tears run down your cheeks and legs! Whitney Dineen is one of my top favorite rom-cm authors, right up there with Alice Clayton, Emma Chase, and Julia Kent." —*A.J. Book Remark*

Also by Whitney Dineen

Romantic Comedies
Relatively Normal
Relatively Sane
She Sins at Midnight
The Reinvention of Mimi Finnegan
Mimi Plus Two
Kindred Spirits
Going Up?

Non-Fiction Humor
Motherhood, Martyrdom & Costco Runs

Middle Reader
Wilhelmina and the Willamette Wig Factory
Who the Heck is Harvey Stingle?

Children's Books
The Friendship Bench

Relatively Sane

Whitney Dineen

Relatively Sane
By Whitney Dineen

https://whitneydineen.com/newsletter/
33 Partners Publishing

Made in the United States of America

March 2019

Print Edition
ISBN-13: 9781090643322

This book is dedicated to my mother Libby Bohlen, who was my inspiration for so much of the crazy. I love you, Mom!

Prologue

As a kid, I had an ongoing fantasy. I'm waiting for the school bus to pick me up in front of my family farm, when a shiny black Lincoln Town Car pulls up next to me. A very attractive woman in the back seat rolls down her window and bursts into tears. She gasps, "Buffy, is that you?" (Note: I might have been enthralled with the television show, *Buffy the Vampire Slayer* at the time. I was definitely a fan of the name.) The woman and her equally handsome husband leap out of the car and throw their arms around me, engulfing me in a cloud of Chanel Number 5 and Versace Man.

Between sobs of joy, she calls to her husband, "Charles, it's our baby. It's really her!"

They tighten their embrace and I become the filling in a Pendleton wool sandwich. This wonderful, loving, perfectly ordinary couple, decked out in city clothes, explains how there was a mix-up at the hospital where I was born. Their baby and another were returned to the wrong bassinets after feeding time. They only discovered the truth when the person they thought was their daughter ran off and joined the circus as it passed through their town.

The woman says, "We knew then and there a mistake had been made. A child of ours would never dream of such nonsense."

In retrospect, I realize I hadn't thought this through very well. I should have wondered what kind of parents wouldn't go after the child they'd raised and save her from a life of carnie living. At the time, I was too involved in my fantasy and the comforting explanation of why I was growing up in a near-insane asylum—a.k.a. Masterton Hall, a.k.a. an old farm house in Central Illinois. It was much easier to convince myself that I didn't belong to the people who laid claim to me. I was Buffy Summers and my real family wasn't embarrassing in the least.

This fantasy got me through some tough times. Like when my grandmother Nan called my little league coach a fukakta screwball who needed his eyes examined, I consoled myself that we didn't share the same blood. As such, the shame I was feeling wasn't really my own.

When my dad showed up to all my school functions wearing a kilt and boasting about the joys of being Scottish, I was comforted that the wrong girl was being called Catriona Masterton. When my mother bought six sauerkraut crocks because they were on sale, even though she hated sauerkraut, I said to myself, "Cat, these aren't your people. Don't lose hope. Your real parents will find you and take you away from all this." When my brother Travis started to walk around the house in my mom's high heels, I reminded myself that Buffy was an only child.

It wasn't until high school that I finally accepted the Summers were no more than wishful thinking on my part, and that I belonged to the Masterton clan, hook, line, and sinker.

Part of my acceptance was because I'd fallen head over heels in love with my childhood playmate, Sam Hawking.

Sam and I frolicked in the mud, learned to play cards, and studied for science tests together before discovering more adult games in the hayloft of my family barn. He gave my life meaning. He was enough reason to give up my dream of belonging to a normal family. If I wanted a life with him, I needed to stay right where I was. Goodbye, Summers Family! Hello, kooky Mastertons.

Sam made me feel things I'd never felt before. My body blossomed under his touch, my heart filled to the point of bursting, and my dreams shot out of the stratosphere. There was nothing he and I couldn't do, be, or achieve as long as we were together. While my family was as odd as they came, around Sam I felt relatively sane. I'd even given us a celebrity couple name, SamCat.

Tragically, as often happens with first loves, we ultimately went our separate ways. The end of high school was the end of us. I was crushed, as it wasn't my idea to break up, but college eventually softened the pain and my life moved on. My subsequent move to New York City propelled me into adulthood, which is where I met Ethan.

For two years, Ethan and I were a good couple. We were grown-ups together. We paid a mortgage, put money away for retirement, and we planned a wedding. Ethan was as different from Sam as I could find in a man. He's what I thought I wanted, what I thought I needed. I was wrong.

I brought Ethan home to meet my family over Thanksgiving, and it didn't quite go according to plan. My parents surprised me by inviting Sam to join us. It had been fourteen years since I'd laid eyes on my first boyfriend. The feelings I thought were long dead, began to revive. The life I had mapped out for myself was sucked into a blackhole, never to be seen again. My past and future collided in such a way a whole new universe was born.

Pet Cemetery

"Cat!" my mom screams from the rafters, "come up here!"

"Where are you?" I holler back.

"In the attic."

The entrance to the attic is in the upstairs hallway, via a skinny staircase that drops down from the ceiling right next to the bathroom. I want to go up there about as much as I wanted to go into strangers' basements as a child—or now for that matter. In general, I'm not a fan of the creepy nether regions of old houses. Upstairs, I see my mom Maggie, or Mags as her friends call her, has started to clear out the garret for the move to town. My parents have finally decided to downsize to a more manageable house. This one is too big for their needs.

Mom's been dropping stuff willy-nilly from the opening in the ceiling and as a result the hallway is full of an array of treasures. I jump aside to avoid being hit by an ancient dressmaker form from the seventies that's still wearing a half-made patchwork skirt. I step around a pile of old Halloween costumes from Travis's and my childhood, and trip over a brown corduroy beanbag chair I don't think I've ever seen before.

I have to shove stuff out of my way to make contact with the floor. I had no idea my parents had such a collection up there. Having said that, my mom recently told me she's storing fifteen banker boxes full of recipes she's clipped from newspapers and magazines, mostly stolen from the library and various waiting rooms around town. The woman is like an onion. You pull back one layer and there's a whole new layer of crazy just waiting to make you cry.

When I finally ascend the rickety stairs to the attic, I'm greeted by a sight so startling, it renders me speechless. Mags is standing next to the oval ox-eye window with light streaming in on her, showcasing a moose head she's wearing. Big, black, shiny marble eyeballs stare back at me. I eventually tear my gaze away from her to look around. The whole space could double for an animal sacrifice scene straight out of a horror flick.

There are squirrels, deer, and even a buffalo head. A beaver with little buck teeth and a demented smile leers at me. "Wow, who knew you guys were this kind of nuts? This is beyond the bounds of even my imagination, and I grew up with you."

My mom pulls off the moose head. "Oh please, this is nothing. Your dad has gotten rid of most of the good stuff over the years. He sold the French mountain sheep when we needed money to repair the tractor and the Indian leopard so we could take that trip to Alaska." She takes a breath and appears to be preparing herself for something. Finally she spits it out, "I thought you might be able to use some of this in the barn when you fix it up for your parties."

Now might be the time to mention I'm the one purchasing my parents' farm. I'm a party planner by trade. Despite having a successful business in NYC, I've realized it's time to build my nest closer to home. A lot closer to home, if you consider that I'll be hanging my shingle on the barn in the field out back. Timing was on my side, as one of my employees was in a position to buy me out, which is funding this adventure of catering to the cool millennial Chicago scene. Barns are the new "it" thing. As long as they don't have dead animals in them.

"How do you envision me doing that? Maybe by prying open the beaver's mouth and stuffing an apple into it before using it as a centerpiece on the buffet table?"

"Don't be ridiculous," my mom sputters. "I was thinking you could hang the heads on the walls and strategically place the squirrels and smaller animals so they're peeking around corners. It would be totally authentic, don't you think?"

"Manure piles and livestock would be authentic as well, but I don't see that working. Thanks for thinking of me though."

"If you won't take them, what am I supposed to do with them?" my mom demands.

"Put them on Craigslist."

"You mean, sell them?" she gasps.

"Actually, I meant you should give them to anyone insane enough to haul them away."

She visibly jolts as if this is the most absurd idea she's ever heard. "Give them away? We have thousands of dollars of preserved wildlife up here. You don't just give that away."

"So, take it with you," I suggest.

"And put it where?"

"Hey, lady, you're the one who wanted to scale down and move to a smaller place."

She smiles at me sweetly. "Do you think we can leave them

up here while we re-home them?"

"Nope." I shake my head. "Because I know re-homing isn't your goal. You're hoping you can leave them here and I'll forget them, but that's not going to happen. Now that I know *Pet Sematary* is right above me, I'm going to have nightmares until it's gone. I may even have to have Reverend Abernathy perform an exorcism."

"Don't be ridiculous." She smiles, trying to charm me. "Can you help me move them downstairs?"

"No can do, Mom. I'll go get Dad for you, though." I have an aversion to touching taxidermied creatures which, I assure you, made my upbringing quite a challenge.

"Don't bother," she snaps. "I'll take care of it myself."

There's a lot to do to get this house into good enough shape for my new venture. Extermination of critters, both dead and alive, has just been bumped up to the top of the list.

The Naked Snow Roll

After graduating college, my childhood friend Sarah, began cultivating her organic farming empire. She now supplies some of Chicago's swankiest dining establishments. Demand for her organic farm-to-table fare has taken off, propelling interest in her farm stand and yurt-style B&B. Her next venture, the vegan café, opens this summer. Her farm has become the mothership for the nutty-crunchy crowd in our neck of the woods.

Sarah calls and asks, "Want to come over and try some of the new recipes I've been working on?"

"I'd love to," I declare. "You would not believe what's going on here today." I tell her about my parents' collection in the attic.

Sarah, a lover of all creatures great and small, says, "Your parents aren't normal. I've accepted your dad's many taxidermied rodent decorations over the years, but really, where does it end? Are they going to stuff Nan when she dies and keep her around for company?"

Just thinking about what my parents will do with my grandmother when she sheds her mortal coil sends a shiver through me. "I know you're kidding, but promise you'll never bring the idea up to them, just in case they glom onto it."

It's a distinct possibility that they would.

"No worries. I was only half-joking. I wouldn't put it past them." She continues, "Come by at noon and I'll have food ready for you to try."

In addition to having an established sustainable organic empire, Sarah also helps people with their health issues by running an alternative, all-natural boot camp. She detoxifies their systems with a two-week diet of pure vegan living. She isn't always vegan herself, just vegetarian, but she claims complete abstinence of animal products is necessary to cleanse impurities from the body and align the spirit. While that's occurring, she walks her guests through guided meditations, aura cleanses, and God knows what else.

"Ethan and his mom have gone back to New York, right?" *Please God, let them be back in New York!* Nerves ping pong across my stomach as I wait for my friend's reply.

As weird as my family is, you'd think I'd have an easier time accepting the fact that my ex has moved in with my friend. Not in a romantic way. More like an, "I just found out I'm on the autistic spectrum and I'm willing to give your alternative therapies a shot at making my life easier" kind of way.

I always knew Ethan was rigid and a bit different, like he counted how many steps it took to get to the subway every morning. There were other things, too. He didn't like to hold hands and was adamant the dinner plates be stored on different shelves than I put them on—like they told him their preference or something. Each thing was of no consequence on its own, but when you put them all together, they definitely added up to something.

It wasn't until I saw him through my family's eyes, at Thanksgiving, that I realized it. The man I once thought exemplified stability, suddenly seemed to be anything but stable. Once he suggested we part ways, he broke down and got the help he not only needed, but turns out, desperately wanted. His obsessive-compulsive quirks weren't unrelated idiosyncrasies. They were a real diagnosis.

Ethan's mother, Natalie, up and left her husband after coming here at Thanksgiving—are you getting an idea of the fun time we had? She met Sarah at that time and decided to stay at her B&B during the holidays to try to map out her future. That's when Natalie got sucked into my friend's web of holistic wonder.

"How big of a problem would it be if they were still here?" Sarah asks.

"You're kidding? They were supposed to leave last week."

"But they're both doing so well. I know if they stay a bit longer, I can help them launch their lives in a healthy new direction."

"So, you're inviting me over for lunch with Ethan and Natalie. That kind of changes my interest level in coming."

"They'll be on the property, but they won't be joining us. They're fasting today and sitting in the sweat lodge. They'll alternate the heat with the naked snow roll."

My friend has mentioned this activity before, but I haven't had the courage to ask about it. "What exactly is the naked snow roll, again?"

"It's meant to shock the system into restarting. Kind of like rebooting a computer. The body needs a jolt to close down the cell memory of preprogramming and the naked snow roll is a very effective technique. When paired with the sweat lodge, it works wonders."

"It sounds like it kills them before bringing them back to life."

"While it doesn't stop their heart, it does halt the old energy flow and allows new energy to be born. It can't take away Ethan's autism, but I can help him exorcise anxiety cast upon him by a society that doesn't understand how his mind works."

"Or send them to the emergency room in shock. Has that ever happened?"

She laughs. "No. Only one guy ever went to the hospital afterward but only because he thought his junk was frostbitten. It wasn't. It was just super cold."

"Did you warn Ethan about that?"

"No way! That guy is always looking for the worst in everything. I don't want to plant ideas that will turn him away from getting the help he needs."

"How's Ethan doing with his need for routine?" I ask. The two years we were together, he was unbending about his schedule. Even going so far as having a Monday lunch, a Tuesday lunch, and so forth.

"Terribly. I change things up every day to purposely deprive him of a sense of order. He hates it and threatens to leave six times a day, but he hasn't gone, yet. My reasoning for doing this is to separate him from his ability to develop habits, so he'll be more flexible when he returns to his normal life."

I snort. "There was precious little about Ethan's life that would have been considered normal. How's he coping with the food?"

"It's hard to say. He says everything tastes good, but he struggles because he misses his regular diet."

I sigh mightily before declaring, "Fine, I'll come over, but I really don't want to run into the Crenshaws." I say this even though just over a month ago I was planning on becoming one of them.

Oh, the bullet I dodged.

"Fear not, you won't even see them. In fact, Ethan hasn't asked after you in three days. That's huge progress."

I don't necessarily want my ex out of my life forever. I still love him like a friend, I just think we need a healthy amount of time apart before we can redefine our new relationship parameters.

Evil Geniuses and Sassy Girls

Nan joins me as soon as I put on my coat. "Can you take me into town to get some of my tissues? I'm all out." Nan has had an ongoing love affair with tissues that have built-in lotion since the day they were invented. She's the only person I've ever met who feels that way.

"Sorry, Nan. I'm off to have lunch at Sarah's. She's working on getting her menu set up for the new café."

My grandmother rubs her hands together. "Yummy! I'd love to come along. Thanks for asking."

She's not being sarcastic. It's how she is and how she usually gets herself included on outings she's interested in. I was so worried Nan was going to die last month when her brain aneurysm burst that I don't have the heart to tell her she wasn't invited. Instead, I warn, "It's a vegetarian café, so no complaining about the food."

She smacks her hand against her heart in shock. "Complain, me? Well, I never."

Uh-uh! She's not fooling me with her innocent-as-a-lamb routine. I'm one hundred percent on to her little tricks and I'm watching her like a hawk. She's behaved herself for the most part since coming home from the nursing home, but I know she could crack at any moment and go right back to her questionable ways.

My grandmother is a force of nature. She immigrated to the US from Scotland when she was only three. She claims to have *the sight*—her term for someone who can prophesy the future—though we've never seen any evidence of this ability. And for lack of a more delicate word, she's mean. I've only recently discovered that her foul-mouth outbursts, which have been occurring for over twenty years, are not the result of the many mini-strokes she's suffered, as previously believed. She just got tired of people not paying attention to her and decided to reinvent herself as an old lady to be feared.

She confessed this to me at the care facility where she was recovering from her brain surgery. Now that I know the truth, I'm making it my mission to get her to clean up her act and channel her angst into kindness. You know the old saying *you catch more flies with honey.* I'll let you know how that goes.

"Grab your purse, Nan. I'll take you to the drug store after we eat." Once we're in the car, I announce, "Ethan and his mother are still out at Sarah's, so if you run into them, no name calling or anything."

"Filthy Sassenach," Nan mutters under her breath.

"Nan," I warn. "I'm not engaged to Ethan anymore, so there's no point in being rude. If you can't be nice, I won't take you to the pharmacy." My family could not understand why Ethan and I were together and viewed Thanksgiving as their last opportunity to show me the error of my ways before we got married.

They were successful.

She demands, "The question is, *why* were you engaged to him? That boy isn't right in the head."

"Just because he's not like everyone else doesn't mean he's not right in the head. He's aware of his differences, which is why he's staying with Sarah. He wants help and the fact he's willing to try some of her alternative therapies proves how much he wants to change. So, be nice."

"Fine," she grumbles. "But I'm still your grandmother. You might want to remember I could put you over my knee if you keep sassing me."

"You and what army?" I laugh.

"Don't tempt me, little girl. You know I'm meaner than I look." The plain truth is, she doesn't look mean at all. But like Sam once said, he wouldn't bet against her in a street fight.

Nan changes the subject by asking, "When are your mom and dad moving out of the house and leaving us bachelorettes on our own?" Nan doesn't want to go with them. She wants to stay put, and that's perfectly fine by me. I love having her around even though she's not the most predictable creature.

"They close on their new place next month, right after I become the official owner of the farm. Do you think you can wait that long to start partying?"

She gives me the side-eye. "I think I can last." Then she asks, "Are you planning on staying in the basement apartment or are you moving upstairs with me?"

I was actually thinking about asking her to move to the basement. I could relocate to the master bedroom and that way we could both have our privacy. I ask, "What do you think I should do?"

16

"I think you should move upstairs with me. I'll be lonely with your parents gone." So much for privacy. But I guess I can see where she's coming from.

I change the subject without confirming anything. "The plumber is starting on the new pipes Monday, so we might have a week or so of inconvenience." Our plumbing is so outdated that when anyone flushes the toilet, they have to yell, FLUSH! right before they do, because scalding hot water simultaneously pours out of any open faucet.

"Good thinking," she comments. "By the way, I have a great idea."

I can only imagine.

I shoot my eyebrows up in question to indicate she should share it. So, she does. "I was watching a show on House to Home Television the other day. You know those cute brothers who renovate people's homes for them?" I don't because I don't watch much TV and when I do, it's only to binge watch something on Netflix. My latest was *Ozark* and now I feel totally schooled in laundering money for the Mexican drug cartel. If I don't make a go of my new party business, that might become my retirement plan. Just kidding. I now have a healthy fear of the Ozarks and I don't care how beautiful they are, I'm never visiting that part of Missouri again.

Nan continues, "Those boys are just darling! Anyhoo, I think you should ask them to come out and help fix the place up. I thought it would be great advertising for your new business."

My grandmother is nobody's fool. That's actually a fantastic idea and I'm going to take her advice and check into it. It's going to be a hard sell to lure couples from Chicago out into the country, two hours away, for their weddings. But it'll be a slam dunk if they've already seen the place on national television.

"Nan, you're brilliant! I'll look into it as soon as we get home from Sarah's."

She seems very pleased with herself and replies, "You're only now figuring that out, huh?"

I shake my head and tease, "I think I've always known it. But up until now I would have classified you as more of an evil genius. I like that you're finally using your powers for good."

She smacks my arms. "Sassy girl. Now hurry up and take me to lunch. I'm about to waste away here."

Nan and I drive down Highway 47 in contented camaraderie. Moments like this are the reason I came home. I plan on enjoying them to their fullest.

The Vegan Pig

"It's a vegan BLT," Sarah declares.

"Girl," Nan says, "were you dropped on your head somewhere along the line? Bacon is from a pig. There's no such thing as vegan bacon."

My friend laughs. "There is if you make it from eggplant."

Nan shakes her head. "That would be an ELT, not a BLT. You kids don't know what you're talking about anymore."

I want a piece of this. "Eggplant bacon sounds disgusting. Couldn't you just call it a veggie sandwich?"

"I could, but here's the thing you need to know about vegetarians, and that includes vegans." We wait expectantly for her mystical insight. "All of them, who have ever been meat eaters, miss bacon. Bacon is the singular item that derails most people from successfully becoming vegetarians. I guarantee having a BLT on the menu will appeal to them enormously."

"Even if it's an ELT and not a BLT?" Nan demands.

Sarah nods in affirmation. So, my grandmother asks, "Why not serve 'roasted pork loin'"—she does the whole finger quotation thing—"made out of mung beans?"

"Because no one ever falls off the vegetarian wagon out of a love for pork loin."

The next thing we try is a vegan omelet. Bewildered, I ask, "How can you make an omelet without eggs?"

"Red lentil flour, baking powder, and almond milk."

"I'd rather lick the floor," Nan gripes.

I shoot my grandmother a warning look and ask Sarah, "Do you have any bread and butter Nan can eat before her blood sugar drops and makes her nastier?"

Sarah leans over and grabs some naan and a plate that holds something that kind of looks like butter but it's a deeper yellow. "I have vegan butter, will that work?"

I assure her it will, but Nan rolls her eyes. "If I don't like it, I'm going to go milk a goat and see if you have any varmints on the property I can roast up."

"Nan, if you can't behave, you're going to have to go sit in the car," I warn. She grouses but does so while tearing off a piece of bread. Hopefully, once her mouth is full, she'll settle down.

Next Sarah serves stew, and while it's pretty good, two things come to mind. One thing is, vegans must always be hungry— there's no way they can eat enough fruit and vegetables to ever feel full (you need bacon, cheese, and ice cream for that); the other thing is, they must be extremely gassy. The bean consumption alone could propel a person into space.

As I make comments like, "Oh, I like this one!" and "More beans, huh?" Sarah looks at the clock and declares it time to roll Ethan.

"What's that mean, 'roll him'?" Nan demands.

Sarah gives a short explanation and my grandmother looks positively appalled. "You starve him, sweat the life out of him, and then make him roll nekkid in the snow? And he pays you for that? Girl, are you one of them dominatrixes I've heard about?"

Surprised, I ask, "Where exactly have you heard about those?"

My grandmother snorts with feeling. "I've got the Google and the Netflix, Cat. I know a thing or two about a thing or two."

Dear God! I can only imagine what she thinks she knows. So, I explain, "Nan, Sarah is an alternative healer. She helps people reprogram their thinking and their health through holistic means."

My grandmother looks unconvinced. "By starving them, sweating them, then rolling them buck nekkid in the snow?"

"Exactly!" my friend answers. "I also brush their auras, take them through past life regression, and perform third eye intervention."

Nan grins mischievously. "Sarah, girl, are you smoking weed? Cause if so, I want to give your stuff a try before I give it up for good."

Nan used to smoke pot with my brother, claiming it helped her keep her mean-spirited outbursts at bay. Being that we now know those were on purpose, we also know it did no such thing. Hence, I've cleared the house of all marijuana paraphernalia left by Travis when he moved to Chicago.

Sarah shakes her blonde head. "No, Nan. Drugs aren't my thing, but I have some amazing stinging nettle tea you might want to try. It's good for high blood pressure, anxiety, diabetes, and inflammation. I bet you'll love it."

"You put any scotch in it?" she asks.

"Not yet, but I'm not opposed to trying it sometime." She pours us each a cup before running outside to tend to Ethan.

Nan takes one sip of the drink and spits it across the room. "Gah! It's tastes like grass!"

"How do you know what grass tastes like?" I ask.

She shoots me a look. "Don't be cheeky with me, young lady. Everyone knows what grass tastes like."

Why did I bring my grandmother with me? I knew beyond a shadow of a doubt that she wasn't going to like the food. She's completely devoid of a politeness filter—like the governor in her head had been poisoned and dragged through a pit of boiling tar before being shot point blank between the eyes. In other words, stone cold dead. Yet, here we are, sitting in my friend's kitchen drinking grass-flavored tea together.

Nan looks like she wants to keep complaining but is trying valiantly to keep her mouth shut. She appears constipated. I'm about to tell her we should get going when a scream rips through the air that sounds remarkably like the sound I made during my first bikini wax.

We run outside to see my ex lying in the snow wearing only his birthday suit. My grandmother dashes into the kitchen and is back in record time with both cups of nettle tea. Before I know what she's planning to do with them, she throws them at Ethan.

He shrieks, "Oh, my GOD!!! Why did you do that?"

"To warm you up, lad. I didn't want your man business to freeze off."

My ex stands up while unsuccessfully trying to cover himself with his hands. "I think you burned … *it*!"

She doesn't look the least bit contrite. Instead, she says, "I was helping you shock your cell memory, like Sarah says. Did it work?"

By the look on his face, I would say mission accomplished.

Epithets and Apologies

The day's trials aren't over. When we leave Sarah's and finally get to the drug store, I lean across Nan, push her door open and almost shove her out of the car. Nan declines, "I'll wait for you here."

"You're going to let your seventy-nine-year-old grandmother, who's recovering from a burst brain, go out there on her own? I could slip and fall on the ice and break my frail hip."

I shoot her a dirty look and growl, "Fine. One box of tissues with the lotion, one Mr. Goodbar, and one Scottish romance set in the Highlands?"

"Yes, ma'am. And make sure the boy on the cover has a good butt. I won't believe the story one bit if it doesn't look like you could bounce a quarter off his keister."

I almost swallow my tongue. "Bounce a quarter off his keister?"

"A firm butt, high in his kilt. Not some saggy lifeless thing."

"Nan, have you ever known romance novels to use saggy-butted models?" This conversation is ridiculous.

"I'm just letting you know I have standards and I want you to keep them in mind when purchasing my reading material."

"Gotcha. One Highland lad in a kilt with a tight can coming up!"

Dorcas Abernathy, the retired Presbyterian minister's wife, holds the door open for me as I enter the pharmacy. I warn her to not go out to the parking lot until I leave; Nan's out there. My grandmother has spent over twenty years relentlessly terrorizing Mrs. Abernathy. Nan, Dorcas, and my grandfather all went to high school together. My gramps asked Dorcas to marry him first, and Nan has never recovered. When she flipped her biscuit a couple decades ago, Dorcas became the main target of her ire.

Mrs. Abernathy rolls her eyes at my warning. "I'm sorry, Cat. I know that woman is your grandmother, but she's a nemesis to polite society. I thought I was finally rid of her, but no, she had to go and recover. Well, I'll tell you what, I'm sick to death of it. I'm going to confront her once and for all."

My God, as if today hasn't been trying enough. I quickly gather the items on Nan's list and chase after Dorcas, who's slowly making her way to the car. I nearly get to her side, when I slip on the ice and go down like newborn foal on ice skates.

Nan unrolls her window and yells, "That could have been me!"

Dorcas looks back at me before shouting at my grandmother, "I wish it had been you, you wretched woman! I wish you'd fall and break every bone in your damn body and then die a slow, painful death!"

It's not like Nan doesn't have it coming. She's called Mrs. Abernathy every horrible name in the book, often in public, almost always with an audience. I'm surprised her old classmate didn't snap long ago. But still, it's a shock to hear the woman who was my church choir director for my entire childhood, as well as the pastor's wife, say such shocking things.

I try to get up but slip again. Maybe if I'm lucky someone will back their car over me and put me out of my misery. Before I can right myself, Nan gets out of the car and smiles beatifically at her enemy. "Dorcas, you look a treat! You don't look a day over fifty. I bet you've been exfoliating, haven't you?"

I recently had a stern talk with my grandmother, telling her point blank that her days of tormenting people were over. She seems to have taken my words to heart and now poor Dorcas has no clue what's happening. I motion for her to come over to me. By the time she reaches me, I've managed to roll myself to my knees. While groaning in pain, I tell her, "She's a new woman after her surgery. She doesn't say rude things anymore."

Poor Mrs. Abernathy. Her face turns red with shame and she looks like she's just been struck by lightning. I bet she feels cheated, too. All those years she's put up with the worst verbal abuse and now she can't even seek satisfaction.

Nan shuffles over to us and further confounds the minister's wife by saying, "You sing like an angel, Dorcas. I swear your voice is enough to make the heavens open up and cry for joy!"

I shoot Nan a look that indicates she's laying it on a bit thick, but she doesn't take my hint. Instead she declares, "Dorcas here, was homecoming queen two years running. This little gal had a rack that wouldn't quit." Then she elbows her old classmate, winks, and says knowingly, "Didn't you, honey?"

Dorcas is totally mute. The most hateful woman in town has just complimented her skin, her voice, and basically told her she had boobs for days … really, what's the right response? I open Nan's bag and offer the befuddled woman the Mr. Goodbar as a reward for having survived the last three minutes. She shakes her head in confusion.

Nan grabs the bag and hands over the romance novel instead, confiding, "Dorcas, you would not believe what goes on between the sheets in these books. Please, take it with my compliments."

Mrs. Abernathy looks down at the cover of *Highland Harem* and turns seven shades of red, but she doesn't give the book back. Instead, she smiles at my grandmother, "That's very good of you, Bridget, thank you." She walks off with a newfound bounce in her step.

My grandmother grins at me mischievously. "That was fun. Now go get me another book."

When we finally get back home, I'm ready to handcuff her to the radiator so she can't cause any more trouble. She seems to realize I'm peeved and makes a beeline for her bedroom. I jump at the opportunity to go downstairs and take a long, relaxing shower. I have a date with Sam tonight, and I want to make sure I look my best.

Romance Novels and Renovations

I was once so in love with Sam Hawking I couldn't imagine surviving a day without him—until he was gone. Then there were over five thousand days without him, but who's counting? How I managed to draw so many breaths away from him is anybody's guess.

To be loved by Sam was like housing another life force under my skin. My whole being was vibrant and full when we were together. I was bigger, stronger, more determined, more everything when we were a couple.

As I dry my hair, I have a vision of a teenage Sam rubbing my ponytail across his cheek. He told me it was like silk. We were sitting in his parents' old farm truck, Betty, the first time he did it. It was one of those moments when you'd swear time just stopped. Every one of my senses had been working on overdrive. I could tell you the exact color of the sky—a deep, cerulean blue with wispy white clouds stretched out in long horizontal lines as though they were lying down to take a nap. The autumn air smelled crisp and clean, and the leaves on the trees ranged from a burnt gold to deep blood-red, the orange so intense it looked like little bits of sunshine had fallen out of the sky to grace our landscape. Hints that winter was right around the corner. Sam Hawking has turned me into a poet.

It has been less than two months since I laid eyes on him again, after a fourteen-year-long hiatus. I haven't known Sam as an adult for long, but I can tell you this: I know *him*. I know his heart like I know my own. He might have a few new lines and a bushel of new experiences, but his core is the same. I strongly suspect his soul is the other half of my own. Nan's aneurysm brought me clarity that only one man made me feel like this. Unfortunately, it wasn't the man I was pledged to marry. It was Sam. It's always been Sam.

I've agreed to let him court me, but not picking up where we left off as teenagers. He needs to get to know the adult me. Our breakup changed me in ways that has rendered me a different person. Even though we share our entire childhoods and our lives are entwined on an almost microscopic level, we are not who we once were.

The day of our high school graduation had felt like the pinnacle of my life. My brain hummed with the untapped possibilities for what was to come. So much living was ahead of us. The hours between accepting our diplomas straight through our family parties flew by with supersonic speed. When everyone finally went home, we lay snuggled on a blanket together under the stars. I wanted to talk about our future. So did Sam.

I let him start. That's when I found out he wanted to go off to college unencumbered. He said he wanted to find out who he was without being tied to who he's always been. It was my first experience with the old "*it's not you, it's me*" excuse for being dumped. That experience put me on my guard for any other romantic entanglement. Until that night, I thought we had planned a life that totally revolved around each other. Secretly, he'd made other arrangements for himself and it broke my heart.

As the years passed—and I grew up—I understood Sam's motivation. Even though I didn't agree with him at the time, and I certainly didn't condone how he went about it, our breakup was a gift to me. I learned how to stand on my own feet, tapping into strength I didn't know I possessed. I realized potential I might not have otherwise known.

Sam knocks on the basement door just as I'm pulling my sweater over my head. I call out, "Come on down! I'm almost ready."

I hear his footsteps on the stairs and my heartbeat accelerates in anticipation. I hadn't thought my body could still react like this until my parents invited him to Thanksgiving dinner.

My first response wasn't favorable. I was livid he had come. How could he possibly think I could want him back in my life after the way things ended? Not to mention the fact that I was engaged to Ethan, who was sitting at the same table with us.

My second reaction was another animal entirely. Let's just say every cell of my body remembered Sam. I'm achingly in lust with his six-foot-tall frame, hair as dark as bittersweet chocolate, and eyes as blue as the ocean. He's as gorgeous as you'd expect from a soap opera doctor. Although he doesn't play a doctor on TV, he is one in real life, at our very own small-town hospital.

When I see him, I throw myself into his arms and attack him like a jungle cat. I wrap my legs around his waist and my arms around his neck. My hands pull his face as close to my lips as possible, without biting them. "You're here."

"Wow!" he laughs. "I could get used to greetings like this."

"You'd better. This is one of the milder ones I have planned."

Sam waggles his eyebrows and inquires, "Want to stay in tonight?"

I smile coyly. "Sure, but not here. Let's go to your place. Nan is riding my last nerve and once she knows you're in the house, she's going to be sniffing around like a hound dog hot on the trail of a meaty bone."

Nan loves Sam like one of her own grandchildren. After I moved to Manhattan, and he moved to Chicago, she visited him twice a year. The two had made a project of eating at every pizza place in The Loop together. Of course, that was just their excuse to see each other. Sam even took Nan and my parents to the Highland Festival sponsored by the Scots of Chicago every summer. He and my dad lost the caber tossing contest and he and Nan danced the reel. Not only is Sam ingrained in every fiber of my being, he's laid claim to my family, as well.

"Nan seems to be recovering like a champ," he says.

I tell him all about my grandmother's day and he's nearly hysterical as I regale him with the tale of the drug store parking lot. "Poor Mrs. Abernathy!" he exclaims.

"Nan gave her a romance novel, promising raunchy goings on. Dorcas was all over it like white on rice."

Sam winks. "Maybe I should borrow one of Nan's books and check out how life in the Highlands used to be."

"She gave me a couple of them for Christmas once," I confess. "You would not believe how explicit they are. I wore a perpetual blush for a month."

"Just think of the easy access with both the men and women wearing skirts."

"Oh, believe me, they make the most of that particular convenience."

"Just remember, Nan may exhibit some odd behavior as she recovers from her surgery," Sam explains. "Brain trauma can cause people to act in unexpected ways."

"How will we ever know if it's Nan or the surgery then?" I laugh.

"That'll be the trick." Sam takes my hand. "So, a night in at my place with take-out and a roaring fire. How does that sound?"

"What kind of take-out were you thinking of?" Our little town, population thirty-two hundred, doesn't offer a huge variety of cuisine to-go.

"We could get submarine sandwiches, we could do fast food, or ..." he lets the third option hang in the air for a moment, "we could get a pizza from Monicals."

"Ding, ding, ding, we have a winner!" I love deep-dish Chicago-style pies and I have a real passion for New York-style pizza, but Monicals is the pizza of my youth. It's thin crust with the perfect amount of toppings, the perfect seasonings, and it's cut in squares rather than triangles. It's just the kind of comfort food I need after a vegan lunch and a day with my grandmother.

In the car, I tell Sam about Nan's idea of applying to HHTV to have the Renovation Brothers come out and revamp the house and barn as one of their projects. I watch his whole body go rigid as I say this, but I don't make anything of it. I just tease, "Yes, I know, Nan says they're adorable and may have mentioned they have nice bums, but you're safe. I'm not going to dump you for either of them."

He makes an undefinable growling sound in the back of his

throat. Then he warns, "Don't get your hopes up. I bet they have thousands of applicants for every episode they film."

"I'm sure they do, but I've learned a thing or two about sales during my years in New York. I'm pretty sure I can work my voodoo on them."

My answer doesn't seem to please him. I don't know if I'm being fanciful, but I swear the idea makes Sam nervous. I take a moment to relish my ability to make him jealous. It's a feeling of pure, delicious power.

Lost and Found at Sea

Sam has been renting a house in town since returning to Gelson two years back. He claims to have taken a job locally in hopes of running into me again. If that isn't the most romantic thing ever, I don't know what is.

He lives in an older part of town where the properties are bigger, the homes are set farther back from the road, and the trees are mature enough to offer great shade in the summertime. It's a charming, established neighborhood. I'm not in love with new construction like so many people are these days. I like houses that have stood long enough to have a story to tell, ones that are individual and don't look like every other one on the block.

His house is where my childhood friend, Bethann, grew up. She and I used to play for hours in the backyard, climbing the huge oak trees. I owe my first and only broken bone to that experience. My arm still hurts when I look at the tree tops, at the horizon, or at food on the top shelf at the grocery store.

When we walk through the front door, I go to the kitchen to fetch some plates, while Sam gets to work on the fire. His whole setup has a temporary feeling. The furniture is mismatched, and there isn't enough of it. When I asked him about it, he said, "I've been waiting for my forever home with my forever woman." I melted like a chocolate bar on the dashboard of a hot car.

Sam puts on some classic Jamie Cullum and we cuddle on the couch. He turns toward me and stares deeply into my eyes. I could drown in their depths. Then he leans in and brushes his lips across mine. A jolt of yearning shoots straight through me, enticing me with the softness of his lips, the brush of his five o'clock shadow.

The song "All at Sea" comes on and it washes over me causing a waterfall of emotion. My scalp tingles and I blink away unexpected tears. The feeling is so intense, I momentarily forget to inhale. It's how I felt before Sam came back into my life—like I was lost in the middle of the ocean.

I felt alone when I was with Ethan. My ex was so busy trying to tolerate life, he never had enough time or inclination to really live it. Working with Jazz, my best friend and business partner, was the only thing that made me feel like I was part of something bigger.

Sam kisses my glistening eyes. "Penny for your thoughts," he says.

"I was just thinking that you've rescued me. I didn't think I needed it, but I did. And you're the last person I ever thought would be my savior."

"I'm so sorry for being such a jackass when we were kids. I promise you, I'll never do something like that to you again. I'm here to stay."

He holds me for a moment before pouring me a glass of cabernet. He says, "Why don't we start going over your plans for the house and barn? We can DIY as much as we can before contracting out the rest."

I make a dismissive grunt. "I don't want to DIY any of it. I want to put my energy into forming my business plan and letting the Renovation Brothers do the rest."

"Even if they do come, it might not be for another several months. Surely, you don't want to wait that long to get started?"

I eyeball him intently and my hands get sweaty in frustration. It's a weird reaction for sure, but my palms always sweat when I'm vexed. He really doesn't like the idea of me applying to this program. "Sam, the exposure would be phenomenal for my new business. Don't go getting all negative on me about this, okay?"

He lightens his mood, smiling. "Fine. You go after national fame, and I'll be on hand to help fix any problems that arise." I have no idea what he's talking about. Professionals will come in, do all the heavy lifting, and leave me with the fun bits like designing my business cards and ordering china.

I change the subject. "Remember when Alton Brown, from the Food Network, came to town? He did that special on corn."

"Do I ever. Most of Gelson brought a dish to the audition in hopes of being on the show. My mom made her corn pudding and a pickled corn frittata."

"There were a few tweaked noses when the producers chose Phil Pickman's corn moonshine and Bitty Manfield's cornpone hotdogs." A sigh escapes me. "I love that we come from a town like this. I love that we're back, too. People who've never lived in the sticks don't realize the innate charm the experience holds."

He raises an eyebrow in question. "Charm like Nan and Dorcas Abernathy, or charm like your dad's love of taxidermied animals and kilts?"

I lean into him and inhale his spicy scent. "Charm like quiet nights and roaring fires in the arms of my first boyfriend."

Sam pulls me in closer. "Well then, yeah, I can definitely appreciate that kind of charm." Then he asks, "What do you think of your parents' new house? Have you been inside yet?"

"Not yet, but I've driven by and it's adorable. It looks like the gingerbread cottage in *Hansel and Gretel*," I tell him.

"My piano teacher, Mrs. Keller, lived there until she passed in October from a heart attack. Do you remember her?"

"Yep, the little old lady with the blue hair and the walker. I thought she was a hundred years old when were kids. I can't imagine that she didn't die years ago."

"She'd had rheumatoid arthritis since she was a teenager. It deformed her when she was quite young; that's the reason she used a walker. I have no idea what was up with her hair color, though. I think she used to let the girls at the beauty school in Paxton experiment on her for free haircuts."

"Note to self: don't accept free haircuts now that I'm home." Then I add, "Although, if you think about it, Mrs. Keller was ahead of her time with her blue hair. She'd totally fit in now."

Sam turns to me suddenly with a very serious expression on his face. "*Now that you're home.* Those words are music to my ears."

My stomach flips in anticipation and perhaps from a small amount of trepidation that my life in New York is behind me. I left Gelson as soon as I could and ran as far as I could imagine. But I was never going to find myself in a big city full of noise and strangers. I had some great adventures there, but even though it was my home for a full decade, I never completely settled.

Apparently, I needed to come back to Illinois and soak in my history to remember who I am. I'm a daughter, granddaughter, sister, friend, and girlfriend. I'm Cat Masterton, small town girl who made a name for herself in the big city, before realizing life wasn't about my career alone. I'm home to stay and it fills me with not only joy, but purpose.

Sam and I spend the night in the glow of reconnected love. We snuggle, talk, and make out like a couple of horny teenagers. My body vibrates with a feeling I haven't experienced since high school. It's a mixture of lust, hope, contentment, and sureness that everything is exactly as it's supposed to be.

We eventually get tired enough to know it's time to call it a night. On our way back to my place, Sam stops at the only traffic light in town and stares at me like he can see right through me. "Kitty Cat, this *is* home." On the surface it might sound like he's talking about our little town, but I know differently. He's talking about us.

Sam and I have begun to spend a fair amount of time together. We feel like two pieces of a puzzle. No matter how much time we've spent apart, we still fit. Even though being with him feels like home, I've vowed to take things slowly. It took my heart years to mend the last time he broke it and I don't ever want to go through pain like that again.

Squabbles and Cherry Pitters

Checking my email, I see the usual offers: shapewear, Russian brides, and a Nigerian prince eager to share his fortune. What I do not expect is an email from the producer of *Renovation Brothers* fewer than twenty-four hours after submitting my application. My eyes jump as I read the words:

> *Dear Catriona,*
>
> *We were delighted by the pictures and stories of your old farmhouse. As luck would have it, we just had a cancellation for our February project. We know this is short notice, but if we could arrange an immediate date to survey the project and hammer out the details, we could start on your renovation in the next few weeks. We hope this is convenient for you.*
>
> *I look forward to hearing from you soon.*
> *Ashley Croner*

Wow and wow! I'm so excited I cheer. Wait until I tell Sam. Forget his warnings of *thousands of applicants for every spot* and *you may need to wait months*. I'm just sliding into this reno like a preordained home run.

But first I call Ashley. I let her know my calendar is wide-open and I'm available to meet with her at her convenience. We set up a tentative date for this coming Friday. She's based in Chicago, so she's excited not to have to get on a plane to do the preliminary interview to audition a new project.

I search out my parents and Nan to tell them the good news. I find them all in the kitchen. My dad holds up a weird plier-like device and asks, "What's this for? Removing unwanted molars?"

My mom looks up and snorts, "Don't be a wise apple. That's a cherry pitter."

"Don't you just spit the cherries pits out after you eat the cherry?"

My dad loves to spit stuff out. I mostly refer to pistachio nut shells and the game he's invented called the *Shuck and Chuck*. The rules are you have to put a minimum of ten pistachios in your mouth at once, then shuck the nuts with your teeth, before spitting out the shells into various spittoons. The winner is the one who gets the most shells into the receptacles in the shortest time. Spitting out cherry pits runs a close second for him. I know. I've watched him do it a thousand times.

Mags rolls her eyes. "Not if you're making a cherry pie or cherry conserve, you don't. You need cups and cups of pitted cherries for those."

"Have you ever made either of those?"

"No, I have not. But just because I haven't done it yet, doesn't mean I won't," she huffs.

It seems to me that while they've been playing their little game of, "What Kitchen Gadget is This?" for some time now, there aren't too many items in the charity box.

I interrupt, "I have some news."

My dad looks up, eagerly. "Please let it be that you've decided to allow your mother to store everything she wants to keep but doesn't want to move."

"Dream on, mister. In fact, it looks like we might need to completely clear this house out. I just got word from *Renovation Brothers* that we might be their February project."

Mags looked panicked. "You're barely waiting until we're out of here to start tearing the place up?"

Wait, what? "I'm not kicking you out, Mom. I just made plans around the date you decided to move." I can't get a decent read of what's going on with her, so I ask, "Are you upset I'm making changes to the house?"

"No. Yes. I don't know!" she answers. She finally settles on, "Maybe."

I approach her to offer a hug of comfort, but she abruptly leaves the room before I can get to her.

My dad tries to undo any hard feelings Mags might have left in her wake and says, "I'm excited for you, honey. I've seen that show a couple times with Nan. Those boys really know what they're doing. What projects are you planning to have them work on?"

"I'd like them to remove the wall between the kitchen and dining room and make one big industrial kitchen. A lot of the caterers will want to cook on site. Then I want them to rework the barn so it's party ready." I sum it up, "I want them to do as much as they can within their time constraints."

My practical father asks, "Do you have enough money for all that?"

I shrug my shoulders. "I should. I was hoping to buy this place mortgage free, but if I have to carry a small loan, it'll be worth it to have all the work done."

All the while we're talking, my grandmother is eyeing a shelf of picture frames located next to the counter my mom uses as a desktop. She looks at the photos, then surreptitiously at me, then back to the pictures. If this were a department store, security would probably suspect her of shoplifting.

I turn to inspect the paltry collection my mom has set aside to give away. Out of the corner of my eye I watch as Nan grabs a photo of me and Sam from our senior prom and shoves it under her sweater. She is a shoplifter!

"Nan, what are you doing?" I ask, without looking directly at her.

She hems and haws like she's desperately trying to think of an acceptable answer. She settles on, "I like this picture."

"I do, too. Why don't you leave it where it was so we can all enjoy it?"

"Well, you know what they say on those decorating shows? It's best not to have your house look too personal."

I haven't the vaguest idea what she's talking about. I don't watch decorating shows. "Then why are you leaving the other twenty pictures? They're just as personal, if not more so." After all, what could be more personal than a woman nursing her baby?

"I just love this one of the two of you. I want to keep it by my bedside. Do you mind?"

"I guess not," I answer. But then I see her walk into the living room and grab another picture of me and Sam off the sideboard. What's this woman up to?

Bare Feet and Breakthroughs

I decide to drive over to Sarah's to see what she thinks of the idea of renting her yurts out to the HHTV people. There are no local hotels within twenty-five miles since the Sleep Eazy closed down last year.

Ethan is the first person I see when I pull in the driveway. He's wearing shorts and walking barefoot in the snow. He looks like a zombie. He doesn't even notice I'm there until I get out of the car and slam the door.

He trips over his foot as he looks up. "Catriona! How are you?"

"I'm fine, Ethan. How are you?" He's been here for nearly three weeks and I haven't spoken to him alone in all that time. Sarah's kept him on a tight schedule of meditations, sweat lodges, and behavioral management exercises. Also, we've just broken up. It's not like we were searching each other out for an awkward exchange.

He looks uncertain how much to tell me. After several moments, he says, "I'm changing. I see things in a way I never have before."

"Like what?" I ask.

He tilts his head as though trying to figure out how to articulate his thoughts. He finally manages, "I've always compared myself to other people and felt so different from them. Everyone I came into contact with made me feel that because my brain didn't work like theirs, I was flawed. It's not like they set out to do that, but you can tell by the looks people give you that they think there's something wrong with you. Sarah is helping me see that everyone has their own unique path, and just because mine isn't typical doesn't mean it's wrong or bad."

"That's wonderful!" And I mean it, I really do, but I can't help but ask, "Do you think you might be heading back to New York soon?" I try to keep the blatant hope out of my voice.

He suddenly looks very worried. "I don't know if I can ever go back there."

"What? Why?" My skin prickles like a colony of fire ants is on the march. "You're not planning on staying here in Gelson, are you?" I mean, what couple breaks up only to move to the same small town to start their lives over? That doesn't seem at all prudent.

Shrugging his shoulders, he responds, "I don't know. I just know that I want to keep working with Sarah for as long as she's willing to help me. She doesn't judge me unless she thinks I'm being ill-mannered and then she points that out. She leaves it up to me if I want to change my ways or not. She's helping me understand how others view my actions, so I can make an informed choice about how to behave."

Ethan and Sarah did not start out on good footing. My ex was intolerably rude to her and her hackles nearly reached the moon in response. It wasn't until my friend received a visit from her spirit guide—her words, not mine—that she changed her thinking about him. Apparently, her guide told her it was her duty as an enlightened being to help those in need, whether she personally liked them or not. After that, Sarah's bent over backwards to help Ethan.

I remind him, "New York has been your home forever. Why would you leave? Wouldn't you feel more comfortable in a place where everything is familiar to you?" In my head I'm chanting, *go home Ethan, go home, go home, go home.* "How are you doing with your need for routine?" I ask.

"Horribly," he answers. "I miss it so much I can taste it. But the thing is, I *am* living without it. I never know what I'm going to eat from one meal to the next. I never know what time Sarah is going to wake me up. I don't know the day's plan until it unfolds. I'm learning how to live in the moment, which is something I don't think I've ever done before."

I'm truly glad to hear this. Ethan is a good person and deserves the best life has to offer. I only hope he's not setting himself up for disappointment. "Good for you, Ethan. I'm proud of you."

He beams like a toddler who's just taken his first steps. "Thank you, Catriona. That means the world to me. Even though we're, you know, not together, you're still important to me."

"I feel the same way. Good luck."

He nods his head and says, "Thank you. I'll always be grateful for what we had." Then he walks away.

Sarah opens the door and calls after him, "Time to warm up your feet, Ethan. Go on back to your mother's yurt and have a cup of lemon balm tea with her. Don't forget to thank the tea leaves for their sacrifice."

He follows her order without question. When I get to the

porch, I say, "This place is starting to feel like a cult. Please don't offer me any Kool-Aid."

"I can see why you might say that, but I'm trying to deprogram him, so he can reprogram himself. I don't want control over him, I just want him to learn to be the one in charge and not to let everything around him dictate his actions."

"And there's no chance he can do that back in New York?"

"Ethan hasn't cramped your style in anyway by being here. In fact, this is the first time you've even talked to him alone since he got to my place."

"Yeah, but just knowing he's here makes me uncomfortable."

"Only if you let it. I'm going to tell you the same thing I told him. Your path is yours alone and it's up to you how you interpret it. Ethan's only a problem for you if you let him be one. The ball's in your court, my friend."

Gah! I hate when she gets all deep and philosophical on me. My only response is to push her into the house and announce, "I have news. The *Renovation Brothers'* producer will be here in two days to discuss redoing parts of the house and barn. What do you think of that?"

She claps her hands together and cheers, "Fantastic! What can I do to help?"

I share my plan to get her yurts rented. She's all for it. She tells me Natalie should be gone in another week, and if Ethan isn't, she'll keep him in the house, freeing the four remaining structures for whoever needs them.

It appears this was meant to be. Now, I just need to keep my mother calm and break the news to my boyfriend. That should be easy, right? Yet the sharp pain stabbing my temples indicates that might not be the case.

Gift Shop Candy and Gratitude

I suffer from a little thing I like to call "Perpetual Optimism." It's escalated to the point where I confess to sulking a bit when I play the lottery and don't win. I know what the odds are, but *someone* wins, so why shouldn't it be me? I feel that same way about *Renovation Brothers*. Real people are booked on the show every day, so they might as well make over my life as opposed to someone else's. Even the naysayers must admit the odds are a heck of lot better than winning the Powerball. Plus, I've already made it through the first step, so boom, baby! I'm on my way. I cannot wait to rub Sam's nose in how easily this is all coming together. Good thing I'm meeting him for lunch. It'll be the perfect opportunity.

Driving into town takes me back. Sam recently told me that everywhere he goes in Gelson, he's haunted by memories of us. I'm starting to experience this for myself. When I pass the Tolstons' farm, I remember Mrs. Tolston's corn-shucking parties. When the harvest came in, she'd invite a load of high school kids to come over. There were probably a hundred bushels for us to prepare for canning, freezing, or drying. Sam and I went every year. We'd stay for hours and then she'd feed us as much steak and corn on the cob as we could eat, followed by fresh-baked peach pies with hand-churned ice cream. We positively stuffed ourselves. My heart warms at the sweetness of the memory.

I briefly wonder if my newfound love for my hometown is a passing fancy. What if I wake up one day and I'm over it, just like I was when I left for college? I don't think that's going to be the case. I've seen a lot of the world, and even though I've enjoyed it, it's made me yearn for the simplicity of life in a small town. I can still travel and explore, but I predict coming home will always be a thrill.

I park my car and walk through the automatic doors into the hospital waiting room, stomping off the snow that's collected on my boots. Somewhere around March I'll probably be so sick of the weather I could spit, but as of now, I appreciate the novelty. While we got walloped with snow a couple times a year in NYC, it was nothing like what we experience in the Midwest. Something about being surrounded by water keeps temperatures milder and the environs less extreme.

I text Sam to tell him I'm here and he responds that he'll be down in five minutes. In the meantime, I sit on the couch and flip through a *People* magazine. Lo and behold, the Renovation Brothers are on the cover. Wowza, they *are* cute! They look like they're about my age. One of them has blond hair and the other black. Their faces are almost identical, and I wonder if they're twins. Sam arrives before I can delve into the article to find out.

He pulls me into his arms and lifts me off my feet as he hugs me. He smells spicy and citrusy and I want to take a bite of him. I could get used to this kind of welcome. "What have you been up to today?" he asks.

With a grin that resembles the Cheshire cat, I blurt out, "I talked to the producer from HHTV today. Guess who has an appointment to meet with them on Friday?"

"You?" I nod my head as he shakes his. "Really?" he asks as his eyebrows jump toward his hairline.

"Why are you so surprised?"

"I don't know. I guess I assumed it would be a lot harder to get on one of those shows."

"Have you ever known anyone who's been on one?" I make a saucy face.

He thinks for a minute before answering, "I don't think so." Once again, he doesn't look at all pleased by my news. In fact, he looks concerned. What in the world does he have to be worried about? He can't honestly believe I could be interested in anyone but him.

Before anything more can be said, my mom and Nan come through the front door. My blood starts to pound in my ears like a stereo with the bass turned up high. My first thought is that something's wrong with Nan, but she looks fine. I run over to them and demand, "What are you guys doing here?"

My mom smiles somewhat painfully. "Nan wanted to stop by and thank everyone who took care of her while she was recovering from her aneurysm."

I look to see if my grandmother is carrying cookies or flowers, but her arms are empty. So, I ask, "Did you bring them something?"

"Why, is it their birthday?"

"It's just a nice gesture, that's all."

"So is stopping by to say thank you," she grumbles. "I'm not made of money, you know. Honestly, they were just doing their job." Then she crosses her arms and shifts her position. "Are you saying a thank you isn't good enough?"

"No, no, no. A thank you is just fine, quite lovely as a matter of fact." Nan's a bit unpredictable today and I'm not quite sure how to navigate around her. She's been moody since her surgery. Sam says this is normal behavior for someone recovering from a brain trauma.

Without a word, my grandmother turns around and takes off for the gift shop. I look at my mom, who just shrugs her shoulders. Nan is back in short order carrying three bags of peanut M&Ms. She snaps, "Are you satisfied now?"

"I'm not sure. What did you do?"

"I just spent the last five dollars in my wallet and bought all the candy I could with it."

Sam intervenes, "What are you going to do with it, Nan?"

She gives him a look that suggests he's not the brightest bulb in the socket. "I'm going to give it to the people who took care of me when my brain burst." Then she tears open a bag. "Being that you were one of them, put out your hand."

She proceeds to pour seven M&Ms into his palm and says, "Thank you, Sam. I'm much obliged for your care."

A bubble of laughter escapes before I can stop it and Nan shoots me a dirty look. "What now? Isn't that good enough for you?"

"I think it is very nice." She glares at me like she doesn't believe me and grabs my mom's arm. They walk away without even saying goodbye.

With a twinkle in his eye, Sam puts his hand out, palm up.

"I'll split them with you. I'll even let you have four."

I take three yellows and an orange. "One thing's for sure, that old lady is going to keep everyone on their toes."

Sam grabs my hand. "Let's go upstairs and watch her hand out candy."

"I'm not sure. Remember, she's my new roommate. I don't want to make her mad."

"Oh, come on. If she looks upset, I'll just kiss you and remind her we're back together."

I smile and let him lead the way, secretly hoping Nan is peeved enough that I have an extra opportunity or two to lock lips with the hottie next to me.

Boxes and Boils

The nurses in intensive care approach Nan cautiously. Sheila Jenkins is the first. She appears to be performing an archaic dance, like the foxtrot or something—one step backwards for every two steps forward. I'm guessing most everyone in town knows Nan's penchant for saying what's on her mind and is rightly a little afraid of her.

Sheila finally arrives at her destination, four feet from my grandmother and asks, "Mrs. McTavish, how are you feeling?"

Nan orders, "Put out your hand."

The nurse reluctantly does as she's told, as though she's expecting to be hit over the knuckles with a ruler.

My grandmother pours seven peanut M&Ms into her palm and says, "I'm grateful for your care. Thank you for helping me while I was a patient here." The hospital employee looks as shocked as if Nan had handed her a check for five million dollars.

My grandmother expresses her gratitude to six more people before she runs out of candy.

By the time she reaches Elsie Fink, she offers her thanks and a smack on the butt. She says, "Elsie, I'm not gonna lie to you, you've got a big rump on you, girl. But it's good and firm and

51

you're bound to attract a husband soon." She adds, "It's all about the bass, honey."

Elsie, who isn't a day under forty-five, looks very pleased and answers, "From your mouth to God's ear, Mrs. McTavish. I'm mighty pleased to see you looking so well."

Sam invites Mom and Nan to join us for lunch, but Mags declines for both of them. "We need to get back to the house and keep packing."

"I don't need to pack. I'm not going anywhere," Nan grumbles.

Mags stares at her mother impatiently. "That may be, but there's still plenty you can get rid of and being that Cat has that TV show coming, we want everything to look good for them." She shoots me a look that suggests she's still none too pleased about the TV people.

Nan looks confused. "Isn't the whole reason they're coming because things don't look good and it's their job to fix them?"

"Then help *me*!" my mom snaps. "God knows, I need it. Dougal seems to think my things are all that's holding us back from fitting everything into the new place."

I smile at my mom. "I can help too, when I get home."

"No, thank you. You'll just throw everything out without taking time to assess its value." Mags is in a snit.

I point out, "Possessions are only worth what someone's willing to pay for them. If no one wants your boxes of old recipes and dead animal heads, then they aren't really worth anything."

"What about sentimental value?" she demands with hands on her hips and spittle on the verge of flying. "Even you have to admit things can have sentimental value."

Oh, boy. I either need to keep my mouth shut around these

two or keep my distance from them entirely. I try one last time, "Mom, you knew by downsizing you'd have to get rid of stuff. I'm just trying to help."

She looks defeated. "I know, I know. It's just a lot harder than it looks. We've been in the same house for thirty years. Things have a way of accumulating."

"Why don't I pack Travis's stuff for him? That ought to help some," I offer.

"I'd appreciate that. You'd better call your brother and let him know you're not going to store his things for him and that he needs to come home to pick them up. Lord knows your dad and I won't have any room."

What my parents really want is for me to let them move out of the house with just their clothes and favorite furniture. This way they can have two homes and only be responsible for one of them. That's not going to happen. If I'm going to turn the farm into a business as well as my home, I can't store their whole life there, too. I have to stick to my guns on this one.

Once Mom and Nan leave, Sam and I head to the cafeteria. I comment, "When Nan was a patient here, I noticed the food was really good. Not at all what you'd expect from a hospital cafeteria."

Sam asks, "Do you remember Emily Rickle from high school? She was a year behind us."

I nod, and he says, "She took over the cafeteria two years ago. She's really whipped the place into shape."

"She should open her own restaurant." And I'm not just saying that. Our little town could use some variety.

"I think she wants to but doesn't have enough money. The

idea was to make a name for herself here and then branch out."

I make a mental note to call Emily. She might be a good person to recommend to clients who rent out my barn for their parties. It's been on my mind to investigate local caterers. I didn't really expect to find someone in town and thought I'd need to look in the Champaign/ Urbana area. But if Emily's up to the challenge of doing weddings, I might be able to help make her dream of opening her own restaurant happen sooner rather than later.

Sam gets a page and cuts our lunch short. He pulls me into his arms one last time and whispers into my ear, "I love you, Cat. Thank you for stopping by to see me." His hot breath sends shivers racing straight to my extremities. I feel like my bones are melting and won't hold me up for much longer. Just being in Sam Hawking's presence turns me into jelly.

I grasp the back of a chair to keep from falling. Even though he's recently started telling me he loves me with regularity, it's fresh enough that it makes me feel lightheaded with joy. I answer, "Any time. Now go save someone's life." I push him away before I climb him like a tree. "I'll see you tonight."

"I'm not saving a life, just lancing a boil."

And with that, I've totally lost my appetite and decide to head back to the farm and work on my business plan.

Sequined Gowns and Table Runners

I head into the house with the intent of scouring the internet for a list of established caterers within a thirty-mile radius. While Emily might be a good candidate, I need to give prospective clients a choice.

I walk through the kitchen and see Mom and Nan hard at work. I begrudgingly put my business plans on the back-burner in order to honor my pledge to pack up Travis's belongings. When I moved back home, we put most of his things in my old room. But there's still plenty of stuff in the junk room in the basement. I decide to start there.

The junk room started out as my mom's craft room. It's where she stores all her failed projects, like her golf babies, which are no more than golf balls painted to look like heads. They're stuck on popsicle stick bodies, adorned in the Masterton plaid. She was convinced these bizarre creations were going to make her rich, claiming that if pet rocks, Mexican jumping beans, and bottled water could be a thing, so could golf babies. Turns out, not so much.

My brother has several boxes marked T. Masterton Designs. *What in the world?*

I discover multiple sketch pads and hesitantly pull one out. I wouldn't normally look … but, I can't resist opening one of them. As I peel the cover back, I hesitate. Oh God, what if it's some kind of pornographic drawing or something that might render me blind?

What I discover is even more shocking than what I feared. The books are full of drawings of women's clothing. Gorgeous sequined gowns, feminine business suits, frilly summer dresses, and even swimsuits. In the bottom right corner of each page is his signature, T. Masterton. Travis did these? I quickly grab the other boxes and find they're all full of stunning images, some dating back five years.

Up until Christmas, I thought my brother was nothing more than a stoned loser living in my parents' basement. While Mom and Dad were giving him the time he needed to "find" himself, they secretly thought he was a drug dealer. They'd recently decided enough was enough and they were finally going to kick him out and force him to become a productive member of society. Then Nan's aneurysm burst.

Her illness was a wake-up call for all us. It made me realize I wanted to move home. It made my parents decide to sell the farm for a more carefree life in town, and it forced Travis to come out as a lover of women's clothing. Apparently, he'd been yearning to dress in drag since seeing Nathan Lane in *The Birdcage* when we were kids.

Travis isn't gay, just a lover of feminine attire. I'm not sure if he dresses like a woman every day, I just know he's started to explore that side of himself and didn't feel he could allow his fantasy to become a reality until we almost lost our grandmother.

That's when he finally made the choice to be true to himself.

In addition to my brother's YouTube channel—where he teaches men how to do their makeup and dress convincingly in drag—he's been learning how to play the bagpipes. Apparently, he's also been designing one fabulous line of clothing after another. Will wonders never cease?

I repack his twelve boxes into a more organized six and wonder why my only sibling never pursued his interest in fashion design. I know it's probably not an easy road, but holy heck, from what I just saw, he could really make a name for himself. I'm going to talk to him about this when he comes to pick up his stuff.

While I'm down here, I decide to help my mom do some packing, whether she likes it or not. I put her golf baby paraphernalia into two boxes and label them accordingly. I hope she'll just throw them out and won't bother looking through them. Sometimes it's easier to toss things when you aren't reunited first.

Once I'm done, I organize a boatload of fabric squares from the time my mom was going to learn how to quilt. She gave it up before she got started. Of course, that didn't happen until she'd amassed thousands of quilting squares that "spoke" to her. Calicos, ginghams, solids, florals, and plaids aplenty. The more I look at them, the more I think they can be turned into something useful for my new business venture. Maybe I can hire some women from church to put them together as table runners, or even quilt them as originally intended, so I could use them as wall hangings in the barn for more rustic events.

As excitement for my new venture builds, my mind starts

racing with possible business names. In New York, Jazz and I made our name as Cat Jazz Productions, but here in the country I need something that's going to vibe with the rustic setting. So, Cat Productions is out. I toy with several other ideas, but nothing quite seems to nail it until I spot a bolt of Masterton plaid sitting on a stainless-steel storage shelf. Then as bold as you please, the name pops into my head: Masterton Country Barn. It tells you exactly what you're going to get, a barn in the country owned by a Masterton. It's perfect.

I sit down and start to doodle out the logo. Then I start another list of things that need to be done. I'm so full of anticipation and purpose I can barely stand it. But the first thing I'm going to do is go upstairs and offer to help my mom. This business can't begin until my parents are out of here, and by the looks of things, that's going to be a Herculean undertaking.

The Art of Decluttering Your Life

As I walk into the living room, I spy my mom on the floor amid an enormous pile of books. These tomes have been on the shelves for as long as I can remember, even though I've never seen anyone read them. They're old leather-bound works from Scotland, so obviously they're considered nearly religious relics in our house.

"Hey, Mom, you want some help?" I offer.

She glares at me like I've just offered to boil her pet bunny. "No." Nothing more.

"How 'bout if I start packing up the china cabinet for you?"

"Fine," she answers with a dismissive wave of her hand. My mother is historically not a woman of few words. In fact, more often than not, she'll spin you an epic tale when only a sentence is needed. This move is rattling her to her very foundation.

As I walk toward the entry hall, I hear Nan say, "This little gal on Netflix says you should only keep things that spark joy in you."

"Shut up, Mom," my mother answers.

Nan grumbles, "I'm just trying to help. I figure if you only keep things that make you joyful, you'll be able to pack up this house in no time flat."

"I would certainly be leaving with one less person. Dougal is dancing on my very last nerve," she says.

"Don't be a baby," Nan admonishes. "Just let me show you what she says to do." My grandmother proceeds to take a book out of her daughter's hand. "She says you gotta hold the object in question and if it doesn't bring you joy, you need to thank it for its service and then put it in the giveaway pile."

"These books belonged to your grandmother. She brought them over on the ship when you all moved here." Then she taunts, "They bring me no personal joy, so I guess I better just chuck them all."

Nan shrieks, "Good Lord, Maggie, I didn't mean these books! I was just showing you what the little Japanese gal was talking about. You absolutely cannot get rid of my grandmother's books!"

"I have no intention of throwing them out, but I've decided to give them away."

"Margaret Fay, you may *not* give away these books. Do you hear me?"

My mom smiles feverishly as she goads, "But I'm giving them to someone who they'll spark joy with."

"Who in the world would that be? No one can even read most of them because they're in Gaelic."

"I'm giving them back to you, Mom. I no longer have room for them, so if they mean so flipping much to you, you can find a place for them here."

Uh-oh. I'm witnessing what could turn into an alarming trend. Mom giving Nan everything she wants to keep but doesn't want to store. If I don't intervene quickly, Mags is going to have her way and walk out of here leaving most of her worldly possessions behind.

I pop my head in and interrupt, "Nan, can I see you in the hallway for a minute?"

"Can't," she responds. "I have to figure out where I'm going put my books."

"It's about Sam," I taunt.

She's on her feet in no time flat, nearly charging at me. "What's going on with my dear boy? Is he coming over for a visit?"

"Nan," I hiss quietly so only she can hear me. "You may not let Mom give you everything she wants to keep but doesn't want to store. "

"Don't be bossy with me, girl. I'm not about to let your mother get rid of family heirlooms."

I enumerate, "No taxidermied animals, no kitchen gadgets, and no recipes. In fact, nothing under sixty years old. You got that?"

She sticks a bony finger in my face and demands, "Or what?"

"Or you can go live with her."

I didn't really mean to say that, but I have to be firm if I'm ever going to turn this farm into *my* home and not my parents'.

My grandmother gasps, "You'd think I didn't almost die or something the way you're talking to me."

"Nan," I say, "I'm sorry you were sick, but you're fine now and there is no way you can keep everything Mom is going to try to give you." She silently stares holes through me. "Nod if you understand," I demand.

Of course, she doesn't. She just walks away mumbling, "Sassy girl better watch her step."

Mean Girls and Dances

As I bubble wrap my parents' wedding china, my mind is full of Sam. We were playmates and cohorts in mischief when we were little, good friends and confidants by the time we were in middle school, and madly in love through most of high school. We have an amazingly full history.

The boy who taught me how to make fart noises with my armpit and burp on demand also covered for me when I peed my pants during our second grade Christmas concert. He co-wrote my term paper on *The Brothers Karamazov* and he even helped put highlights in my hair for senior prom. We've been entwined in each other's lives for as long as I can remember.

One memory stands out above all the others. It was the beginning of tenth grade, when I'd just realized I liked Sam as more than a friend and hadn't figured out a way how to let him know. I was in the loft, trying to understand why Margie Bingham was being so nasty to me. We'd never been friends, but we'd been in school together our whole lives. In a small town—where your entire graduating class is under a hundred people—if you don't get along with someone, you simply stay out of their way. All-out war is unnecessary drama that could go on for forever. Margie seemed bent on it.

Sam had interrupted my thoughts when he called out my name. "Kitty Cat, you up there?"

I yelled down, "Yeah. Come on up."

So, he did. He lay down right next to me, putting his arms above his head and supporting it on top of intertwined fingers. He was wearing a light-blue flannel shirt, Levi 501s, and a smile. I could have eaten him up. He opened with, "A penny for your thoughts."

I sighed, "I'm wondering what's going on with Margie. She's been an absolute cow lately and I don't know why."

Sam made a sound low in his throat like he knew the answer, but didn't know how to tell me, so I pushed. "What? What do you know?"

"The Sadie Hawkins dance is next month," he answered, apropos of nothing.

I knew that only too well. I'd been dying to ask Sam but didn't know how he'd receive the invitation. He was such an important part of my life, I didn't want to lose his friendship by declaring feelings that might not be mutual. It was my biggest frustration and it consumed a fair number of my waking hours. I answered, "Yeah, I know about the dance."

"Are you going?"

Oh my gosh, this was my big chance. I could feel the heat between us as we lay there. The hair on my arms stood on end like I'd just stuck my finger in an open socket. I thought Sam felt something, too, but I couldn't be sure. I was too chicken to declare myself in case my feelings weren't reciprocated. I answered, "I don't think so. I mean, who would I ask?" *And what did this have to do with Margie?*

"Margie asked me to go and I said no."

I wasn't surprised. Every girl in our class had been sniffing around Sam since the school year began. His transformation from boy next door to super stud was impossible to miss. Even the older girls, eleventh-graders, had started to flirt with him. I prodded, "Why? I mean Margie's gorgeous. Why wouldn't you go with her?"

He hemmed and hawed and finally confessed, "I like someone else."

I felt like an anvil had been dropped on me. "Really? Who?" Even though I'd asked the question, I didn't want to know the answer. I was blindly jealous at the thought of Sam having a crush on someone. Knowing who would only make it real.

"I'm not sure she feels the same way, so I don't want to say."

Good. I didn't really want to hear. I asked, "Do you think she's going to ask you to the dance?

He shook his head. "No way. She's out of my league."

No one was out of Sam's league, but he didn't know that, yet. He still saw himself as a band geek, which only made him that much more attractive. Too many guys knew they looked good and acted accordingly. Sam's appeal increased exponentially because he wasn't cocky and arrogant.

"What are you going to do?" I nervously asked, chewing on my bottom lip in fear.

"I thought you could ask me and then we could both go to the dance and have fun without worrying about real dates."

"Really?" I responded.

"Only if you aren't planning on going with someone else."

He was the only one I wanted to ask, but I wanted the date to be real. Barring that, going with him in any capacity was too good of an opportunity to pass up. I turned to him with an expression of pure joy and asked, "Sam Hawking, would you like to go to the Sadie Hawkins dance with me?"

His smile was so big the corners of his mouth nearly touched his ears. "Yes, ma'am, I sure would."

I didn't realize until later that he hadn't explained how Margie asking him to the dance related to me. Then Sam cornered me in the school hallway the following week and confessed, "Turns out the girl I like asked me to the dance, after all." That's when it all came together.

I bravely told him, "Turns out I asked the boy I wanted to ask all along." Then we shared our first real kiss and it was pure heaven. In that moment I knew I was where I belonged.

In Sam's arms.

Childhood Bologna

Being with Sam is like spending time in a hot air popper. We float here and there and sometimes pop right out and do something totally unpredictable. Take tonight. He called about an hour after I left the hospital and told me he'd pick me up at six. He didn't say where we were going, only that I should dress in something I wore in high school. As I don't own anything I wore during my teenage years, I plan to recreate the look with items from my adult wardrobe.

When he arrives at the house, he's wearing a pair of heart stopping 501s and his letterman jacket. "Hello!" I tease, "Are you taking me to the big game and then out for a milkshake?"

He smiles mischievously. "Just you wait and see." Then he grabs my hand and pulls me to the front door. We've finally gotten to a place where my whole family doesn't sprint to greet Sam when he arrives, so we're able to sneak out without getting waylaid by any of them.

He's brought his parents' old truck, and when I get into the cab, I see a picnic basket. I reach over to look in and Sam playfully smacks my hand away. "No peeking. I don't want the surprise ruined." Then, he pulls out a bandana, folds it over on itself lengthwise, and instructs, "Close your eyes."

"You're blindfolding me?" Talk about handing over control. It's a sign of how completely I trust this man that I do what he says without further question.

The last thing I see before doing Sam's bidding is his beautiful boyish smile. "I'm surprising you," he answers.

So, I let him cover my eyes right after he slips a Maroon 5 CD in the player. "This Love" booms through the speakers and I flashback as surely as if I'd just stepped into a time machine. I've always thought music and scents could transport a person faster than any vehicle ever created. And this song, it transports me. It plays a memorable part in Sam's and my relationship. It was the first one we danced to after declaring our true feelings for each other.

I didn't know what the lyrics were about, I just knew that with Sam's arms wrapped around me, combined with the music, that my spirit soared to places it hadn't been before. I lean my head back and let the memory envelop me while my first boyfriend drives me to a secret location.

We arrive two songs later. When the truck stops, I reach up to take off the mask, but Sam won't let me. "I don't want you to know where we are until we get inside." I hear him jump out and run around to the passenger side to get me. He leads me carefully across the snowy ground, the crunching under our boots keeps time with the increasing cadence of my heartbeat.

We must be somewhere in Gelson because we didn't drive far enough to be in another town. We walk for about a minute before entering a building. Something about it smells familiar—hamburgers meets disinfectant with a side of sweaty socks. Yet it can't be, because how would Sam be able to get us into this building after hours? He leads me a short distance, opens another door and gently pushes me through it.

I immediately know we're in the high school gym. I pull my mask off to confirm my suspicions. There aren't any lights on, but in the middle of the floor is a blanket surrounded by battery-operated candles. "How did you do this? How did you get in here?"

He laughs. "I'm on the school board. It's one of the many perks of the job. That is, if you think being able to get into your old high school after hours is a perk."

"You're still the big man on campus, aren't you?"

"I even have change for the vending machine if you want something I didn't pack in my trusty basket." He jangles some coins in his pocket before leading the way to our destination. I follow along, a starving wanderer.

When we're seated, he opens the basket and takes out a bottle of red wine and two glasses. He fills them and toasts, "To us."

I lift my glass high and add, "To the boy who stole my heart." After taking a sip, I lean back on the throw pillows Sam has scattered around the blanket. As he unpacks dinner, I ask, "What are we having?"

He hands me a plastic baggy. "Bologna sandwiches with sliced pickles, lettuce, and mayo."

"You're joking." It was our favorite childhood lunch to share.

"Nope. I once knew a little girl who told me bologna was the perfect food and that one day, when she was married and had her own house, she'd eat it at every meal."

"We were eight when I said that. How do you know I still

like it?" The truth is I haven't eaten bologna in over a decade, but I'm not opposed to having it tonight.

He continues to pull out plastic containers from the basket. "I don't, which is why I also brought along some pâté, cheese, olives, and a baguette."

"Always a Boy Scout," I tease.

He reaches in and brings out a can of our favorite childhood potato chips. "It's true. I'm always prepared."

I flirtatiously say, "Oh yeah, well, we'll see about that when it's time for dessert." Sam's eyes light up in anticipation. "Not that kind of dessert, naughty boy."

"A man can dream, can't he?"

Chinamen and Possibilities

Today's the day. I wake with a feeling of excitement previously reserved for Christmas mornings when my age was still in single digits. The *Renovation Brothers'* producer will be here in a few hours. There are boxes everywhere, making it obvious my parents are doing more packing than purging. I have no idea how everything is going to fit in their new place. Luckily, that's not my problem as long as Nan doesn't accept any more of their gifts.

By the time I make it to the kitchen, the gang's all here, dressed in their finest. Or what they consider their finest. For Dad, it's his best kilt. Mom is also wearing a skirt, but thankfully they're not a match set. True to her love of vintage fashion—as in clothes she's owned and worn for many decades—Nan is adorned in an Asian-inspired outfit that isn't entirely—or at all— politically correct. But far be it from me to point that out. My grandmother is from another era that doesn't always vibe with the changing tides of time, like respecting the cultural heritage of non-Scots. If you look at her tunic closely, you can see what she calls "little Chinamen" embroidered on the bodice. Silk thread ponytails dangle from the fabric, the only hair on otherwise bald heads. She's even drawn black eyeliner on her eyelids to make them look slightly slanted. I don't ask.

My family follows me into the living room to await the producer's arrival. Nan glides around the room like a creeper. I see her pick up a couple of picture frames and turn them over. I don't know what's going on with her, but she's up to something.

Before I can ask her, a car pulls up to the house. I press my face against the living room window like an eager puppy waiting for her people to come home. The woman, who I assume is the television producer, is dazzling. Her long, shiny hair is the most gorgeous shade of auburn. She's not a true redhead, but there's enough red, you wouldn't classify her as a full brunette, either. She's tall and slim and very stylish. Not that I can tell too much with her winter coat on, but she carries herself like a queen. My average height, blond self, feels a tiny bit intimidated.

I open the front door before she can knock. She immediately puts her hand out and warmly says, "You must be Catriona."

"I am. And you must be Ashley."

I welcome her in, take her coat, and discover she's just as elegant as my first impression led me to believe. She's wearing a beige cashmere dress, accessorized by a thick, brown leather belt and riding boots. I usher her into the living room where my family awaits. Ashley greets them, and to my relief they don't say anything embarrassing. Once the pleasantries are over, she focuses her attention on me. "Tell me about your house."

"What do you want to know?" Then I can't help myself, I gush, "I'm thrilled you were able to come out so soon!"

Her smile is infectious and makes her look very approachable and more beautiful than I first thought. "I want to know what your life here is like. Are there any structural issues we need to consider? Anything you can think of. I need to know your house as well as you do, so we can be as prepared as possible."

"I'm a party planner from New York City," I explain, "but I grew up here. I've recently moved back home and I'm buying my parents' farm. I want to use the barn for events."

She explains, "While the program makes renovations look like they happen very quickly, it often takes several months. The brothers, Jeremy and Josh, only stop in occasionally to film their segments. The majority of the labor is outsourced to local contractors, whom I supervise."

I nod my head. I still haven't watched an episode but plan to binge-watch right after our meeting is over. Finally, as we walk out to the barn, Ashley mentions, "I've actually been to Gelson before."

"You have? Why in the world?" Because the plain truth is, we're not exactly a destination location, unless you've read about Sarah's place and want her to reboot your cell memory by depriving you of bacon and rolling you in the elements. I can't imagine the naked snow roll ever hitting the big time, as entertaining as it is. Poor Ethan.

Once my business is up and running, I hope to help put us on the map in a mainstream kind of way.

"I drove through with a friend from college once," she replies.

I want to ask who. If she's from Gelson, I probably know her or went to school with her or one of her siblings. But something in her demeanor suggests she wants to get back to business, so I don't push. Instead, as we approach the barn, I explain, "We don't house many animals anymore, so it's just a big empty space begging for use."

"Is this the sole area you plan on using for your events?"

"For the guests, yes. The house will need to be open for caterers and the like. Other than that, I don't really want to have a lot of strangers traipsing through."

"So, who lives with you? Do you have a husband and children? Because if so, I should warn you, it can be very stressful residing here during renovations."

"No husband and children. Just me and my grandmother. My parents are moving into a smaller place in town."

She nods her head. "That shouldn't be too bad, then." After a brief tour of the barn, she announces, "We'll have to plumb for bathrooms. With the number of guests you'll be hosting, you should have at least two."

I don't know why I hadn't thought of that. If porta-potties were the only facilities available, I'd probably limit the kind of events I could have to purely casual ones. I suggest, "The bathrooms should be nice enough to support elegant affairs."

We discuss plans to enclose part of the loft for storage and to build an actual staircase to replace the old rickety one. Ashley takes notes and does a little calculating before saying, "We can probably do the barn in one episode. Then swing a two-part arc and do the kitchen and whatever other house renos you want done in the second."

I gasp, "Two episodes? That's pretty exciting! Wow. I guess I'd need an idea how much money we're talking before I can commit to it. I know the barn will be pricey, and I'm sure the kitchen won't be a small project, either."

"True. But because we're filming this, we provide the labor at no charge and all supplies are purchased at a wholesaler's discount. If we say on-air that the project is a sixty-thousand-dollar renovation, you only need to have approximately twenty thousand of that. We tweak the numbers so viewers will have an idea of how much the same design would cost them."

"In that case, if you could get me some quotes, I'm sure I can come up with more that needs to be done." I brainstorm, "Perhaps the basement can be turned into a prep area for the party hosts, provided they have their own entrance to the outside. That way, if it's a wedding, the bridal party has a place to get ready before the event."

Ashley nods her head. "I love that idea." Then she explains, "Okay, so the next step is for me to get in touch with local contractors and get bids. Being that it's winter in a small town, I'm assuming people will be hungry for work and exposure. I'll make some calls and get back to you in the next day or two."

This is going a heck of lot faster than I could have ever imagined. In my eyes, it's more proof than ever that it's meant to be. What could possibly go wrong?

Eucalyptus Flogging

As soon as Ashley leaves, I start a list of what has to be done. First up is a full plumbing remodel. Other than the kitchen, barn, and basement, I should probably have them do the bathrooms. They haven't been touched in the thirty years my parents have lived here and probably not before then based on the 1940s décor and hideous plumbing situation. I have no idea what this is all going to cost, but if I have to, I'll open a home equity line of credit to pay for whatever I can't cover.

You'd think I'd be nervous about spending so much on a house I could probably never resell for enough to recoup my investment—as in, no one in Gelson would pay so much—but I'm an all-in kind of gal. Once I've determined to do something, any obstacles better either step out of my way or get mowed down in the process.

When I told Ashley about Sarah's place, she took the info. She was relieved there were accommodations in Gelson, as it would cut down on commuting time. I pick up the phone to call my childhood friend. "Sar, it's me." Then I proceed to relay my exciting news.

She's nearly as giddy as I am. "Fantastic! OMG. Cat, this is going to be epic! Just make sure that if the renos go into the spring, you have them put in a beautiful garden. Not only will you be able to grow food, but it'll be an awesome backdrop for wedding photos. Can't you just see the bride and groom peeking out of the corn stalks?"

I laugh at the image. "Maybe we should add a nice flower garden, too. You know, in case they want something a bit more traditional. Can you help with the design?"

"You know I will. Oh, and by the way, Ethan's mom left today. She went back to Westport."

"Is she still leaving Jason?"

At Thanksgiving, Ethan's mom Natalie told me a story about the boy she was engaged to in college and how she broke it off with him because they were such different people. She used that tale to warn me against marrying her son, assuring me he wasn't going to change and would probably only get more stuck in his ways as the years progressed. At the time, I was angry at her interference, as I thought she was doubting my love for Ethan. In retrospect, it was the best advice I could have received. It opened my eyes and got me out before it was too late.

Natalie must have started thinking about what might have been in her own life. From the outside, it looked like she and Jason had had a good marriage, but you never know what's really going on between people in their private lives.

Sarah answers, "I'm not sure if she's leaving her husband or not. All I did was help her regroup. She hasn't shared any personal information with me."

"Man, someone trusts you enough let you roll them naked in the snow, you'd think they'd open up to you," I joke.

"I know the work I do sounds intrusive, but it's not. I don't get involved with my client's personal problems. I just help them on the track to discovering their own journey." She adds, "Which doesn't include me."

"Sar, how did you get into this stuff, anyway? I mean, you always marched to your own tune, but I did not see this coming."

"I'll tell you someday. But before I do, you have to come out here and experience it for yourself."

Sam and I had talked about doing just that only a couple weeks ago, but that was before all the *Renovation Brothers* stuff came up. "I'm not sure when I can make that happen, but I promise to make some time this year."

"Yeah, you've got a bit on your plate right now. But don't worry. I'm not going anywhere."

"What do you roll me in if I come during the summer?" I ask.

"Mud," she replies.

"You do not!"

"Mud is extremely therapeutic," my friend answers. "Especially if there's a high clay content, which I always add. As it dries, it pulls toxins out of the body. You can never go wrong with a good mud bath."

"I'll have to keep that in mind," I manage. "How's Ethan doing?" I know it's not my business anymore, but old habits die hard.

"I'm flogging him with eucalyptus branches after his sweat lodge today. That will help stimulate his mental functions and clear his brain of old thinking."

"By flog him, do you mean hit him?"

"It's more of a firm tapping."

I joke, "Someone needs to give you your own television show, you know that?"

"No way!" she replies. "What I do is serious business. A TV show would just play on the sensationalism of it. That would definitely not be the way to help people."

"But you could reach the masses."

"I'd become a spectacle. That's not for me. I genuinely want to help people and that has to be done one-on-one, in a private and safe environment."

My friend is truly committed to this unconventional life of hers and it's obvious her intentions are honorable. I respect her for that.

Before hanging up, Sarah and I promise to get together for lunch sometime this week. It's nice to have such a good friend nearby. Even though I miss Jazz, I have yet to miss New York. My city life couldn't be farther behind me.

Unconscious Raccoons and Kisses

The week flies by at a breakneck pace. My parents have been packing nonstop while Nan has been working against any headway by ignoring my warning. She's been setting fires wherever she can to halt their progress. Whenever my mom puts something into the charity box, my grandmother walks by and says "You can't get rid of that! Remember when …?" —insert random memory here.

My favorite was over a rolling pin Mags was finally willing to part with. Yesterday, my dad tried to convince her that four rolling pins was three too many. She disagreed, but ultimately compromised and agreed to let go of one. Once she'd decided which to relinquish, Nan shouted, "Not that one! That's the one I threw across the kitchen to hit the intruder. Remember? He snuck right through the kitchen door!"

The unwanted guest was a raccoon that she had knocked unconscious. The same one my dad unsuccessfully tried to nurse back to health. The three of them paused looking misty-eyed at the memory.

Dad sniffles, "He's still up in the attic, you know?"

"I'm pretty sure I could have taught Mickey Mantle a thing

or two about throwing," Nan says.

Not to be left out, Mags adds, "We're taking all the rolling pins! They're all so special in their own way."

The entire living room is now stacked floor-to-ceiling with moving boxes. Only four of them are destined for St. Vinnie's. I had to force myself not to engage in their process. It was either that or lose my thready grasp on sanity. Also, if things were packed in boxes that meant they were leaving the house, and that right there was my ultimate goal.

My parents start moving today. Can I get a hallelujah? They've decided to economize and do it themselves, no hiring professionals to help. Normally, I'd support such a decision, but now that I'm home, witnessing it in person, I'd have to say it wasn't the best choice.

Sam and my dad are loading their possessions into the moving truck, Mags is fluttering around waving her hands in panic and yelling out orders, Nan is sitting on the living room couch reading a magazine, and I'm trying to figure out how they're going to get everything out of here before the setup crew from *Renovation Brothers* arrives in two days.

The producers have decided to start on the barn first because they want to repair the leaks in the roof before more damage can occur. As a result, we can store everything from the house out there when they're done. My big challenge now is to get my parents to take everything in the loft with them.

I walk out the front door to make sure the contents of the barn haven't been forgotten and run right into Sam. He immediately wraps his arms around me and gives me a tender kiss. Then he picks me up caveman style and moves me out of his way. "Got to keep moving or we're never going to get them out of here."

"What are the chances it's going to happen before Valentine's Day?" I ask.

"Be optimistic. I'm pretty sure if we work nonstop for the next twenty-six hours, we might make it."

"You're a saint to be doing this, you know that?"

"Oh, I don't know. I might have an ulterior motive." He smiles wickedly.

A shiver runs up my spine. "I hope you don't think I'm going to repay your efforts, somehow."

With a slow wink, he responds, "That's exactly what I think." Then he adds, "In all seriousness though, I'm not going to be around while your fancy Renovation Brothers are here. I have to make up the time I'm taking off from the hospital. Then Doc Miller is going on vacation and I'm covering for him."

I can't help but wonder how much of that is true and how much it is Sam not supporting my decision to do this television show. "Why are you so against the Renovation Brothers?" I demand.

"I just worry it won't be quite the experience you want it to be."

"I have no idea what you're talking about. All I expect them to do is renovate my house. You make it seem like they have some ulterior motive or something."

He sighs. "You picture this being a nice, easy experience without any problems. I'm just saying there are bound to be obstacles and some of them may be insurmountable."

I shake my head and smack him on the arm as I head to the

barn. Over my shoulder, I call out, "Just you wait, Mr. Party Pooper! This reno is going to go so smoothly I'll make you eat your words."

A flash of worry crosses his face and I hear him mumble, "I hope you do."

Schweer the Queer

Travis shows up just as my dad and Sam pull out of the driveway to take the first truckload to my parents' new house. He strolls through the front door in a red boucle sweater dress with gold button details and a thick strand of pearls around his neck. If it weren't for his flaming red wig, he'd be a dead ringer for a younger Barbara Bush.

I approach him with outstretched arms and a joyful smile on my face. "Travis, thank God you're here!" Travis likes to be addressed by his female moniker, Rhona, when he's in drag, but as this is a new development, I sometimes forget. I grab him in a full-body hug and hold on tight, catching a whiff of his perfume. He's wearing my favorite—Eau d'Hadrien by Annick Goutal. Its fresh, citrusy fragrance is one of my happy triggers.

My brother is a giant in his four-inch, black patent leather pumps. He must have bought them from Fredrick's of Hollywood, where the drag queens shop, as no department store carries women's shoes in a size 14 wide.

I'm about to ask him if he designed this particular ensemble, when I see he's not alone. Scottie Schweer pops his head through the door. "Scottay! Get over here and give me some love!!!"

Scottie lets out a glass-shattering shriek of excitement which does not fit his physical appearance and launches himself at me. "Kitty Cat, come here and purr for me!" Then he growls like a jungle cat before picking me up and twirling me around the room.

"When did you get back in town?" I demand.

"I came down with Trav for the day."

My brother teases, "Now that my big sister is officially throwing me out, he's going to help me schlep all my crap back to the Windy City."

"You're more than welcome to visit any time you want. But if I store your stuff, Mom and Dad are going to be butt-hurt that I won't store theirs."

He rolls his eyes heavenward. "I can only imagine. How's Mags holding up? Has she been able to unload anything?"

"As far as I can tell, she's gotten rid of less than one percent of her earthly belongings. I'm pretty sure she and Dad are going to have to pitch a tent and sleep in their new yard. I don't think there will be any room for them in the house once they've unloaded the moving truck."

Scottie interjects, "Speaking of junk … can you believe your brother is stuffing his in pantyhose now? I thought we gay boys were the only ones brave enough to flirt with our inner She-Ra. And even then, not all of us do."

Travis replies, "No one expects you to dress in drag."

"It's just so strange!" Scottie declares. "I mean, how are we supposed to hang out in public together now that you're out of closet, as it were? Other men will assume I'm straight with a great big hunk of woman like you, and the eligible ladies will think you're as queer as a three-dollar bill. We'll never be able to troll for hook-ups together."

"So, we'll drink beer and burp the alphabet like we've always done," my brother replies.

"Works for me."

Scottie and Travis's friendship goes back to when they were in kindergarten together. My brother was the first person his friend came out to when he realized he was gay in the sixth grade. Trav didn't so much as blink an eye at the declaration. He merely said, "I don't care who you're crushing on, as long as it isn't me."

Scottie was so relieved to have a true friend and confidant that if he ever did pine for my brother in a romantic way, he had the good sense to keep it to himself.

Scottie spots Nan sound asleep on the couch with a gossip magazine across her face. "How's the old lady holding up? Trav told me about her aneurysm."

I grimace. "Well, she's still Nan, albeit a tiny bit less mean."

Scottie dramatically throws his hand to his heart and declares, "Mean Nan is the only Nan I've ever known! I don't want her changing on me now."

My grandmother groans in response to all the noise in the room. Her eyes open slowly and when she sees our guest, she hollers out, "Is that Queer Schweer here?!" It may sound like Nan is disparaging Scottie's lifestyle, but that couldn't be further from the truth. Nan found out Scottie's secret shortly after my brother and her only response was to tell him that in life you had to be proud of yourself and let your freak flag fly. She'd advised, "Own your story, young Scott. It's the only one you'll ever have to tell."

He complained, "The guys at school call me Schweer the Queer."

"Then I'm going to call you that too!" my grandmother had proclaimed. "After all, I think you're pretty wonderful, so if that's what I call you, you won't associate the name as a negative."

Scottie trots across the room and picks Nan straight up off the couch like she's a bride being carried over the threshold and croons, "My favorite fruit fly!" Then he sets her down gently and asks, "Seriously, how are you doing, old lady? I hear you gave everyone quite a scare."

Nan smiles adoringly. "Yes, well, they weren't paying enough attention to me. I needed to get them back on track."

Scottie nods his head in response. "Good. They should never take you for granted."

After a few more minutes with Nan, Travis changes out of his high heels, and the men get to work hauling my brother's boxes up from the basement. When I see the one containing his fashion designs, I demand, "Why didn't you ever tell me you designed clothes?"

"Because I designed them for me. I figured once that secret was out, I couldn't keep the rest from you."

"You're an idiot, Travis. I would have been so proud of you. I am so proud of you. I'd have begged you to make me clothes, too."

"Liar! You would have blamed my designs on the pot and told me to stop getting high. The last thing you would have done is trusted me with your wardrobe."

He's right. I hate being called out when I'm trying to sell myself as righteous. "What are you going to do with your sketches?" See how I changed the subject to save face?

"I'm going to make myself a new wardrobe."

"I'll submit my measurements, so you can start on mine, as well."

"Me too!" Nan yells out.

My brother laughs. "Fine. Now will you let me pass so I can move out of your house?"

When my dad and Sam get back, we all sit down to take a break to gather our strength. My mom serves a batch of her famous shortbread cookies that had been pressed into a pan etched with mushrooms—which is somehow fitting as we're kind of a psychedelic lot. My dad and brother being the only ones in skirts and all.

Scottie lifts his tea, doctored with a shot of scotch, and toasts, "To the best family I know. May the next phase of life be everything you dream it will be!"

Mom fills her cup to the top with Glenfiddich and nothing else and adds, "May the next phase get here quickly before I drop dead from the transition." We all toast to that one.

Nan lifts her cup and proclaims, "To my favorite queer. It's good to see you again, boy." We all toast to that one, too.

Pictures Without Frames

I wake up the next morning to find Sam passed out on the living room couch. He's still wearing his clothes from yesterday and he looks delicious. His dark hair is mussed like he's been sailing in gale-force winds, and his morning stubble makes him look like a rogue pirate. It's all I can do to not jump on top of him.

I don't do it for two reasons. One, it might lead to something I'm not ready to let happen, and two, if I did let it happen, I would not want it to be in full view of the household. So, I go into the kitchen and start a pot of coffee instead. When it's brewed, I pour two cups and carry them over to Sam.

His eyes pop open and he smiles. "There's my girl." Then he sits up and pats the spot next to him. "Come here and caffeinate me, woman."

I cuddle into his warmth and take a moment to inhale his manly scent. I want to stay right here all day and do nothing but smell him. Okay, maybe I want to do other stuff too, but we've got to stay on schedule. "Do you really think you'll be done moving my parents out today?"

"Yup." Then he confides, "Your folks didn't want me to tell you, but they rented a storage unit in town so they can keep everything without fighting about it."

"Well, that's a waste of money. What's the point of holding on to things if you're not planning on using them?" But I silently applaud their choice. Things were starting to get really tense around here.

"It's part of the letting go process. Your mom and dad have had their possessions for years. They identify with them so much it defines them. I think once they get used to the new place, they'll start to let go."

I smile at his innate sensitivity and understanding. "You're a sweet man, you know that?"

He waggles his eyebrows at me and croons, "Sweet like a cup of sugar." Puckering up his lips, he offers a kiss, "Want some sugar?"

After a quick smooch, I stand up and declare, "I'm off to kick dead animals down from the attic. Make sure you pack those before anything else."

As I climb the stairs and see the spots on the walls where pictures once hung, I start to feel a little giddy. This house is mine and I can finally make my own mark on it. Once the wallpaper comes down and everything has a fresh coat of paint, I'll rescue my paltry belongings from the basement and start hanging my own pictures and making my own memories.

Climbing the attic stairs, I wonder what I could use the space for other than storage. During my years with Ethan,—the minimalist—I weeded my possessions down to a very few boxes. Personal storage is one thing I don't need.

As I hit the top step, I see my mom sitting on an old rocking chair by the garret window. She looks eerily like Norman Bates' mother in *Psycho*. She's just rocking away, staring out at the world below.

I make a noise to alert her to my presence before greeting, "Hey, Mom."

She grunts in acknowledgment but doesn't bother turning around.

I ask, "How are you doing?" I'm not sure what to say to her as I'm currently not her favorite person.

"I'm okay," she finally answers. Then she turns to me with tears in her eyes. "Truth be told, I'm a little bit jealous of you right now."

"Of me? Why?"

"Because you're just starting your life, honey. I came to this house as a young woman full of hopes and dreams. I raised my babies here and made all the memories that made me the person I am. All of that was done here on this farm, in this house. And now it's your turn."

I'm silent in response as there doesn't seem to be anything for me to say. After several long moments, she adds, "Don't get me wrong, I'm ready to go. It's just that I feel like I'm a picture walking out of its frame. Does that make any sense?"

I nod my head. It makes a lot of sense, and I don't think I could have put it better myself. "You'll always be part of this house's picture, Mom."

She smiles up at me. "Thank you. That means a lot." Then she adds, "There's no one I'd rather see here than you."

I walk over and pull her out of her chair to give her a hug. She holds on tight and whispers, "I wish I could hit the pause button and enjoy this moment forever."

I feel so fortunate to finally be home to enjoy all the moments. I only hope they're all as sweet as this one.

What Quiet Moments?

As my parents' worldly possessions leave the house, they find an odd array of items they once thought lost forever. My mom discovered her missing antique diamond brooch she suspected Travis stole to buy drugs. Dad came upon four misplaced rodents still dressed for Valentine's Day, circa 2004. And when they cleaned out the chest freezer in the basement, not only did they unearth fifteen-year-old meat, but they also found the last remaining piece of cake of their wedding. They defrosted it and each took a bite before spitting it. Then they transferred the rest to a box so they could put it in their freezer in the new house. It's almost like they were reconfirming their vow to stay together on the next part of their journey. It was sweet, but gross.

When my mom saw me cringe at their sentimental moment, she declared, "It's bad luck to throw it away." Salmonella is also bad luck, but I didn't bother to point that out. My parents will do what they'll do regardless of common sense.

Today is the day Ashley is bringing over the crew she hired to start work on the barn. We're having a production meeting at nine sharp, which means I have twenty minutes to pour a gallon of coffee down my throat and get dressed.

When I walk into the kitchen, Nan is already there wearing black cropped pants and a satin jacket à la nineteen fifty something. She looks like a geriatric Pink Lady from the movie *Grease*. "I've never seen that outfit before," I say on my way to the coffee pot.

"This old thing?" she declares. "I wore this on Halloween, nineteen eighty-one. It's cute, huh?"

Apparently, my grandmother has reached the stage in life where the line between Halloween costumes and everyday clothes has blurred to the point of not existing. At least she's not wearing Travis's old clown costume from his clown college days.

There's a sharp knock on the back door before Sam lets himself in. He hands over a dozen red roses nicely displayed in a tall vase with baby's breath and ferns. "I stopped by to wish you good luck today." Then he gives me a lingering kiss before pouring himself a cup of coffee.

"You're the most thoughtful boyfriend in the world!" I gush. "I'm happy you're here. I want you to meet Ashley before we get started this morning."

Sam looks at the clock and stops in his tracks. He proceeds to the kitchen sink and pours his cup down the drain. Then he notices Nan and gives her a peck on the cheek. "Whoops. The time has totally gotten away from me! I should be at the hospital right now." And without further ado he walks out the door yelling, "I'll call you later this afternoon."

Just when I thought I might have been misinterpreting his reaction to my doing this show ... I have no idea why he's so negative about it, but at this point it doesn't matter. I'm committed and my house and barn are going to be gorgeous! That'll show him.

As Sam exits, the doorbell rings. I don't give him another thought as I let in the local contractors who are going to do the lion's share of the work around here. Before I can drink my first cup of coffee, Ashley arrives, dressed in designer jeans and high-heeled boots.

"Are you ready to get this party started?" she asks.

"Absolutely. Just let me run upstairs and grab my sweater. It's kind of cold in here with everyone coming and going."

At nine o'clock on the nose, we're assembled in the living room. The television producer announces, "I want us all familiar with the ins and outs of this project before Josh and Jeremy arrive tomorrow to shoot their segments. The Renovation Brothers will be here for four days beginning tomorrow, to film their opening spots. After that they'll be here two days a week until the final wrap up."

Marcus Frost, the local plumber and quarterback of the varsity team the year Sam and I were freshmen, asks, "Are they going to do any of the work?"

Ashley answers, "The brothers are the front people. We'll film them hammering nails and talking about the design plans, but they're the hosts. Your job is to get the work done; they explain what's happening to the audience."

She spends the next twenty minutes going over the schedule with everyone and answering questions before announcing, "Okay, all of my construction people need to follow me out to the barn. I'll finalize demolition plans with you."

Mr. Sharp, our town's only electrician asks, "Are you done with me? I promised the missus a breakfast out to celebrate our lottery winnings."

All eyes open wide in surprise. The Sharps have been playing the same lotto numbers since I was a kid. It's about time they won something. "How much did you score, Mr. Sharp?" I ask the question everyone wants the answer to.

"Seven dollars and eighty-nine cents! Can you believe it? We're pretty excited."

That's not the best return on the thousands they've put into it, but if it makes them happy, who am I to rain on their parade? I've got enough on my plate.

The Right Lighting

In a word, Jeremy and Josh Reynolds are scrumptious. They're meticulously coiffed and groomed. I prefer a more carefree look myself, but you've got to give them props for execution. They're Hollywood shiny with an almost airbrushed feel to them.

Jeremy, the blonde, is the first to acknowledge me. He thrusts his hand out to shake mine as he exclaims, "You must be Catriona! Thanks for letting us come and work on your place. We're pretty pumped to get to reno a barn."

Josh, the dark brooding one, looks like he could have played Heathcliff in *Wuthering Heights*. He doesn't seem quite as excited as his brother. Yet, he offers a truly knee-melting smile in lieu of words. Good lord, I can see why Sam might feel intimidated by these guys, even though he hasn't come right out and said it. They're inhumanly gorgeous.

Before their coats are off, Nan strolls in wearing a dress straight out of an old *I Love Lucy* episode—full skirt, Peter Pan collar, the works. She must have unearthed a bunch of stuff during my parents' exodus as she's recently been sporting fashions I can't remember ever seeing before. Props to her for still being able to fit into them. She takes one look at the show's hosts and her eyes pop open like she's on the receiving end of a live cattle prod. "Hello, boys!" Then she throws her arms wide open as if to say, "Come to Mama!"

They approach her graciously and Jeremy goes in for the hug she's angling for. Josh takes her hand and kisses it. Nan looks like she might faint but is forcing herself to stay conscious to enjoy every moment of the godlike attention cast her way.

Ashley walks through the front door, thoroughly unfazed by the brotherly duo and announces, "Jeremy, Josh, we start filming in an hour. Come with me, and I'll show you the barn." Then she trains her eyes on me and Nan and hands us both a sheet of paper. "You look great. Why don't you check out the script, so you're ready when we shoot?"

"Script?" Nan demands. "What do we need a script for? This ain't no movie, girl."

"Of course not, Mrs. McTavish. We just put together a loose idea of the exchange we'd like to see between you and the brothers. You'll use your own words, but we've found a script cuts down on the number of takes and helps keep us on schedule."

Nan grumbles without offering any other response. I lead her over to the couch, which happens to be the only remaining piece of furniture in the living room. She sits down right in the saggy middle and declares, "I don't say anything in this script! That can't be right. I have things to say, Cat."

I'm sure she does. I look at the piece of paper Ashley handed me and read:

Camera pans across rural farm scene before following Jeremy and Josh to the front door of the Masterton House. Brothers stomp the snow off their feet, rub their hands together, etc.

Jeremy: Wow, Josh, this is a cool one, huh?

Josh: Straight up. I can't remember the last barn we did. (Pause.) Have we ever even done a barn?

Jeremy: (Shakes head.) Not that I recall, bro. (Knocks on door.)

Catriona: (Opens door.) Hi, there! Welcome to my farm!

The script goes on to benignly introduce the niceties of my remodel. It's all pretty generic stuff, but Nan isn't having any of it. "Why don't I get to say anything?"

"I guess because they're remodeling the barn for my business. They must be focusing on that." I wonder what Nan wants to say, but I don't ask. I've learned there are times when it's best not to know.

Ashley and the Renovation Brothers are outside for at least twenty minutes before they come back in. Josh, looks positively aglow and enthuses, "That's one cool space!"

Jeremy's beaming as well. "Nice job finding this one, Ash. Our viewers are going to love it." To me, he adds, "There's only so much suburban banality you can shove down people's throats, you know?"

I still haven't watched more than a handful of episodes as I've been focused on getting my parents moved out, but he's right. The ones I saw were pretty much cookie cutter copies of one another. Young couple with mundane jobs and a surprisingly large budget needs to make better use of their space. They inevitably take down walls for an open-concept feel.

If the walls are load bearing, they install new five-thousand-dollar support beams. They do bathrooms and kitchens, too, but it all has the same kind of feel—granite, subway tiles, new cabinets, voilà! The transformation is complete. Everyone lives happily ever after.

I smile as I gush, "We're thrilled you're here. The barn will primarily be used for wedding receptions, so it needs a lot of work. I hope you're up for the challenge."

Ashley gushes, "They're up for it all right. I'm going to get the camera guy on the front door. Cat, if you can stand by it so he can get the lighting right, that would be great."

"Where do you want me?" Nan demands. Her tone is a bit caustic, even for her.

"You can stay right there on the couch, if you'd like."

"You gonna come over here and light me, too?"

Ashley looks confused. "No. I just thought the couch would be a good place, so you'll be out of the way when we start filming."

"Out of the way?" Nan yells. "Listen here, girl, this is my house too, and I'm not planning on getting out of anyone's way. I've got things to say!"

Ashley looks and me and I explain, "Nan wants in on the action."

"I guess she can stand next to you." Before she can even finish her sentence, Nan jumps up and is the first to take her place. Let the show begin!

Coleslaw and Stability

Sam cancels our dinner plans because he needs to stay late to monitor a heart patient. "Mrs. Jenkins had surgery today, and I want to sit with her as long as I can."

"She's lucky to have you," I say, even though I'm totally disappointed. Mrs. Jenkins was the grade school lunch lady when we were growing up. She always gave Sam extra coleslaw. By doing so, she won his undying devotion. I'm sure he would have taken excellent care of her either way, but you feed a kid his favorite food, especially when it's a weird food for a kid to like, and you have a champion for life.

"How did it go today?" he asks.

"Oh my God, you don't want to know."

"That bad?"

I don't want to give Sam the satisfaction of thinking he was right about me doing this show, because he wasn't. I answer, "Everyone from HHTV is great. It's just that Nan's gotten it into her head she's the star. She's interrupting every take by going off script and monopolizing the scene." I add, "It's thrown us off schedule. Ashley says if I can't rein her in, she won't be allowed to be there when we film."

"I'm sure that's going to go over like a lead balloon."

"I haven't told her, yet. Poor Nan is so excited they're here, what with it being her idea and all, I don't want to rain on her parade."

"If it gets too bad, she can come hang out at the hospital with me. I can put her in the break room with a TV remote, or she can visit with anyone who wants the company. She probably knows everyone here."

I laugh. "Oh yeah, I'm sure she'd rather be at our local hospital with a bunch of sick people than on television with Jeremy and Josh."

"You underestimate my draw. I'm willing to bet your grandmother would way prefer my company to those pretty boys." He sounds annoyed like I don't think he's as exciting as the Renovation Brothers. The green-eyed monster of jealousy looms like a storm cloud.

"I know *I'd* rather be with you, but those guys are the reason my new business is going to launch with a boom, so I'm grateful to have them here." I'm trying to assure him there's no reason for him to be jealous while still affirming the rightness of my decision. It's quite the tightrope walk, let me tell you.

"Fine."

"What's that supposed to mean?" I demand.

"It means, fine. Enjoy your time in the spotlight." He's making it sound like I'm doing something indecent.

"Sam, I thought we were past this. I thought you understood why it was important for me to do this show."

"Just let me know if you need me to cover Nan for you."

Right now, I don't want him doing anything for me. He

cancels plans and poops on my renovation parade. Quite frankly, he's not giving me the support I need.

His voice suddenly softens, catching me off guard as he says gently, "I missed you today, Kitty Cat. Any chance you can meet me in the hospital cafeteria for lunch tomorrow?"

"Nope. I'm supposed to be here in case anyone has any questions about what they're doing. I won't be free for three more days." Yes, I'm sticking my tongue out at the phone. I'm not sure I even want to see him right now, with the attitude he's flashing.

"In that case, maybe we can schedule another night for dinner. I'll call you tomorrow and check in."

"Fine," I reply. "I need to take everyone over to Sarah's and show them where they're staying."

"I love you, Kitty Cat. Sleep tight." I hang up with Sam without telling him I love him back. Not that I don't, I'm just a little piqued by his juvenile behavior. I need my loved ones to have my back.

Ashley walks into the kitchen and hands me three more sheets of paper. "We have a big day tomorrow if we're going to get back on schedule. Have you talked to your grandmother yet?"

I shake my head. "I haven't had a chance. I promise I'll do it tonight."

"I'm not trying to cause any trouble here, Cat, but as they say, time is money and we can't afford to lose either."

"Gotcha." I grab my keys. "I'll meet you out front and lead the way to Sarah's."

As soon as I reach my car, Jeremy waves, "Would you mind if I ride with you?"

"Not at all." I wait as he runs over and hops into the passenger side of my banana-yellow rental car. I still haven't gone car shopping yet. I need to make that a priority, but with the renovation, it's going to have to wait awhile longer.

I climb in and take a peek in Jeremy's direction. He doesn't look any different from how he looked nine hours ago. I can't help myself; I demand, "How can you still look so good after putting in a full day of work?"

He winks. "I've a got this great face mask I use every night. Seriously, it sucks every impurity out of my pores and makes me look fresh twenty-four-seven."

"I'm going to need the name of that mask," I semi-joke.

He asks, "What in the world made you leave the Big Apple to move back to the house you grew up in?"

I explain it all to him. I share the whole tale about Ethan and Sam and even mention that Ethan is staying at Sarah's to reboot his thinking and hopefully help his ASD. Then I tell him about Nan's aneurysm and how it forced me to prioritize my life.

"Wow. You don't hear stories like that every day, do you?"

I shake my head. "Nope. But the truth is, I think I was always destined to come home. Not just because of Sam, but because I feel like me here. In New York I was always trying to be this bigger version of who I really am. You know what I mean?"

He doesn't respond right away but I see his shoulders slump a little as he finally replies, "I totally know what you mean. You don't get your own television show without becoming a different person. I mean, I'm essentially me, just not the same me I would have been if there weren't cameras around all the time."

"It must be hard."

"You're one of the few people who's ever thought that. Most think I should be upbeat and ready to go at a moment's notice, like I should always act like the person they see on television. It's plain exhausting."

"How about Josh? Does he feel the same way?"

"Not really. You've spent some time with him now, so you know he's naturally more reserved than I am. He keeps pretty true to himself."

"How did you guys end up in this business anyway?"

He answers, "We grew up in a construction family, so we came by our love of renovating honestly. In college, I took a theater class and got hooked on the acting bug. After Jeremy and I graduated, we shared an apartment in Wrigleyville for a few years. I auditioned for commercials and plays while he worked as an accountant. Then one day, I met a casting agent who started asking me all kinds of questions. When I told her about growing up with a contractor for a father, she asked if I'd ever wanted to follow in my dad's footsteps. Once she heard I had a twin brother, she told me about a program she was casting for HHTV. The rest is history. We've been doing this show for nearly six years now."

"Do you guys still live in Chicago?"

"That's where we're based. Although thirty weeks out of the year we're filming all over the country. During that time, we're only home on weekends."

"It must be hard to date with a schedule like that."

"It's give and take. Right now, I'm taking the money and all the stability it offers. Hopefully somewhere down the line, it'll lead to finding the right person to spend my life with."

I'm enjoying getting to know Jeremy. He seems like a really good guy and I hope he gets everything he's searching for. In the meantime, I'm grateful for what he's doing to help me make my dream come true. I'm just not sure my relationship with Sam is going to come out of this unscathed. I don't know what his problem is, but I do know I need him to get on board with my dream.

Compost to Mushrooms

Sarah runs out of her house as soon as she sees our little convoy pull up. Jeremy and I lead the way, with Ashley and Josh behind us, and the camera crew picking up the rear. My friend's arms are flapping in the breeze and she calls out, "YAY!!! You're finally here!"

Jeremy laughs, "She's pretty excitable, huh?"

"Not normally, no. Sarah's the most chill person I've ever met." I hop out of the car and hug my friend. "You back on caffeine or something?"

She performs a little dance. "No. Ethan's had a breakthrough and I'm just super-jazzed about it!"

"What breakthrough?"

She doesn't answer my question. Instead, she calls out, "Ethan, come out here." My ex opens the front door and there he stands wearing two things I have never seen him in before. The first is a pair of sweatpants. Ethan's always claimed sweatpants were the clothing equivalent of Fritos. Which essentially means he finds no value in them.

I couldn't disagree more on both accounts, but I digress.

The second item is by far the more surprising. It's a red

sweater. Ethan hates red. It makes him feel anxious and nervous. In fact, my red afghan is part of what led to our breakup. Turns out he took it off the sofa and hid it in the closet whenever I was away. I felt like he was hiding me before I understood it was the color he couldn't handle.

I call out, "Ethan, you're wearing red!" I'm so excited I totally ignore the HHTV group—and the fact that I've been trying to keep my distance from him. I run up to him and throw my arms around him.

He hugs back tentatively—as he doesn't like to be touched a lot— and unsuccessfully tries to stifle his emotion. "It's amazing, right?"

"How did you do it?"

"Sarah had me go through a bunch of colored film sheets until she found one as close to red as I could tolerate. It was a kind of burgundy. Anyway, for the last few days, she's had me carry it around and when I saw an uncomfortable shade of red, I'd put it up in front of my eyes, so the color was muted. My brain seems to have adjusted so now it mutes the color on its own."

I look at my friend and gush, "YOU are amazing!"

"It's true, I am," she answers with a laugh. "But I swear I've never used this technique before. My spirit guide, Taraz, told me about it, so I knew it would work." *Taraz is a genius.* I've always poo-pooed some of my friend's more out-there beliefs, but I'm starting to think there might just be something to this otherworldly instructor of hers.

I finally realize Ashley, Jeremy, Josh, and the two camera guys are all waiting, staring at us. I say, "Sarah, Ethan, this is Ashley,

Jeremy, Josh, Ben, and Tyler. They're from *Renovation Brothers*."
Then I add, "This is Sarah, my best friend from childhood and
my … um … Ethan." I had told Jeremy that Ethan was my ex,
but it felt weird saying it in front of a group of people. I don't
want to make him feel any more uncomfortable than he must be.

Sarah jumps down from her porch steps and announces,
"Follow me and I'll show you the yurts." She opens the door of
the first one and ushers us all in. "I've started all the wood stoves,
so the temperature should stay around 65 degrees inside even
though it's twenty-eight outside. If you get too hot, just turn
down the thermostat nob. The whole room is only sixteen feet
across, so it holds its heat well."

She walks to the far corner and motions for everyone to look
behind the screen. "Each yurt has a compostable toilet. If you're
doing a number one, proceed as usual, but if you have to poop,
you have to flip this handle on the side and then shovel a scoop
of sawdust on top when you're done. The toilet will do the rest."

Ashley visibly pales. "What about toilet paper? Do we just,
you know, throw it in the toilet?"

Sarah nods. "Yup. It'll break down."

The younger of the two cameramen, Tyler, asks, "What do
you do with all the waste?"

"I empty it between guests. If the guests are male, I pour the
urine on the blueberry bushes because it has a higher acid content
than female urine and the blueberries really love it. Otherwise I
just add it to the compost heap."

Remind me to never eat Sarah's blueberries again. Blurgh.

Ashley cringes. "Do you use the compost in your garden?"

"I have a special hole dug for human waste. I'll let it age for

107

about five years, adding organic elements like straw and peat moss. Then I'll burn it with some dried leaves. After that, it'll make its way into the farm compost." She sees the look on Ashley's face and adds, "Human manure is very beneficial to the soil when processed correctly. And let's face it, poop is poop, right? I mean, we don't think twice about using steer manure. Why should we be freaked out by human waste?"

Josh speaks for the first time since we arrive. "I think it's pretty cool you do this. I'd like to look around a bit during daylight hours, if you don't mind."

"I'd love to show you around," Sarah gushes like a proud mother. She finishes her tour by explaining how the electricity is hooked up to the solar battery at the main house. She assures everyone the rain catchers are attached to a water heater, so they can have a hot bath if they choose. "Every yurt has a hip bath." She indicates a three-quarters metal tub like they used in old western movies.

Jeremy, Josh, and Ashley all have their own yurts, and Ben and Tyler share one. Once everyone's moved their luggage into their lodgings, my friend announces, "You're welcome to follow me to the café for dinner. I made a vegetarian welcome feast."

Over a meal of warm goat cheese salads dressed in a vinaigrette made from dried mushrooms (which Sarah foraged herself), a butternut quinoa stew, and hot naan bread, we celebrate the end of the first day of filming. It could only get better from here, right?

Day Two

People have vastly different reactions to being in front of a television camera. Some fear it like a Sasquatch intent on giving them a full body hug after a long hot summer. Others turn into seventh graders, determined to steal the attention for themselves. I cite all the YouTube videos where perfectly upstanding citizens feel the need to sneak behind news reporters on location and perform lewd hand gestures hoping for a cheap laugh.

At seven thirty on the dot, my parents park in the driveway. My father jumps out of the passenger side holding a medium-size taxidermied beaver posed to look like it's chewing on a stump of wood. "Good morning, lass! We're here to rescue you."

I expected my dad to be in full Scottish chieftain regalia, so I'm not surprised by his kilt, but the beaver? "What's up with your little friend, Dad? I thought we were ridding the place of your entourage."

"You mean Chip here? I brought him along for good luck." He explains, "I doubt this old homestead has ever been creature-free and I thought you could use a little good fortune." How a dead beaver equals good luck is beyond me, but whatever, things can't get worse.

My mom hops out of the driver's side as she pops open the trunk with her remote. She's wearing a grass skirt and God knows what else under her winter coat. "You on your way to a luau?" I ask nervously.

She laughs merrily. "You mean my pa'u? I just found it and thought I'd bring it over to show Nan. I have my real clothes on underneath." She pulls a large plastic container out of the back and joins us on the porch.

"What did you bring?" I ask hoping to all that's holy it's not haggis.

"Just some pecan tassies and shortbread. I thought we could make those TV people forget about Nan's unruly behavior yesterday."

"Nice, Mom, thanks." I take the container out of her hands. "Why don't you come in and have some breakfast. The crew isn't due to arrive for another thirty minutes."

Mom steps over the threshold and stops dead in her tracks. "It's very strange to see this old place empty. Kind of sad and exciting at the same time."

Dad pushes her through the door and begins to look around for the perfect location for Chip. He tries him on the stairs, then moves him to the fireplace. He even places him on the couch for a moment before picking him back up and tucking him under his arm. "Ah, the right place will come to me. It always does."

In the kitchen he puts his furry friend on the table next to Mom's cookies before heading to the stove to fry up some eggs. "You have a toaster, honey?"

"Mom left me three just in case. I think the stainless steel one with the black trim actually works."

He pulls out the toaster and busies himself gathering eggs and the like out of the refrigerator. "Too bad you had to give the hens away. I always like fresh eggs in the morning."

"They're only on loan to Sarah until I can have a hen house built. I can't keep the girls in the barn while renovations are happening, and certainly not once the events begin."

"Too true, dear, they'd be too nervous to lay eggs there," my mom says. "What about Heather? Is she coming home at some point?"

Heather is my parents eighteen-year-old donkey who performs no necessary farm task other than beautifying the landscape. "I won't have any place to keep her, Mom. Mr. Ryan, next door, says he'll hang on to her. She's keeping his old horse, Marvin, company."

Nan walks in looking remarkably normal for her. She's wearing slacks and a wool sweater. She glares at me, "Is this boring enough for your fancy television people?" Then she shakes her head forlornly. "Not that they're even going to let me be on the TV."

"Nan, it's not my decision." I feel horrible saying this to her as she so desperately wants to be in on everything. "The producers only want so much interaction with us, and I'm sorry to say, most of it is with me because I'm the one who owns the house."

She scoffs and mumbles, "Just a bunch of filthy Sassenach know-it-alls. Probably couldn't find their own arses with two hands and a map."

I giggle under my breath. I love sassy Nan. Unfortunately, she's getting in the way of real progress and that won't do. I'd be lying if I said I wasn't nervous that this sudden good behavior of hers wasn't going to create a bigger boomerang of acting out. Thank God my parents are here to intervene.

Bloody Band Aids and Hitler

When the *Renovation Brothers* crew arrives, they have Sarah and Ethan in tow. Sarah, I wouldn't mind, but what is my ex doing with her? My left eye begins to twitch involuntarily. More people getting in the way is the last thing we need right now.

While the TV folks head straight out to the barn, my friend comes into the kitchen and drops a tray of flax seed muffins next to my mom's goodies. Then she removes her coat and instructs, "Ethan, take your shoes off and go on out back. Walk through the field for a while. I'll call you when it's time to come in."

"Sar, I'm surprised to see you here." Then I lean in and whisper, "Why in the world did you bring *him* with you?" I point to Ethan.

"Jeremy and Josh invited us. They thought it might be fun for us to witness the action firsthand."

My whole family watches as Ethan obeys Sarah's orders. Other than Nan, they weren't rude to him over Thanksgiving. They just didn't think he was right for me, which is why they bent over backwards to throw Sam in my path. They all seem a bit uncomfortable to have my ex around.

When the back door slams, Sarah senses the change in

atmosphere and says, "Ethan is doing fine. He's better off without you, Cat." My eyebrows lift in question and she explains, "You were enabling him to maintain a semi-comfortable life without getting the help he needed. Ultimately, it would have all come crashing down on him."

"What would have?" Nan demands.

"His world, Nan," she answers. "If people don't face their problems, they're just putting Band-Aids on gaping wounds. That only masks the problem. You have to address the injury from within for permanent healing to occur."

My dad says, "I feel bad for him."

My friend shakes her head. "Don't. He's making remarkable progress, which would have never happened if his life wasn't shaken up in a big way."

"Maybe you can introduce him to a nice girl, Sarah," my mom suggests.

"Sorry, Mrs. M. The last thing Ethan needs is a love interest. This is his time to focus on himself. When people are part of a couple, they automatically consider the other person's needs when making decisions. Ethan has to be completely selfish right now and only take care of Ethan."

"Why didn't you leave him at your farm?" I ask.

"He's vulnerable. I want him to always feel like he has support in this process. Leaving him alone wouldn't have helped him feel safe."

I want to ask why she didn't stay with him. I mean, heck, that seems like a better choice to me. Apparently, no one in my life, except Sam, can resist the lure of a television camera. And he's the one I really want here with me.

Jeremy and Josh come through the backdoor. Jeremy is all smiles. "Good morning!" He greets my parents, "You must be Mags and Dougal. Cat's told us all about you."

I did, too. Last night at Sarah's I spilled the beans and warned everyone to be on their guard with my parents. I have no idea what mischief they might get into, but being their child for over thirty years has definitely taught me something out of the ordinary is bound to occur.

My mom greets him with a hug and my dad shakes his hand enthusiastically. Josh steps forward almost shyly and puts his hand out, "Josh."

My mom nearly mauls him and gushes, "The dark brooding type always gets me right here!" She beats on her solar plexus like a female Tarzan.

My dad claps him on the shoulder and confesses, "It's true. I used to be just like you before marriage and kids turned me gray." Josh seems to take it all in stride. He's been warned.

Ashley walks into the kitchen and it starts to feel a bit crowded. She greets my parents and announces, "Here's the drill. We start filming in twenty minutes. Cat, we'll need you by the front door to retake yesterday's opening scene. Everyone else can stay in here or the living room, but we're going to need you to maintain absolute silence. We have a lot to do today." She casts a meaningful look at Nan.

My grandmother purposefully ignores her by turning her head, but not before saying, "Hitler was bossy, too."

CUT!!!

Camera pans to the door as Cat opens it.

Cat: Welcome to my farm.

Jeremy: Thanks! What a cool place.

Josh: Seriously, we can't remember the last time we renovated a barn. We're totally excited.

Brothers walk in and take off their ...

"CUT!" Ashley yells. "Mr. Masterton, *what* are you doing?"

"Just running upstairs to use the bathroom, lass."

"Sir," the producer explains, "we're right in the middle of a take. I thought I told you all to stay out of the scene."

"Can't stop a runaway train!" He continues his mad dash up the stairs.

"Can't he use the bathroom under the stairs?" Ashley asks no one in particular.

My mom answers this one. "He could, honey, but the water pressure isn't very strong in there"—her meaning hanging heavily in the air.

Ashley looks at my family and announces, "No one move. No one say a word. Okay?" They nod their heads mutely.

"Take two!"

Camera pans to the open door as Cat opens it.
Cat: Welcome to my farm.
Jeremy: Thanks! What a cool place.
Josh: Seriously, we can't remember the last time we …

"FLUSH!" my dad shouts from above our heads.

"CUT!!!" Ashley yells. "Mr. Masterton, will you please come down here?"

My dad peeks at her as he tentatively descends the stairs. "Sorry about that."

"Listen, we don't have time for all these distractions. I need everyone who's not part of the crew to leave the house. Cat, you stay." When no one moves, she barks, "NOW!"

I smile contritely and offer, "I'm sorry about this."

Ashley raises her hand like she really needs me to quit talking, so I do. When we hear the backdoor slam, she says, "Okay, third and final take. We're using this one no matter what."

Everything goes according to script until I look out the window next to the front door and see Chip peeking in through the bottom pane. I nearly burst out laughing. Luckily, I'm able to contain myself until Ben, the cameraman yells, "Aaand scene!"

There is no way I'm going to tell Ashley what my dad was doing out there. After all, she said she was using this take no matter what, so there's no point upsetting her any more than she already is.

I'm not in the second scene where Jeremy and Josh walk down the path to the barn. I call everyone back into the kitchen to threaten them with bodily harm if they don't straighten up. But as soon as they walk in the door my dad apologizes, "I'm so sorry, lass. I'll never do it again."

"What's that dad? You'll never run through a scene again or you'll never have Chip peek in the windows?"

"You saw that, did you?" he asks with a proud air.

Unable to stop myself, I start laughing. "Yes, I saw it. Thank God, Ashley didn't though." Then I try to look serious. "I can't afford to have them back out of this renovation."

My mom reaches over to take my hand and gives it a reassuring squeeze. "Don't you worry, honey. Now that we know how this is supposed to go, we won't cause any more trouble. Will we, Dougal?" she adds with a pointed look at my father.

Just as I start to feel like the bumpy start of the day is behind us, I hear Ashley yell, "Cut! Ethan, get out of the path and put your shoes on! What's wrong with you people?"

Nan looks oddly pleased with herself. She smiles smugly and sits down to help herself to some shortbread. "Looks like I'm not the problem anymore."

When the Boys Roam Free

Once Ethan's back in the house warming up his feet, the rest of the morning rolls by without complication. When I go out to the barn, I'm amazed by how much demo has already taken place. The horse stalls have been torn down, as has most of the loft. When I question why that is, I learn the upstairs is going to be repositioned toward the back of the barn, so the front two thirds can be vaulted. It will show off the original beams while making the space feel incredibly large.

All the wood is being saved, and the planks in good enough shape will be repurposed and used for tables and benches.

Right before lunch, Ashley approaches my father and says, "We'd like to film a scene with you and the brothers, Mr. Masterton. We're going to use it as a teaser for the episode." All previous upset seems to have been forgiven, if not forgotten.

My dad is delighted by the suggestion. "Why, thank you, lass. I'd love to chat with the boys on camera."

"Do you have a script you'd like him to follow?" I ask. I hope the answer is yes because heaven knows what my dad will say without guidance.

Ashley shakes her head. "No, we'll just wing it and use the

good bits." God help us.

HHTV has a craft services budget which allows us to cater meals in every day. Sarah feeds the crew breakfast at her place and from now on we'll be serving lunch and dinner here at the house. I've asked Emily Rickle from the hospital to do the honors. If I'm going to suggest her as a potential caterer for future clients, I need to make sure she's up to the task.

Emily is on the quiet side, but she's remarkably competent in the kitchen. While she's laying out various salads and sandwiches on the counter, she announces, "There's a pot of sweet basil and tomato soup on the stove for anyone interested. The drinks are on the counter next to the sink."

Nan sidles up to Ashley and demands, "When do you want to film my segment?"

"I don't think we're going to need you, Mrs. McTavish," the producer answers curtly. Clearly, she's not forgiven Nan for the upset she caused yesterday.

I intervene before my grandmother is the source of any bloodshed. "I'm sure they'll use you in the big reveal, Nan, if not before." I send Ashley a look over Nan's head that suggests she should go along with this statement if she wants to keep my grandmother out of her hair.

She nods her head tentatively. "Absolutely. We have fun plans for the final scene that include the entire family."

Nan seems temporarily placated and goes downstairs to take a nap.

"Mom, don't you need to go home and unpack?"

She shakes her head. "If your dad is staying, so am I. I'm not doing all the work by myself."

"Sarah, don't you need to get Ethan back to the farm for a sweat lodge or flogging of some sort?"

"Nope. We're good."

Jeremy sidles up to me, "Relax. They're a hoot. Plus, it's a lot of fun watching them tick off Ashley."

"I thought you liked Ashley."

He shrugs his shoulders in response. "I do, about eighty percent of the time. She just gets tightly wound sometimes, and it's fun to watch her squirm."

"You've got a devil on your shoulder, don't you?"

He winks. "Maybe. But hey, this job can get dull. You wouldn't believe some of the boring people we renovate for. You can't begrudge us some fun with your family."

"As long as you don't go so far that Ashley quits the project before it's completed. I need this renovation for my new business."

"Josh and I are the executive producers as well as the stars. Ashley works for us. If we say the project is a go, it's a go."

I exhale. "Okay. Just promise me you won't encourage them. They're outrageous enough on their own."

He winks across the room at my dad while answering, "Don't I know it. Dougal couldn't wait to tell us what he's wearing under his plaid."

I feel my face turn red. "Oh my God, not that whole bit about letting his boys roam free?"

He mimics my father, "Ah lass, you can't go wrong when you go native." Then he adds, "He's offered to lend us some tartans for the segment we're shooting with him."

I shake my head in response. "You think that's going to work for your show?"

"Not the way it's currently structured. But Josh and I have plans to liven things up a little and move into a younger demographic. The network is trying to court viewers in the twenty-five to thirty-five age group. We think the wacky Masterton family might just be our path to making that happen."

I feel my stomach drop to my knees. They have no idea the can of worms they're opening.

The Doodle Sack

Ashley and the brothers have a network meeting in Chicago today, so we have a day off from filming. It's a relief, as the pressure of a household full of people and construction noise is starting to take its toll on my normally cheerful disposition.

Coincidentally, as soon as I told Sam we weren't shooting today, he suddenly became free to come over. It's possible it's a fluke, but I'm a little suspicious as this is the first time he could fit me into his busy schedule all week. I'm trying hard not to be annoyed by this.

When I wake up, the house is blissfully quiet. Nan is either sleeping in or watching television in her room. I told my parents and Sarah that under pain of death they are not to come over today. I need a break from the chaos, plain and simple.

The good news is the barn is looking amazing and they're only four days into the reno. At this rate, they'll be ready to take on the kitchen in a few more weeks.

There's a knock on the back door while I'm heating up a couple of sesame seed bagels in the toaster. I turn and my heart melts to see Sam's gorgeous face pressed against the glass. It's nearly impossible to stay mad at this guy. His intense baby blues alone are enough for me to surrender all rational thought.

I open the door and greet, "Hey, stranger, glad you could stop by."

He pulls a bouquet of tulips from behind his back and gives me puppy-dog eyes. "Don't be mad. I took unscheduled days off work to help your folks move, and I needed to pay back some favors. Otherwise, I would have been here a lot sooner."

No fair! He's turning this around on me. I pull him in for a welcome smooch because let's face it, I haven't seen him in three-and-a-half days, and I really need a fix. I inhale the freshness of his minty breath and the spicy citrus of his aftershave. A wave of hormones rushes over me like a tsunami bent on destruction. I want to devour this man for breakfast and keep going until I've had my fill.

As I wrap one leg around his waist, with the other about to join it, he pushes me back slightly and gasps, "Cat, if you keep doing that, I'm not going to want to stop."

I'm not sure I want him to stop. My parents have finally moved out, Ethan is out of the picture for good, and my business plans are heading in the right direction. Now might be the perfect time to jump in with both feet and throw caution to the wind by celebrating my rediscovered feelings for my first love.

Before I can give him the green light, Nan walks in. She takes one look at the scene in front of her, checks out Sam from head to toe before briefly stopping at the hem of his shirt, and announces, "Looks like someone's happy to see me."

Sam blushes. "Nan! That's not something you should even be thinking, let alone saying."

"Psh, you kids think you invented sex. I'll have you know, I was doing the horizontal hokey pokey long before you were even in a glint in your father's eye."

"Horizontal hokey pokey?" I blurt out.

"Unless you prefer riding the bologna pony or dipping the corn dog," she continues. Sam and I are rendered completely mute, which she takes as encouragement. "Of course, there's always Mr. Wobbly hides his helmet, the slap-and-tickle, or souring the kraut."

A horror-induced burst of laugher escapes me. "Nan, stop it!"

She waves a dismissive hand in my direction. "What is it with you kids? Just because someone is old and gray and gets a touch of the rheumatiz, you think they were never vital or sexual. I'll have you know, your grandfather and I used to dip the wick three times a week, and that was after your mother went away to college."

I'm torn between pure jealousy and a disgust so intense I may never be able to eat bologna or corn dogs again, not to mention sauerkraut.

The amorous mood in the kitchen has most definitely been killed. Sam no longer looks happy to see anyone and Nan settles down at the kitchen table like she's going to be there for a while. She pulls her crossword puzzle book out of her robe and says, "I need a ten letter Old English word for bagpipes. Actually, I think it's two words."

"That seems like one you should know, Nan," I answer.

"You'd think. But the truth is I can't remember what I ate for dinner last night. Help me out."

"You had pork chops, homemade apple sauce, and green beans."

"That's not what I meant! What's the word I'm looking for?"

Sam speaks up, "Doodle sack."

Nan beams. "Yup, that's it. Doodle sack fits perfectly." Then she looks up mischievously and asks, "Don't you just love when the doodle sack fits?"

The Taj Mabarn

Despite his previous behavior, Sam can't help but be impressed with the progress on the barn. He lets out a long whistle before saying, "This place is going to look awesome!"

I walk him around, showcasing how I imagine everything looking when it's all finished. There's going to be a large bar toward the back that will hide a prep area for the caterers. They'll be able to store extra plates, silverware, glassware, and bins for bussing dirty dishes. You know, all the stuff they won't want to run into the kitchen to get every time they need it.

Pointing to the far-left wall, I say, "The stairs for the loft will be there. We'll use it for storage for chairs, linens, candles, and other odds and ends."

Then I show him the pictures of the wagon wheel chandeliers we're ordering. They're designed to look like candle light, even though they'll be electric. "Aren't they gorgeous? We'll have five hanging down from the center vault, so they'll still be a good ten feet above everyone's heads when they're standing."

"I'd imagined a more rustic look, but you're going to have the Taj Mahal of barns by the time you're done here," he exclaims.

"That's the plan. I want this to be the most elegant outbuilding our side of the Mississippi." Then I show him where they're putting in a stone fireplace—dead center on the right wall. "It's going to be big enough to roast a boar for country-style events, and for fancier affairs, it'll throw enough heat that ladies can wear strapless dresses in the dead of winter."

"This is really impressive. How many tables can you fit in here?"

"We can comfortably fit fifteen seventy-two-inch rounds, which will easily seat a hundred and fifty people, or we can run three rows of long banquette tables all the way to the bar which will accommodate a hundred and eighty. We can squeeze in more if they don't want a dance floor."

"Where are the guests going to park?"

"They're going to clear a half acre on the side of the property for a parking lot."

"I'm kind of speechless."

I squeal, "I know. It's totally exciting!" Then I pull his sleeve and tell him how we're going to knock out french doors on the left side of the barn that will bring in natural lighting and offer ventilation. "They're going to pour ten feet of concrete all the way around the building and extend the roof, so the area is covered, creating a transitional space. We'll use it for dancing or extra seating in warmer weather. I think when I have pictures taken for the brochure, I'll have it set up with tall cocktail tables and hanging fuchsia baskets to create a perfect balance that will appeal to people hosting all kinds of events."

His shakes his head. "You're going to single-handedly boost the economy of our little town. You know that?"

My heart fills to the point of bursting. "I sure hope so. I figure all the parties will need caterers, flowers, musicians, parking attendants, bartenders, and servers. That should be an easy twenty people right there. I'll have the tables, chairs, basic china, glassware, silverware, and linens already here. That way I can make the money on the rentals and they won't have to be schlepped in from Champaign or Bloomington."

"What if you can't get enough parties to support this kind of space?"

I smack his arm. "That's what the TV show is doing here. Not only are they saving me two-thirds the cost of renovating, but they're going to get the word out, and this big, gorgeous place is going to start booking the minute the show airs."

He looks a little overwhelmed, which I totally get. This *is* a major endeavor. I add, "Worst case scenario, no one wants to have their party here and we fill it back up with animals."

He shakes his head. "Everyone is going to want to have their event here. This is amazing, Cat. I'm impressed by the scale of what you're doing."

"Do you finally understand why I need the Renovation Brothers to take this project on?"

He doesn't seem happy about it, but he seems to realize the importance of me doing this TV show. He answers, "I do. I really do."

"So, you're going to come around and meet everyone and be a part of the fun?"

He looks like I've just asked him to eat a huge plate of haggis and wash it down with a pint of pig's blood. Instead of answering my question, he takes my hand and sighs. "I love you, Cat."

My stomach lurches like I've just eaten old sushi. I know he loves me, that's not what I was asking. What in the world is Sam's problem? I can't for the life of me figure out why he can't support my dream. And more importantly, if he can't support me in this, is he going to abandon me at other times when I need him? I love him and I know he loves me, but I'm beginning to have doubts about our long-term future together if this is the way he's going to act.

The Show Must Go On

Sam and I wound up having a nice weekend, despite the fact that he's been acting like a poop. We drove through the countryside and had brunch at a darling place in Urbana. I even managed to forget all the excitement happening at my house for a couple hours.

Sarah and Ethan aren't with the crew when they come back this morning. Thank God. If I'm honest, it's been a little stressful having Ethan around so much.

I don't see Ashley anywhere, so I find Jeremy and demand, "Did she quit? Is my family really that bad?"

"No and no. It turns out the network likes the direction Josh and I want to take this episode and Ashley does not. She feels the formula we have works, so why would we upset the apple cart?"

"So, she quit?"

He shakes his blond head. "Again, she didn't quit. Josh and I asked for a week with a different producer who hasn't worked on our show before, in order to fully present our new vision to the network. We've given Ash the week off. If HHTV likes the footage, we'll give her the opportunity to come back on board and finish out the season, but in the way we want."

"OMG, you fired her?"

"You're a lot of work, woman. Would you just relax and let us work our magic?"

I sigh. "I like Ashley."

"Why? I mean I like her too, but what's she done to make you such a fan?"

"I don't know. I guess I feel a sisterhood with her. We're around the same age, living in the same part of the country, working in fields that aren't considered the norm. Plus, she picked my farm over others who would have loved to have had their houses chosen."

Jeremy points and says, "There's our new producer now. Tad, get over here!" he yells out.

A young guy, probably in his mid-twenties, heads our way. His level of *hipsterness* makes the Renovation Brothers look like cavemen. Seriously, he has an immaculately groomed beard and mustache. There's enough mousse in the front of his hair to sculpt a four-inch pompadour and he's wearing cropped pants with loafers. He's also sporting rimmed glasses that may or may not actually have a prescription. He's the kind of guy that has people my grandmother's age worrying about leaving the world in the hands of a younger generation.

Tad throws out his hand in enthusiasm. "Heya, I'm Tad. *Hundo P* excited to be here!"

At my confused expression, he explains, "Hundred percent, totes stoked, TBH I'm like, so sure, we're gonna hit this one out of the ballpark, I can taste it."

I take his hand briefly and give it a slight shake. "Great! Listen, you see that old lady over there?" I point to Nan. "You totes have to go meet her."

When he walks away, I turn to Jeremy and demand, "What's he smoking?"

"Ah, come on, you know how it is with kids these days. You've got to look beyond their fashion and language to find the brilliance."

I snort. "I thought I was young. This guy makes me feel like I'm a hundred. Or should I say a hundo?" I roll my eyes for emphasis.

Josh walks over and hands me a paper bag. "Sarah asked me to give this to you."

I take it having no idea what's inside and say, "Thanks. How are you doing, Josh? Are you as excited as Jeremy is about Tad the Rad?"

As I've mentioned before, Josh is way more reserved than his brother, so I'm taken aback when he laughs out loud and answers, "He's not as big of a doofus as you might think. Let him do his thing and I promise you won't be disappointed."

It appears that Tad's first mission, to endear himself to my grandmother, is successful. I thought Nan would turn him into a trembling mass of drool, but he has her laughing her head off at something. I feel like I'm standing in the middle of that old fifty's series, *The Twilight Zone*.

When the brothers walk away, I open the brown paper bag from my friend. Inside is a bunch of dried herbs wrapped tightly with twine to hold them together. There's a note that says: *This is for the barn. I'll explain later this morning when I get there.*

Damn! Sarah's coming back, which means Ethan will be here, too. Add Nan, my parents, and Tad, and I'm starting to wonder where I can go to get away from everyone. I decide to head into town while they set up the first scene. Maybe I'll stop by the hospital to see Sam.

Maybe his reticence about coming to the house has nothing to do with me. Maybe he's afraid of cameras or something. God knows he wasn't growing up, but people change. I resolve to give him the benefit of the doubt and try not to be irritated. I'm almost positive that's the right move.

Lies and Slips

I stop at the hospital cafeteria to grab a cup of coffee before calling Sam to let him know I'm here. I run into Emily and share, "The crew loves the meals you've been bringing us."

She smiles brightly. "I'm glad. I really enjoy catering. I'm ready to do more than work in a hospital cafeteria."

"I'll throw a couple smaller parties your way when we start out to see how you do with crowds. If you're comfortable with those, we can move you up to full-scale weddings. You know, the kind with a dozen bridesmaids and groomsmen?"

She claps her hands together in excitement. "I can't wait!" Then she asks, "Are you here to see Sam?"

"Yup. I had a few minutes to kill so I thought I'd stop by and say hi."

"I saw him in the parking lot. He was leaving when I pulled in twenty minutes ago."

I grab my coffee and move out of line to give him a quick call. The phone rings twice before I hear his sexy voice. "Hey, babe, what's up?"

"I stopped by the hospital to see if you wanted to hang out for a few minutes."

Before I can say anything else, he answers, "I'm swamped right now. Mr. Philips broke his hip this morning and I'm keeping him company while his wife grabs a bite to eat. Sorry about that. Call or text before you come next time, and I'll let you know if I'm available."

"Sooooo, you're here at the hospital?" I ask.

"Course I am. Where else would I be?"

I have no idea. According to Emily, he's left the building. According to Sam he's still here. "Um, okay then. Let's catch up later. Bye." I hit END.

My stomach starts to roll around like I'm on a raft in a category-five hurricane. I want to know what's going on, but I don't want to alert Sam I'm having trust issues. That's why I don't go upstairs in search of answers. If he's there, he'll wonder what I'm doing there after telling me he was busy. If he's not there, someone else might mention I stopped by, and he'll know I caught him in a lie. That's why I head out to the hospital parking lot.

I drive slowly up and down the aisles looking for either Sam's SUV or his parents' old truck, Betty. No luck. In a fit of pure crazy, I decide to go by his house to see if he's home. His car isn't there, either. That's when I become a borderline stalker/infuriated girlfriend and decide to drag Main Street looking for him.

On the third block I spot him. He's parked right in front of Betsy's diner. He could have told me he was there, and I would have come to meet him. I park in the first empty spot I see, so I can go in and find out why he lied to me.

Peeking through the front window, I scan the crowd. Once I'm through the door, I begin to feel light-headed, almost like

I'm having an out-of-body experience. I'm sure Sam must be at the counter because it's busy this time of morning. Most tables are taken by couples or larger groups of people. When I don't see him there, I glance around the main dining room. Luckily, I spy him before he sees me because he's not alone. Sam's sitting with a woman. Her back is to me, and they're both leaning toward the center of the table in a very cozy tableau, which of course makes me wonder what in the heck is going on.

Part of me wants to storm over there and go all single-white-female on them, but Sam spots me before I can. He jumps up and rushes to my side. "Cat, what are you doing here?" He sounds nervous, and rightly so. I just caught him in a mother of a lie.

He leans in as though to kiss me, but I push him away. "What am I doing here? What are you doing here?" I demand. "I thought you were tied up with Mr. Philips."

"I am. I mean, I was. I mean, I had this appointment with a drug rep, then I'm heading right back to the hospital after I grab a quick bite to eat."

"Why didn't you say that on the phone? Why lie?" I demand.

"I just figured it would save time." He seems super nervous.

I stare him down trying to discern if this is another untruth, or if he's on the level. "If you lie about small things Sam, you're sure to lie about bigger ones. I don't like liars."

He tries to grab my hands, but I put them in my pockets. "I ... I'm sorry, Cat. I really am."

"You should be," I say, before turning and storming away.

Once I'm back in my car, I sit for a moment trying to still my erratic heartbeat. Should I wait for Sam to come out? To what end? The only reason to wait is to get a better look at this drug rep. If that's what she really is. I only have Sam's word for it, and at the moment, that's not worth too much to me.

My phone pings as soon as I turn on the car, but I don't answer it. Once I have the heater turned up full blast—to warm the non-weather-related chill that's taken over my body—I check it out. It's from my mom:

We're going to be late coming over. Your dad fell on the ice at the new house, and I'm trying to get him up. Any chance you can pop by and help me?

I'm not sure what good I'd be. I'm a hundred and thirty pounds soaking wet with an alarmingly low muscle mass. But I text her back:

On my way. My decision has been made for me.

Little does she know I'll be there in three minutes instead of thirteen because I'm already in town. I temporarily push my thoughts of Sam onto the back burner, and I say a silent prayer my dad hasn't seriously hurt himself. He's only sixty, but isn't that the time people start to slip and fall and break stuff, like Mr. Phillips ostensibly did? I wonder if our old gym teacher's hip is really broken and make a note to ask around.

Bruised Bums and Kitty Litter

My dad is sprawled out on his icy new driveway with his kilt flipped up above his knees. It's a good thing I arrive so quickly, or he might have gotten frost bite. When my mom sees me, she helps him adjust his tartan and calls out, "You got here fast."

I step out of my car and answer, "I was just up the road. Nan ran out of her tissues." No sense telling her what I was really up to. She'd only take Sam's side. After working so hard to get us back together, I can't see her wanting to believe the golden boy is a liar.

My dad looks like he's in a lot of pain. "What happened?" I ask as I get closer.

"I was just coming out to throw some kitty litter behind the tires, so your mom and I could get out of the driveway. I must have hit a patch of ice because I went down hard. Oh lass, I think I did a real job on my keister."

"Do you think you broke something?"

"No, but I'm sure to be black and blue for a good while."

I kneel next to him and ask my mom, "Can you run inside and get some of those rag rugs you used to keep in the laundry room?" Having grown up with firsthand stories of the Great

139

Depression, Nan had been taught to save every old sheet, piece of clothing, or dish towel that no longer provided its intended purpose. Her mother had instructed her how to weave these things together into rag rugs. My parents probably have forty of them in various sizes.

My mom jumps up. "On my way!"

She brings back five in short order and I lay three of them next to my dad. "Okay, try to move off the ice onto the rugs. If it hurts, stop."

He rolls over gingerly, without too much trouble. "That certainly feels a lot warmer on my bum. Thank you, lass."

"You know what else would be warmer on your bum?" I ask. "Underwear!" I'm not even kidding. My dad has an underwear aversion that just isn't normal. It wouldn't matter as much if he wore pants, but it's a little odd to have all his business hanging out under a skirt. It's not like he goes around showing it off. Just the knowledge is enough to make most people uncomfortable. And he makes sure to tell them.

As soon as he's situated on the rugs, I lay the other two on the spot he just vacated. "Okay, now see if you can get onto your knees. Mom and I can help you up from there."

With a few grumbles and groans, he follows instructions, and we're able to get him back on his feet in short order. I announce, "I think it's time you hire someone to come plow the drive."

My dad shakes his head. "Total waste of money. What's the point of shoveling out the snow when it's just going to fall again?"

"That same line of thinking makes me wonder why you bother to clean, when it's only going to get dirty again." Two things can happen here. Either my parents will agree with me and stop cleaning, or they'll realize shoveling the driveway isn't going to destroy all logical reasoning in their lives. Not that they're known for logical reasoning.

My mom sighs, "I just got a flyer on the door the other day from that Heinz boy. He's has himself a snowblower, and he wants to make money for his junior trip to Washington D.C."

My dad grunts but doesn't veto the idea. I guess a bruised butt is a small price to pay to avoid a bigger accident like a broken bone. I hope I have as easy a time healing my bruised ego. I don't know what's going on with Sam and the woman in the diner, but I'm sure as heck going to find out.

Burn, Baby, Burn

Tad is a whirlwind of energy. As soon as I pull into the driveway, I see him virtually leaping across the front yard toward the barn. It makes me miss Ashley. I liked seeing her non-bizarrely groomed self with clipboard in hand. It made me feel like this reno would go off without a hitch. Tad makes me nervous, like watching a toddler run with scissors and a lit firecracker.

When the new producer sees me, he changes course and does a little cha-cha-cha in my direction. "There she is!" he exclaims to the trees. "I was just about to call you. Are you ready for your scene?"

"I didn't think I had one until after lunch," I answer.

He looks confused before declaring, "Ah, old schedule. You left before I had a chance to give you the revised one."

I take the offered piece of paper and look it over. "It says here that Sarah and I are both in it. Does she know that?" So far, my friend hasn't been in front of the camera at all.

"She sure does! She's one groovy tassel."

"I'm sure she is," I answer. "Is there something special I should know about what we're shooting? Do you want me to change clothes or something?"

He eyes my leggings and old Pink Floyd T-shirt that once belonged to my dad. "You look totes deck."

I'm only thirty. Having recently moved here from New York City, you'd think I'd be cool enough to understand what this guy was talking about. But I worked in high-end party planning. Most of the hosts who employed me were over forty and exceptionally well-to-do. They were lawyers, traders, and third generation trust fund babies, not hipsters. To be perfectly honest, I don't really vibe with the whole scene. Hence my knowledge of hipster speak is pretty slim. That's why I have no idea if being "totes deck" is a good thing or not. But by the big thumbs up Tad flashes me, I'm going to guess it is.

Sarah and Ethan are on the porch. My ex is rocking back and forth on one of the chairs my parents left, reading a book. He doesn't even look up when I stand next to him. That's an Ethanism I'm used to. When he's left this world for the one between the covers of a good story, he's totally gone. I wish I could be more like that. I have to be virtually in a sound deprivation chamber in order to read.

Sarah greets, "Hey, chick, you ready to make some magic?"

"I guess. What are you going to be doing?"

"Didn't the Tadster tell you?"

"Nope."

"Where's the sack I sent over earlier?" she asks. I open my purse and hand it to her. She grabs it and announces, "Sage. We're gonna smudge the place and release any old energy that's trapped."

I'm familiar with the practice of smudging. I just thought it was something people did before moving into a new house. Not that I believe in it, but it's a nice idea, removing the old energy in a home to make way for the new. "Whose energy are we smudging? The animals?"

"The animals or whatever negative vibes might be filtering in from other dimensions."

"Other dimensions?"

"Yeah, you know, other planes that lay on top of ours. Ones we don't see because they vibrate at a different frequency."

Dear God. These people, whom I love, and have moved all the way home to be with, are making me feel insane. Sarah has always danced to her own tune, but she's gotten way crazier over the years. "Okay, so we're smudging the barn. How does that go exactly?"

"I say a little prayer to Mother Earth and implore her to help the sage absorb any negative energy and then cleanse it away through fire."

"Ooooookay. Anything else?"

"Yeah. Nan is going to say some Gaelic prayer, too. Tad thinks the Scottish element will add real flair."

I know how absurd this is going to look, but honestly, the marketing aspect is brilliant. This will not be a standard episode of *Renovation Brothers*, and it will most definitely have people talking, which is something I want. Because, if they're talking about my wackadoo family, then they'll be talking about my barn.

I briefly worry that I might lose some business from this exposure, as well. The world is full of ordinary people with pretty vanilla lives who might balk at my less-than-normal family. They might choose not to have their reception here as a result. But there's not a whole lot I can do about that.

That's why I don't say anything when Nan walks out of the house wearing her full Scottish holiday uniform of a long plaid skirt, white shirt, and vest. She flashes a nearly hysterical smile of excitement that she's getting back in front of the camera, and announces, "Let's get this party started!"

That's a Wrap!

Camera pans across the corn fields surrounding the Masterton barn.
Cut to Cat, Nan, and Sarah inside the barn with the bros.

Directions: No script. We want pure improvisation. Just smudge the crap out of that place and let yourselves be free!

Ashley would have had a heart attack if she read that. Who am I kidding? I could definitely benefit from a baby aspirin right about now. At least, I think aspirin is what they use to ward off cardiac arrest.

Jeremy and Josh are standing in the middle of the barn when we walk in. They look as adorable as ever. Sarah runs over to them and shakes her bag of sage. Then Tad calls out, "Okay everyone, take your places." Once we're situated, he calls, "Aaand action!"

Jeremy: So, Sarah, you're a friend of Cat's?

Sarah: Yup. We go all the way back to grade school together.

Josh: And you'd like to bless the barn now that the demo is done, and we're getting ready to put this place back together.

Sarah: Absolutely. Renovations have a way of disturbing

146

lingering souls. It's good to clear out their presence and make way for a harmonious new start.

Josh: Cat, what do you think about that?

Cat: (laughing) I'm all for a harmonious new start.

Jeremy: Okay then, let's get to it.

Sarah: (Looking up to the rafters with her eyes closed and palms up): *Hertha, Erda, Jörd, Fjörgyn, Hlödyn, Gaia, Tellus! Etnoah, Ina Maka,* we implore you, bring peace to this space! (She lights the sage on fire and turns to the left) Spirit of the East, bring enlightenment to any who enter within these walls. (She turns left again) Spirit of the North, bring strength to all who dwell within these walls. (She turns again) Spirit of the West, bring open minds to those who draw breath within these walls. (Another turn) Spirit of the South, nurture the hearts of those who abide within these walls. We ask you to release any trapped energy and release it through the burning of sage.

Nan: (Begins a Scottish jig and calls out): *Aireamh na h-aoine, ort iasg mò do bhriogais! Pòg mo thòin! Tha thu cho duaichnidh ri èarr àirde de a' coisich deas damh!* (Grabs the sage from Sarah and proceeds to dance around with it for a while.)

Jeremy: Wow, I'm really moved here. That was beautiful.

Josh: I totally feel the peace. What about you, Cat? Are you feeling anything?

Cat: Oh, I'm definitely feeling something, all right.

I don't say what exactly it is I'm feeling because I cannot believe what my grandmother just did. The only Gaelic I know is what she's taught me, and I'm a bit rusty as it's not a language I hear every day. Also, God knows I can't wrap my tongue around it for anything, but I think she just said, "Damn you, one-eyed trouser snake! Kiss my arse! You are as ugly as the south end of a northbound traveling ox!"

I notice my parents standing in the entrance of the barn, out of camera range, and by the look on my mother's face, my translation isn't far off the mark.

Cat: (Smiles at grandmother) That was beautiful, Nan. Can you tell everyone what you just said?"

Nan: (Looks alarmed) Of course, dear. I said, "Great father in the sky, bless this place and offer protection and grace to all who enter. Amen."

I can't imagine anyone watching this show will speak Gaelic, so I can't bring myself to tell the brothers and Tad what just occurred. As far as I'm concerned, the sooner this is over with, the better. That's when I see Travis and Scottie Schweer peek their heads above my parents. My God, this program is going to turn into a three-ring circus.

So, What Brings You Here?

"Hey, Trav. What are you doing back so soon?" Whoops, I should have called him Rhona today.

"Didn't Mom tell you?" He looks resplendent in a winter white suit with a red silk blouse. Today's wig is nearly the same shade as his blouse, making him quite the picture against the snowy white landscape.

"The *Renovation Brothers'* producer wanted to meet the whole family. Turns out they might want to use me in some scenes." He leans in and whispers, "No hard feelings if you're uncomfortable with that."

"I'd love to have you involved!" And that's the truth. Fewer than two months ago I viewed my brother as a total loser, hanging out in the basement getting high all day, with no direction in life. But I was wrong. He's not only employed, but he's also a designer. I'm prouder than I've ever been.

"Okay, but if you change your mind, I'll understand."

"I won't change my mind. You brought Scottie with you again, huh?"

Travis cringes. "Yeah. His mother asked him to come home. She's trying to talk him into going to some religious bootcamp that's promised to turn him straight."

"And he came back knowing that?"

My brother shrugs his shoulders. "He came back to clear his stuff out of her house. He's going to tell her that until she can accept him for who he is, he's going to be staying out of her life. A self-protection thing, you know?" Then he adds, "Be prepared, we may be adopting him."

Poor Scottie, it's not like growing up gay in a small town isn't hard enough. Thank God he took off for Chicago right after high school. "I'll make sure to tell him we'd be all over making him an honorary Masterton."

Jeremy calls out my name and comes running toward us. "Cat, hey, who's this?"

"Jeremy, this is my brother Travis, although he prefers to be called Rhona when he's in drag." Then to my brother, I add, "Rhona, this is Jeremy. He's one of the Renovation Brothers."

Travis puts out his hand. Jeremy takes my brother's giant paw and doesn't hesitate to kiss it. Travis looks surprised and says, "That was very chivalrous. But, just so you know, I'm not gay."

Jeremy laughs. "Me neither, but it seemed fitting."

Josh joins us and looks Travis straight in the eye, all six-four of him in heels. "Dude, this family is the best! Seriously, our ratings are going to blow up after this episode."

My brother laughingly agrees, "We aim to please. I'm Cat's brother, by the way."

"I'm Josh, Jeremy's brother. So, we had no idea you were a drag queen."

Travis explains, "Not queen, just drag."

"Do you have a wife or girlfriend?" Josh asks.

"Nope. It's kind of hard to meet a woman who's okay with this. I'm looking though."

"Do you want to be on the show in women's clothes or in guy's clothes? Do you ever wear guy clothes?" Jeremy asks.

"I've only started dressing in drag in the last couple of months. I can do whatever you prefer."

Josh answers, "Clearly, we prefer this. I mean, what we love about your family is that you're all kind of out there. If you don't mind me saying, a giant guy in a dress really adds color."

"Don't mind it at all. What is it you want me to do?"

Jeremy answers, "We thought we could tape a scene with you and Cat sitting in the barn talking about your childhood memories. You know, to just bring out the history of the place and show why it's so important to your family."

"I could do that. Do you want to tape it today? If not, I'm going to have to arrange to take some time off work."

Josh asks, "Do you live in Gelson?"

"Chicago," Travis answers.

"Let me talk to Tad and try to fit it in. We wouldn't want you to have to come back if you don't have to."

Tad positively loses his mind when he meets Travis and declares, "You are one crazy *cronkite*! I could bust a *moby* just looking at you!"

Apparently, Travis understands what he's saying and replies, "I appreciate the offer, but I only dance with women."

The producer replies, "Totes get it! My gaydar didn't even ping when I saw you. I promise I wasn't laying the moves on you." Yet, there's a little something in his eye that hints at disappointment.

My brother smiles and offers, "I should introduce you to my friend Scottie. He's inside."

Netflix and Chill

Scottie's taken to my bed in a fit of depression. He says he's going to stay in the basement and eat chocolate and watch Netflix all day. He isn't the least bit interested in meeting anyone *or* being on TV. When the most gregarious guy you know says something like that, you know it's serious. Serious enough that Nan has declared she's going to stay with him and not try to horn in on the spotlight anymore today.

While I'm concerned about Scottie's well-being, there may be a small part of me that wants to kiss him for keeping Nan occupied.

And away from the cameras.

Travis and I hit the barn with the camera crew and Tad to dig up some family memories.

Camera walks behind Cat and her brother into the barn. Cut to filming them from the front.

Travis: Man, this place really brings back memories, doesn't it?

Cat: Remember that time you lit a firecracker in here, and the cow went into early labor?

Travis: Yeah, not my best moment. Remember the time you fell asleep in the loft with bubble gum in your mouth and woke up looking the like the scarecrow from the *Wizard of Oz*? God, that was funny. All the straw you were laying on got stuck in your hair along with the gum.

Cat: Third grade. The only year I ever had short hair. (Quietly walking around together for a few moments.) So, what do you think about me turning this place into a party venue?

Travis: I think it's a great idea. We had such an incredible childhood here. I like the thought of sharing our space, so other people can make their own happy memories here.

Cat: We sure were lucky, huh?

Travis: The luckiest. (Sister and brother sit down next to each other on a bale of hay, each lost in their own thoughts.)

"Cut!" Tad yells out. "You guys are naturals! I don't know how you did it, but I wasn't even focused on the big guy in the dress. You sold your relationship and childhood in such a way everyone is going to want to have their party here. You were totes chill."

"Thanks, Tad," I say. I think the quirky producer is growing on me a little. At least his enthusiasm for our project is.

When Travis and I walk out of the barn, we run into Ashley, of all people. She doesn't look like her normal self. She seems kind of disheveled and angry looking. He hair is pulled up in a pony tail instead of hanging long like it usually does. Her makeup is as impeccable as ever though, and if she didn't look like she wanted to rip someone's head off, I'd even go so far as to say she looks more beautiful than I've seen her. "Hey, Ashley, what are you doing here? I thought you were off this week."

Her eyes are smoking mad. "You could say that. I just wanted to stop by to see how things are going with *Tad*." She says his name like she's referring to Satan.

I don't know how to respond. Clearly, she won't embrace the knowledge that everything is going great. But I don't want to lie. Instead, I offer, "Ashley, this is my brother Travis. You can call him Rhona."

The producer looks at him like he's so far beneath her he might as well be the dirt on the floor. Travis doesn't seem to notice, he just mutters under his breath, "Shwing!"

She doesn't appear to hear him. Instead, she looks appalled and complains, "They're going to turn our program into a freak show! It'll ruin my reputation as a producer!"

Okay, now I'm mad. Who does she think she is calling my brother a freak? I say, "Listen, Ashley, I don't know what's going on with you and the brothers, but you may not stand in front of my house and call my brother names. That crap isn't going to fly here."

She glares at me and snaps, "You." Then she jabs her pointer finger at me. "I would have never signed up your farm if I'd known."

I feel like we're in some twisted soap opera. "Look, I'm sorry my family's oddities are making your job difficult, but this is a cool project and your viewers are going to love it."

"Yeah and make you a tidy fortune as a result. You want it all, don't you?"

I'm not sure what her beef is with me. She knew all along what I was going to do with my barn. "Why don't you take up your problems with Jeremy and Josh?"

I don't want her coming back as producer of my episode after all. Her whole aura feels charged, like lightning is about to strike. The hair at the back of my neck is standing on end and I'm extremely unsettled.

When she walks away, my brother whistles. "I think I'm going to go ahead and take some time off from work. That is one hot tamale."

I look at him like he's totally insane. "What's wrong with you? She just called you a freak!"

"That's okay," he says. "I'd be happy to change her mind."

"How? By showing her how to do her makeup?"

Travis smiles so big his teeth look like Chiclets. "Don't you worry. I'll find a way."

And that, right there, is exactly what concerns me. Seriously, I'm not sure I can handle much more excitement.

More Excitement

Before I left New York City, my best friend and business partner Jazz, said, "You're going to go stir crazy in that tiny little blip of a town you call home. I'm not kidding, Cat, you're going to be bored to death."

Turns out, not so much. I don't think I've been short of excitement once since I've been back. And now with Sam acting out, there's a good deal more drama than I'd bargained for. I can't seem to stop thinking about him and his lying to me over something so piddly. I wonder if I'm making a bigger deal out of it than I should, but it comes back to the lying. Not cool. Not cool at all.

Ashley somehow sweet-talked the brothers into letting her stay to watch Tad at work. She was so steaming mad when she talked to me, she must either be a great actress or have had a quick lobotomy to change her personality. When I see Jeremy at lunch I ask, "So, what's up with Ashley? She seemed pretty peeved when I talked to her."

"Really?" he asks. "I didn't get that vibe at all. She just said she wanted to hang out here this week and see what changes we had in mind for the show. That way if the network green lights us, she's ready to step back in."

"You're not going to let her, are you?"

He looks confused. "Cat, you practically begged me to bring her back this morning. Why the change of heart?"

"She just really wigged me out when she showed up. She was downright rude to Travis."

His eyes widen in surprise. "I'll be on the lookout for that. I don't want her hanging around if she can't be professional."

"Okay, good. I'll let you know if I see anything."

He looks amused like I'm a junior high school girl caught in the middle of an adolescent cat fight. Whatever. I know what happened. I don't have to defend myself.

I decide to check on Scottie when I hear a banging sound and a scream come from the powder room under the stairs. I run over in time to see Ashley exit the room, followed by a gush of water.

"What happened?" I yell.

"I don't know. The toilet exploded and water started overflowing everywhere!"

I don't stop to think, I just start throwing towels out of the linen closet onto the mess and wipe it up before it can soak into the floorboards. I throw some towels Ashley's way so she can help, but she just lets them hit her and fall to the floor, like there's no way she's cleaning up toilet water—even though she's the one who caused the mess.

Travis comes out of the kitchen to help. Once we've deposited the soaked towels in the laundry room, I see him approach her and ask, "Are you okay?"

What the hell? Is she okay? Does he think she's been scarred for life because she witnessed an overflowing toilet?

Ashley pushes him away. "I'm fine. Leave me alone."

But Travis doesn't leave her alone. He follows her around like a lost puppy dog for the rest of the afternoon. It's positively nauseating to witness.

This day has felt like it's lasted the better part of a month and I cannot wait until everyone leaves. When the crew heads back out in the barn, I plop on the sofa and put my feet up, hoping for a moment of solitude. Then Jeremy walks in. "Hey, Cat. I have a favor I need to ask you."

"What's that?" I ask having no idea what he could possibly want.

"Would you mind putting Ashley up? Sarah doesn't have any extra room because Tad took over Ash's yurt for the week."

My mouth hangs wide open like a mounted sea bass. I don't want Ashley invading my personal space for an entire week. It's enough she'll be here all day during taping. But not only is Jeremy the star of the show, he's also one of the executive producers. He's doing a lot to help me. Before I can think of a way out of it, I hear myself answer, "Sure."

After all, how bad can it be?

Full House

There was a light in Ashley's eyes when she found out she was staying here that quite frankly scares me. I don't trust that woman as far as I could throw her.

Travis, still in his winter white suit and red blouse, corners me over dinner and announces, "I think I'm going stay for the rest of the week, if that's okay."

"Here?" I ask.

"Mom and Dad don't have the space. Their spare bedroom is packed floor to ceiling with boxes."

"Of course, you can you stay," I manage. "It's just that Jeremy asked if Ashley could crash here, too. I need to figure out where to put everyone."

My brother's eyes light up like an unchaperoned kid with money to spend in the candy aisle at the grocery store. "Really?"

"Watch out for her, Trav. She's really mad about being taken off as producer of this episode. I have a feeling she's going to take it out on everyone in her path."

"Come on, Cat. You can understand why she's upset. All you've ever done is sing her praises up until today, so cut her some slack."

"How can you say that?" I demand. "She was horrible to you this afternoon."

"I represent the changes she sees taking place in the show, that's all. She's just not used to me."

As far as I know, Travis didn't date while living in my parents' basement. I never saw him with a girl or heard he was seeing anyone. I hate to have him go from a complete lack of social life to an infatuation with an emotionally unstable bully. Having said that, I really did like Ashley up until today. Maybe I do need to lighten up and be more understanding. High road, here I come—kicking and screaming perhaps, but still.

Nan joins us and announces, "I told Scottie he can stay with us until he's ready to confront his mother. Poor boy is a mess."

I love Scottie, but suddenly there are going to be three extra bodies under my roof, and while there's plenty of room for them, I'm not quite sure where to put them. My brother reads my mind. "Scottie and I will take your old room with the twin beds and Ashley can have Mom and Dad's old room. There should be an old blow-up mattress in the basement."

"Ashley's staying here?" Nan asks, sounding none too pleased. "I didn't know she was back. I thought that darling boy, Tad, was taking over." Clearly Ashley isn't Nan's favorite person as she was the obstacle to my grandmother having more camera time.

"Yeah, she's here to observe the changes Tad is making, so if the network likes them, she knows what'll be expected of her when she comes back." No sense poisoning the well by telling Nan how rude Ashley was to Travis. Especially since my brother doesn't even seem to care.

"You should put her out in the barn," Nan says. Then she goes off to fill her plate.

I grab my mug of soup and decide to take it out to the front porch for some much-needed quiet time. Meals are extremely busy with my family, cast, crew, and workers milling about. There are so many people, they've even taken over my living space in the basement.

I need somewhere in this house that's just mine, but it doesn't look like that will be the case until everyone clears out.

A Storm is Brewing

Once I'm settled into bed for the night, my mind shoots straight back to Sam. He's been lurking there all day, but thankfully there's been a lot to distract me. I pick up the phone to call him before deciding against it. He needs to be the one to get in touch with me. He needs to beg my forgiveness and make things right. The ball is so in his court on this one.

I chastise myself. How can I even want to talk to him after what he did this morning? I try to stay awake as long as I can, but the rigors of the day ultimately take their toll, and I fall into a restless sleep.

My eyes suddenly pop open sometime later when I hear a scream. I can't decide if it's real or I dreamed it, so I lie there for a moment until I hear it again. Yup, it's real. I throw my covers off and run up the stairs looking for the source of the disruption. By the third shriek, I know it's originating from the master bedroom. I arrive at the same time Nan does. Travis is already there, wearing only his boxer shorts.

"What's going on?" I demand.

Ashley is sitting up in bed pointing at the closet. She's deathly pale like she's just seen a ghost. Her whole body is shaking as though she's having a seizure. I walk over to the closet to see what's upset her and burst out laughing.

God bless my parents. They left several of their taxidermied pets from the attic for me and even moved them into the master bedroom closet. When I turn on the light, I see a note stuck to the moose's horns. It reads:

> *Kitty Cat,*
>
> *Don't be mad, but we really think these are going to come in handy in the new barn. If you still don't want them once it's finished, we'll find a new home for them. Just try to keep an open mind.*
>
> *Love,*
> *Mom and Dad*

Ashley is full on crying now. "Wh ... wha ... what are those things?"

Travis sits down next to her and wraps his arms around her. "Don't worry, those are just my parents' animals."

"But, they're dead!" she cries, all the while clinging to him like she's covered in super glue.

"Better than alive, I'd think," he jokes.

Ashley looks up at him and abruptly pushes him away. "Who are you?"

"Travis. We met earlier today."

She looks horribly confused. "You're not Travis."

"Pretty sure I am."

"No, you're not. Travis was in a dress. You're a man."

"I was a man when I was wearing a dress, too."

"Why were you wearing a dress?"

"Because I like how it feels. Sort of freeing."

Ashley suddenly hits my brother. "Get out of my bed!"

He jumps up while saying, "I was just trying to comfort you. You were a little out of your head there."

"I can't sleep in here," Ashley declares.

"For the love of God, why not?" my grandmother demands. "Those beasts have gone on to their reward. They ain't gonna hurt ya."

The producer starts to stutter, "I … I … I just can't. I mean, there's a moose in the closet! That's not normal."

Well, she's got us there, but it's not like anyone ever claimed we were normal. I speak up, "You guys figure out where you're going to sleep. I'm going to bed."

I leave the circus behind and head back to my room in the basement where I can be alone. Happily, blissfully alone without a moose, or anyone, for company. When I crawl under my blankets, I close my eyes, but my brain won't shut off long enough for me to fall sleep. Tomorrow is bound to be a long day with Ashley on site.

Sleep Deprivation and Gerbils

My phone rings at seven a.m. If my calculations are correct, I might have gotten a grand total of four hours of sleep. The last time I remember looking at the clock it was 2:57. I sang the same ditty in my head as I did every other time I checked the time. Two, two, bo boo, banana fanna fo foo ... but I don't remember anything else, so I must have finally gone lights out.

I groggily answer, "Hello?"

"Cat, it's me. How are you?" It's Sam. His voice fills me with a feeling of contentment and warmth—until I remember he lied to me yesterday.

"I slept like crap," I snap. "What do you want?"

"I'm sorry about yesterday. I promise I wasn't hiding anything from you. I should have told you where I was, I just really wanted to finish my meeting and get back to work."

"And ..." I prompt.

"I'm sorry. Truly. Cat, I love you and I'd never do anything to hurt us."

"What do mean by that?" I ask.

"I mean you and I together, are all that matters. I'll do everything I have to in order to protect us."

His words clearly have a deeper meaning than what he's copping to.

"I miss you. What are you doing tonight?" he asks.

Gah, tonight. I can barely think of today, yet alone anything after that. "I don't know, why?" I begin to thaw ever so slightly.

"I thought we could go to dinner and movie or something. How does that sound?"

I want to tell him that if he wants to see me, he has to come over here, but even I don't want to be here anymore. "Fine. I'll meet you at your house at six." I hang up before he can say anything else. I'm exhausted and I desperately need more sleep.

I don't wake up until ten. I'm so out of it I'm not even sure where I am. I know I'm not in New York. I finally recognize my parents' basement. Then I remember it's my basement now. I sit up slowly and wonder why no one woke me. The house is dead quiet, so everyone must be outside.

I jump out of bed and throw on some yoga pants and a t-shirt without even bothering to brush my hair or teeth before running up the stairs. There are remnants of breakfast lying around the kitchen, so I grab a muffin and my coat and head out the back door. I hear the familiar sounds of electric saws and nail guns filling the air. Bodies are milling about. Scottie is sitting on the tire swing kicking his feet back and forth under him. He looks like a kid on a playground that no one will play with—in a word, dejected.

I approach, "Hey, buddy. You okay?"

He doesn't even look up. "No."

"I'm sorry about your mom. Travis told me."

"What kind of woman doesn't accept her own kid? It's not

natural." He lets out a big sigh.

I'm in total agreement with him. Sadly, not all creatures were meant to be mothers. Travis and I had gerbils when we were kids and one of the moms, Felicity, used to eat her babies. It was the most unbelievably barbaric thing. At first, we didn't know what was going on. Her offspring just started disappearing. By her third litter, we noticed the father, Jason Priestly, was carrying his kids up the plastic chute at night to the little gerbil lookout. Once he got them up there, he'd scoot them into the corner and sit on them. It turns out he was protecting them from Felicity.

I'm not necessarily comparing Scottie's mom to Felicity, I'm just saying not all mothers excel in the role. "Your mom has never wanted to believe you were gay. Maybe if you tried talking to her and just lay it out for her …"

He finally looks up. "You know, in all the years since I've left home, I've avoided the subject of my sexuality with my mother. I don't know how to begin to communicate with her."

"Why don't you just go over and visit her today and see what comes of it. You can stay here as long as you want, so if it doesn't go well, you can come back and regroup until you're ready to try again."

"Thanks, Cat. You know, you guys have always been more of a family to me than my own."

"We love you, Scottie. Maybe you just need to give your family a chance. They might not let you down."

"Yeah, but I think the odds are they will."

I ruffle his hair. "Then you always have us. Now, have you seen Nan?" I figure if I find my grandmother, I'll locate the center of the action.

"I think she's in the barn with Tad and the brothers."

"Thanks. Hang in there." Then I head toward the barn to see what's happening. The first thing I see are my parents surrounded by a ring of dead animals.

As I get closer, I hear my mom say, "We think you should find a way to use these fellas out here."

Tad claps his hands and lets out an enthusiastic, "Yes! We can put the little guys up in the chandeliers once they're installed." Then as he points to the fireplace says, "And the moose head should definitely go up there." He's in raptures of excitement. I don't even particularly mind that my mom has gotten her way. The animals do sort of fit. As long as we keep them far away from the food, I don't foresee any problems.

Mags catches my eye and offers a tentative wave. I shake my head and roll my eyes in way of surrender. She does a little happy dance of victory, which puts me on notice. Tad loves my family's crazy, and he's only just skimmed the surface.

From the Ridiculous to the Sublime

Emily sets up lunch in the kitchen for everyone before excusing herself. "I need to get back to the hospital and make sure I get the food order in for next week."

She comes back into the house a moment later with the news her car won't start. She asks if I can give her a ride. Before I can answer, Jeremy calls out, "Cat, we need you for the next scene in ten minutes!"

I turn to Emily. "Can you wait until I'm done?"

She shakes her head. "If I don't place the order by two, I won't be able to get it in until Thursday. Do you think Travis can take me?"

"No, I forgot he took my car out to do some shopping. Scottie drove over to his mom's house." My mom took Nan into town to do some errands. The only people left with vehicles are the construction crew.

I'm about to ask one of them to drive her when Ashley walks up and says, "I'll take her. I need to pick up a few things at the drug store anyway."

My eyebrows shoot up in surprise. Ashley has avoided me like the plague today. I gather she's a bit embarrassed about the scene in her bedroom last night, but she hasn't seemed openly hostile which is a good sign. I turn to Emily and suggest, "Why don't you call AAA to tow your car? If you need a ride home tonight, I'm sure Sam can drop you off. I'm meeting him at his house at six."

"Thanks, Cat. I'll do that." Then to Ashley, she adds, "And thank you. I really appreciate the lift."

When they leave, I enjoy a few moments of relative quiet. It's just me, my dad, and the crew left. I eventually saunter out to the barn to see what they need me for.

Tad has a table set up by the fireplace, which is still a work in progress. I join him and ask, "What are we shooting today?"

"I thought we'd get some film of you going through catalogues picking out accessories for the remodel." He explains, "I want to get some teaser footage for commercials."

"You think catalogue shopping will be riveting enough to get viewers?" Maybe he's not the boy wonder everyone thinks he is.

He laughs and decides, "Not even. It's what'll be happening around you that's going to sell it."

"What's going to be happening around me?" That's when Jeremy and Josh walk in with my dad and the construction crew. I burst out laughing. From the extraordinarily handsome Renovation Brothers to the short squat Mr. Simms, every one of them is decked out in the Masterton plaid. My dad has been a busy boy.

He calls out, "Ah, lass, don't they look a treat?" Then he leaves the barn again.

Tad calls out, "Okay everyone, take your places!"

The men scurry about, grabbing their tools, while forming a

half-circle around the table I'm sitting at. I feel like a sacrificial lamb in a B-horror film.

Jeremy comes over and says, "Just pretend you can't see us, okay?"

"I'd have to be blind not to see you. Whose idea was this?"

"Dougal's," he answers.

"My dad has a lot of explaining to do." And as I say that, he comes back into the barn carrying his bagpipes. Sweet Jesus, anything but that. My father's bagpipe skills are nearly non-existent. Travis has turned out to be the real piper in the family, but sadly he's not here.

Tad yells, "Dougal, get in position! On your count we'll start to roll."

My dad gets his bagpipes strapped on and stands to the right of the table facing the camera. He calls out, "On the count of three! One! Two! And Three!" He begins to bleat out the opening strains of "Bratach Bana," which is a lively Scottish country reel.

All the men around me turn to each other and bow before they start locking arms to dance. There's no helping it, I burst out laughing so loud, Tad calls, "CUT!" and then asks, "Cat, what are you doing? I told you to sit there and pretend you can't see anyone."

"Are you kidding?" I ask. "You've got to give a girl warning when you're going to do something this outrageous. I mean, it's like a psychedelic version of *High School Musical* in here."

The producer sighs. "Totes. Okay, sorry about that. Now that you know, you've gotta act like they aren't there. You ready?"

I'm pretty sure I'm not, but I nod my head. The second take

is even funnier than the first because Tom Brooder trips and falls over Josh. They both go down like a ton of bricks. By the fifteenth take, all seems to be going well, if you don't count the excruciating racket my dad is trying to pass off as music.

A few seconds in, Travis shows up wearing the long, red-sequined dress he wore to my parents' Christmas party. He relieves my dad of the pipes, and his version of the jig is so beautifully on point, the men pick their heels up even higher. When the song ends, I'm still poring over lighting catalogs. The men line up in front of me and take a bow, flipping up their kilts to the camera. By the look on Tad's face, I can only assume they're following my dad's lead and adhering to strict Scottish dress code.

That's right, they're all commando.

Flaming Bagels

Something is going on with Sam. He keeps pacing around and looking over his shoulder. He reminds me of a dog right before a storm blows in. "Would you mind if we stayed in tonight?" he asks.

"I suppose that would be okay." I get enough crowds at home. Plus, it'll be easier for us to have a chat about his lying here versus in a noisy restaurant.

I preheat the oven for the orange chicken Sam pulls out of the freezer. He puts on a pot of jasmine rice before leaving to take a quick shower.

While he's in the bathroom, I start a fire and turn on some music, trying to create a calm atmosphere. He comes out a few minutes later, wearing jeans and sweater, looking positively delectable. It's a thought I stomp out as soon as I have it. No lusty feelings until we clear the air.

Sam walks over to the window and proceeds to look out before drawing the blinds. Then he approaches me and wraps his arms around my waist. "Thank you for coming over."

I let him hold me, but I don't lean into him. He still needs to make things right before I return his affection.

He changes the subject. "So, how's everything going at your house?"

I tell him how the brothers have decided to take the episode in a new direction and have brought on another producer. He seems excited. "So, the other one is gone?"

"I wish. She's staying with me so she can witness firsthand the direction Jeremy and Josh want to take the show."

"Why's she staying with you and not Sarah?" He seems as surprised by my new houseguest as I am.

"Not enough yurts. Plus, to be honest, I don't think Ashley ever took to the whole earthy/crunchy scene. She was kind of put off by the compostable toilets."

"It's not for everyone," he agrees. "How long is she staying with you?"

"I think until Friday, I'm not sure. A lot depends on the network."

"Are you still glad you're doing this whole television renovation thing?" he asks.

"Of course. It's been hectic, but this way I get more done, and I'm not responsible for making sure everyone shows up on time to do their jobs."

Enough small talk. We sit down on the couch, not right next to each other, more on opposite ends.

I begin, "Why didn't you tell me you were at Betsy's yesterday?" I stare right at him.

"I thought we worked this out on the phone last night. I told you, I didn't want to get into a long drawn-out conversation. I just wanted to finish up and get back to the hospital."

"Who were you with again?"

He says, "Cat, she was a drug rep. I'm interested in a new statin she reps. I was having a meeting and a late breakfast. I was not cheating on you."

He seems pretty sincere and I'm on the verge of believing him, but I'm still mad we even had to have this conversation.

"I was jonesing for Betsy's waffles and I thought I'd kill two birds with one stone."

Maybe.

We spend the rest of the evening sitting in front of the fire talking. I even let Sam scoot closer toward me, but he seems to understand any further intimacy is off the table for now.

I'm about to top off my wine, when we hear a loud bang at the front door. The sound of squealing tires rips through the air right afterward. Sam jumps up to find out what it is. He opens the door and looks down at a white paper bag burning on his front porch. He starts stomping on it to get the fire out while I scream, "What is it?"

He looks totally perplexed. "It's a bag of bagels." He looks closer. "With a couple rocks thrown in, probably so it would hit its mark."

"Bagels? Who on earth would set fire to a bag of bagels and throw them at your front door?"

"Kids? Maybe it's a club initiation prank or something."

"The Bagel Club?" I can't help it, I start giggling. We desperately needed something to release the tension in the air. I didn't expect it would be a bag of burning bread, but I'm happy for it nonetheless.

"Maybe the kids in Home Ec are hazing a new recruit," Sam joins in.

175

I burst into laughter. "Mrs. Stein is probably upset you didn't remove her hairy mole and she's pelting you with flaming bagels in revenge."

He suggests, "Elaine at the bakery could be mad at me for going to Betsy's so often. I bet she's getting even because I haven't stopped in to buy anything in over a week."

"Stop!" I shout. I'm doubled over from hilarity. My sides feel like I've run a four-minute mile. "Oh my God, I haven't laughed so hard in ages."

"Just shows you that when you come to my house you get dinner and a show."

I look at the clock and see it's already after ten. "I have to go. My house fills up pretty early in the morning, and I need a good night's sleep."

Sam pulls me into his arms lovingly and gives me the sweetest kiss to dream about. "Good night, Kitty Cat. I love you."

I confess, "I love you, too, Sam." I don't say anything more. This seems a big enough declaration, given the hurdle we needed to overcome tonight.

"May I offer you a bagel to go?" he teases.

Old Faithful and Home Burials

I walk into a seemingly empty house. Where is everyone? Flipping the lights on, I call up the stairs, "Anyone up there?"

"Just cleaning up a bit of a mess," Travis yells back.

I don't think anything of it until I hear Nan say, "The rug in my room is soaked through."

Why would the rug in Nan's room be wet? I run up the stairs and find every towel we own, once again, laid across the floor. Scottie is on his hands and knees wiping up a puddle, and I demand, "What happened now?"

Ashley snaps, "This house is a menace! I flushed your stupid toilet and it blew up like the one downstairs. It was like Old Faithful!"

I stare at the producer intently before asking, "How exactly are you flushing the toilet?"

"What's that supposed to mean? I push the handle down like everyone else does."

"Yet you're the only one this has ever happened to, and this is the second time in two days." I want to ask if she's dropping a hand grenade in the bowl before flushing. It's the only way I can imagine her single-handedly destroying my commodes with such precision.

"I can't help if your antiquated plumbing hates me!" She looks like a petulant three-year-old. Which of course my brother interprets as a need for comfort. He drops the towel he's holding and reaches out to put his arm around her. Ashley yells, "Don't touch me, you're filthy! Yuck, now I need to shower again."

Nan says, "Quit being so prissy, girl. It's not like you pooped in there. It's just toilet water."

The producer looks like she wants to cry, like she can't believe someone said the word poop in front her. I'm trying to remember why I ever liked her.

"Ashley, just go to bed," Scottie orders. "You can shower in the morning, unless you want to get down here and help clean up your mess."

The thought is more than she can bear. She pushes my brother off her and runs for the safety of her room.

"When are the brothers starting the renovations in the house?" Travis asks.

"Not until after the barn is done," I answer. "So at least another two or three weeks."

He grimaces and proclaims, "Looks like you bought a lemon, Cat."

"Come on, Trav, we've always known the plumbing here was sketchy at best. I mean who else has to yell out before they flush a toilet, so the person at the kitchen sink doesn't get third degree burns?"

"True enough. But still, you'd better see if you can get Marcus up here tomorrow and find out how we can keep this from happening again. I'm getting tired of washing towels."

I nod. "He's working on the bathrooms in the barn

tomorrow. I'll ask him then. In the meantime"—I perform a little curtsey—"I'll leave you to your task. I'm off to bed."

Nan drops the towel she's holding and begs, "Can I come with you?"

"Why?"

"In case I have to tinkle in the middle of the night. The bathroom in the basement is the only one that doesn't seem to be possessed."

I smile and hold out my hand. "Sure, Nan. You can take my bed. I'll sleep on the couch."

"Nonsense, lass. I'll just crawl in with you." The look on her face suggests she's in need of a little human contact.

"Sounds good, come on."

Once we're finally situated under the covers—I say finally because my grandmother has quite a little stretching routine she performs before getting into bed—Nan says, "I don't want to be put in a cemetery when my time comes." *Oh God, please let her not be thinking of taxidermy.*

"I don't think it's legal to bury you at home," I say.

"Let's look into it. Maybe there's something we can do. I've got a bit of money set aside for a bribe."

"Okay, I'll call the county, but do you mind if we wait until the renovations are done first?"

"I think I can hold off on my harp lessons until then."

I smile and close my eyes. I'm almost asleep when I feel my grandmother's bony arm wrap around me. I love being home. I'm just ready for the chaos to be behind us.

All the Laundry

When I see the pile of towels that awaits me in the laundry room this morning, I resolve to head into town and hit the laundromat. That way I can get it done in one go. I'm walking out the door as the crew pulls up and Tad calls out, "What's the clothesline, tassel?"

I've been around this hipster producer long enough to understand he's asking me what's going on, so I answer, "Another exploding toilet. I'm going to the Soap-n-Spin in town to catch up on the laundry."

He calls out to the cameraman, Ben, "Hey, juicer, get over here and catch some footage of Cat doing the wash." To me, he adds, "We can use it in the next episode when we reno the house."

"Ah yes, nothing says 'watch my show' like filming a woman at the laundromat." Then I tease, "Unless you're sending the dancing Scottish clansmen with me."

"Nah, we'll use this clip to show the drudgery that comes when a house is falling down and in need of help from the Reno Brothers. Trust me, every cool couple watching us at the coin-op will be applying to the show. It'll help ramp up our younger audience."

"You're always thinking ahead, Tad. I'm starting to see why

you're so good at your job." And truthfully, he is. I saw the rough cuts from the barn dance, and they were brilliant—like a comedic, Scottish version of *River Dance*. I can't imagine Ashley ever having the imagination or the creativity to pull that off.

Jeremy walks by and calls out, "Why don't I come along? Tad's going to be filming construction fillers this morning and Josh can handle any scenes we're needed in."

"Good thinking, bro!" Tad says. "Make sure to have Ben scan some Kodachrome of downtown. It's totes retro."

Ben says, "I'll take my car. It already has my camera loaded in it."

"Sounds good. I just need to grab two more baskets from the house."

While Jeremy and I fetch the rest of the soaked laundry, he says, "Dude, we got here in the nick of time, huh? The whole place is starting to fall apart."

"I guess so," I say.

We pass Ashley as we haul our load out to the car. Jeremy asks, "Where're you headed, Ash?"

Her whole demeanor turns sweeter than a truckload of cotton candy when she sees him. "I just wanted to pop into town and pick up some donuts for the crew. I hear there's a great bakery on Main Street."

"We can get them on our way back from doing the laundry, if you want," I offer.

"I'm happy to go now. That way they'll be sure to be here for the morning break."

She seems incredibly conciliatory considering my last couple of encounters with her have been tarnished by overflowing toilets. I merely smile and continue to my car.

Jeremy hops in and asks, "Things all better with Ash?"

I shrug my shoulders. "I guess. In all honesty I've been avoiding her. There's enough going on that we don't need to spend time together if we don't want to." And I don't want to.

On the way to the laundromat, Jeremy says, "We emailed the barn dance footage to the network. They love what we're doing. Since we're coming to the end of our shooting season, they've pushed out our other two projects to next season. They want us here full time to make sure we end this season with a home run. You cool with that?"

"Sure. I mean, the more you're here, the faster things get done, right?" Then I ask, "Does that mean Ashley's going to be staying at my house the whole time, or are they pulling Tad off the show?"

"Can't pull Tad, yet. At least not until he finishes the barn. But the network is going to pay you for housing Ash. That is, if you'll keep her."

"How much?" I'm not desperate for the money, but I really don't want her here, so I should get something out of it, right?

"One fifty a night and she goes back to Chicago on the weekends."

I'm silent for a couple beats before replying, "Seven hundred and fifty bucks a week is nothing to scoff at. I could definitely buy a couple new toilets for that. Okay, you've got a deal." I do the math and realize if that's what the network pays per head, Sarah must be making a tidy sum renting out her yurts. It makes me happy to be able to throw that kind of business her way.

Even though this renovation has proven more stressful than I thought it would be, it's been a win-win for everyone. My parents get their new house in town, I get a completely remodeled barn for my business, Sarah makes extra cash, and the Renovation Brothers get to reinvent their show. Now, if we can only fix the toilets, everything should be golden.

When Mercury Turns Around

"Mother pucking son-of-corn!" I hear Nan yell.

Dear God, what now? I run up to the kitchen to find my grandmother standing ankle deep in soap suds. "What happened?"

"I don't know. I just came in to get a cup of tea and this … this bubble bath was waiting for me."

As soon as the crew had finished lunch, I loaded the dishwasher and started it before going downstairs to work on my logo. Josh knows a guy who's going to make my barn sign, but I need to finish my design concept first.

"Did you put the wrong soap in it?" Nan asks. "That happened to me once when we got our first automatic machine back in the seventies. What a mess!"

I wade over to the kitchen sink and open the cabinet underneath. I pull out the detergent I used, and it says dishwashing soap right on it. "Maybe there was a glass or something with hand soap on it." Which means someone had to put it there, which means sabotage! The question still remains, who?

My grandmother nods. "That'd do it. Cat, I think you need to have Sarah come in and burn some weeds in the house for you. Things aren't going so well around here, lately." She means sage, and I think that might be a good idea.

"How in the world do we clean this up?"

"Go out to the garage and get me that long push broom we use for the porch."

I jump to do her bidding. I'm glad somebody has a plan because the only thing coming to me is curling up in a ball and crying. When I return, I see Ashley sprawled out on the floor right in the middle of the suds.

"What happened?" I ask.

"Your grandmother called me in to show me something and I slid right into this." She looks steaming mad.

Nan replies, "It isn't my fault you didn't watch where you were going. I thought you might want to film the cleanup is all."

Ashley snarls, "How in the world did you manage to create another mess?"

I take exception to her tone. "We didn't do anything. And I'd like to remind you, that you were the one who caused the toilet catastrophes."

"Don't you blame that on me! I just flushed the things."

I've had enough of her attitude and confront her. "Ashley, why exactly are you so mad at me? Ever since you came back from your network meeting, and Tad took over the project, it's like you're out to get me or something. It's not my fault HHTV wanted to go in a new direction."

She glares at me like she's trying to activate some kind of eye laser. Finally, she manages, "I'm sorry you've interpreted my actions that way."

What the heck is she talking about? How else am I supposed

to interpret her actions? This chick is a couple pints short of a gallon.

Travis runs in like a pinch hitter sliding into home plate for the winning run. "I heard Ashley cry out." Then he spots her lying in the middle of a soapy mountain and runs to her side. "What happened?"

"Your sister's demonic house happened," she answers.

He tenderly helps her to her feet and croons, "Poor thing. Did you hurt yourself?"

Ashley looks up at him and takes in his all-boy attire before batting her eyes—!!!—and replying, "I might be bruised."

Travis gently helps her to the other room, and I want to vomit.

Nan opens the back door and starts pushing all the suds outside. I brush past Ashley to get the towels. When I return, Nan has the bulk of the mess out of the house. Then she says, "Your turn."

I throw the towels on the floor to soak up any residual water and add new towels to my ever-growing list of things to purchase. This lot has spent a little too much time on the ground sopping up questionable liquids for me to want to use them on my naked body again.

With the kitchen finished, I call Sam to tell him about Hell Day down on the farm. He picks up immediately, but before I can say anything, he announces, "I'm in the parking lot of the hospital. Somebody soaped my windshield and I can't clean it off enough to see. Can you come get me?"

"Soaped your windshield?"

"I'm guessing whoever was behind the flaming bagel incident, must have a bone to pick with me."

"Did you kill someone recently that I don't know about?" I ask.

"Not even a squirrel."

"I was going to tell you about my wretched day, but you've got me beat by a mile."

"I don't know, misery likes company. What happened to you?" I tell him about all the flooding going on around here. I also start to wonder if his trouble and mine might somehow be related.

He says, "Ask Sarah if Mercury is in retrograde."

"What does that even mean?"

"I'm not totally sure, but I do know Mercury is the closest planet to the sun and therefore its orbit is the fastest. A few times a year it appears to move backwards, and people say that's when bad luck occurs on our planet."

"You believe that?"

He answers, "Not as a rule, but when a string of crappy things happens around the same time, I do wonder."

"What are you supposed to do when Mercury is in retrograde?"

"Near I as I can figure, hide. There's no escaping it other than to do your darndest to stay out of the way of trouble."

"I'm not sure how I'm supposed to do that. I can't very well tell everyone to leave and come back when Mercury starts behaving itself again."

"No, I guess you can't. But can you come here and drive me back to my house?"

"Sure. I'll be there in fifteen." Then I hang up. Mother pucking son-of-corn, indeed. If that Roman god of a planet doesn't start behaving itself soon, I may be in real trouble.

Highland Hussies

After I drop Sam off at his house, I stop by the drug store for Nan. As ever, her list includes a Mr. Goodbar, tissues with lotion, a romance novel that has something to do with Scotland, and this time she's added beef jerky to her demands. Apparently, her last story reminded her of how much she likes dried meat.

Dorcus Abernathy, Nan's ex-nemesis, is in the book section when I get there. "Mrs. Abernathy, how are you doing this fine day?" I always pull out my best manners when addressing adults from my childhood.

She looks slightly flustered to be recognized and instinctively throws something back on the shelf—it's a book, *His Brazen Highland Lassie.* "Nan particularly liked that one," I offer.

"Ah, yes, well, that's good to know." It seems my grandmother helped the minister's wife develop a new hobby—devouring trashy romance novels. "Well, um, dear," then she leans in conspiratorially, "I'd appreciate if we could keep this between us." She looks around shifty-eyed, like she's buying crystal meth or human trafficking Scottish lairds.

"Of course, Mrs. Abernathy. Your secret is safe with me." Then I wink at her reassuringly. She grabs the book she just shelved, along with a copy of *Seduced by a Highland Hussy* and *Forbidden Highland Love* and makes a bee-line for the cash register.

On the tissue aisle, I run into Emily, who seems to have picked up a case of the sniffles. She promises, "Don't worry, I'm not sick-sick. I'll still be making all your meals this week."

I say, "The crew is in love with your cooking, and I'm beginning to fear they may try to hire you away when they leave."

She sighs. "Josh is so mysteriously handsome, isn't he?"

"I think most of HHTV's viewing audience agrees with you." She looks devastated by my comment. "He's on the cover of *People* magazine. People are bound to notice."

"I guess you're right. Too bad we don't have any men like him around here. I'd totally go after him if he was local."

I take her hand and lead her to the book section. I pluck a copy of *Highland Harem* off the shelf and hand it to her. "For the lonely nights until this town gets more interesting. Her eyes light up as she takes the book.

I run into Ethan, of all people, standing next to the beef jerky. He looks slightly perplexed. "Ethan, what are you doing here?"

He seems equally surprised to see me. "Sarah thought I was ready to interact with more people. Strangers." He looks uncertain. "She's tasked me with talking to five people I don't know."

Interesting. "How's it going?"

"So far I've gotten a haircut, purchased some rug cleaner, and bought a muffin. I think I've done well."

"Rug cleaner?" I ask.

He hands me a bag. "For the carpet in Nan's room. Sarah

said there was an overflowing toilet incident."

How sweet. I'm not sure my grandmother will appreciate the gift, but I certainly do. This is Ethan at his most considerate. Most people think flowers or candy are thoughtful gifts, but Ethan always manages to find the thing people really need.

He turns to the beef jerky and asks, "Do you know how much fat and sodium are in those things?"

"I don't think they're known for being health food." I grab a handful. "Traditionally, drying meat was a great way to preserve it. It's perfect for hunters, hikers, and high-energy snacking."

"You actually like that stuff?" he asks in such a way that you'd think it was illegal or made out of raw slugs.

"I'm getting it for Nan."

"Oh, well then." I can tell he wants to offer a warning, but ultimately chooses not to. "It's nice to see you, Cat."

"You too, Ethan. Where are you headed now?"

"I'm off to Betsy's to get a bite to eat. I'd ask you to join me, but I'm supposed to be pushing my boundaries. I'm afraid Sarah would consider it cheating if you were there."

"We'll do it another time then." I smile as he walks off.

One of the best parts of living in a small town is always running into people you know. I used to think the anonymity of a big city was what my heart wanted, but I've changed my mind. I like being surrounded by familiar faces. This little town is like one great big family. Sure, it's a bit dysfunctional, but aren't all families?

Ultimatums and Flings

Marcus, the plumber, hands me a very small, very wet field mouse still wearing his battle tartan with a small dagger super-glued to his tiny paw. "Your upstairs plumbing obstacle."

"You found this in the toilet?"

He nods his head.

"How could a mouse have gotten into the pipes?" Then I have a horrible image of my dad sitting on the toilet playing with his little friend and accidentally dropping it in. He would have had to have done it yesterday though, or the overflow would have happened much sooner. So much yuck on so many levels. "Anything in the downstairs pipes?" I ask.

"About seven tampons."

"What?" I have no words. My mom and Nan are both completely menopausal, and the house has a septic field. There's no way I'd flush a tampon! But this isn't information I can comfortably share with my old high school classmate. I do know I'm going to have a stern talking to with Ashley though.

"Both of the toilets are now fully functional."

"Thank you." I switch topics to get off that whole tampon thing. "Marcus, you're single, right?"

He eyes me with some uncertainty. "Yeah, but aren't you and Sam a thing?"

"Oh, nonononono, I'm not asking for me." Awkward much? "I just ran into Emily at the drug store and she mentioned the night life here was a little dull. Is there someplace for single people to hang out in town?"

"A lot of folks go to Ten Pin, the bar at the bowling alley."

"Still?" I ask. "You'd think someone would have opened another place in town in the last decade."

"Lots of people hang out in Champaign. There're more people there." He doesn't say anything else. He just picks up his tool box and walks out the front door.

This is definitely something I need to think about, but not until after the renovations are over. I can't take on one more thing right now. I realize I haven't been in any scenes today, so I drop my bags and head out to the barn to see what's going on.

As soon as I walk through the large sliding door, I spot my parents standing in a circle with Jeremy, Josh, and Tad. My folks appear to be teaching them how to do the Highland fling. This is not a dance for amateurs as it involves a lot of leaping and twirling, but the TV boys seem to be more than up for the challenge.

My dad says, "It helps if you let out a WOOP! when you jump."

Tad declares, "Amazeballs, daddio! I love this Scottish moby!"

Mags instructs, "You want to make sure you get high enough off the ground that your kilt flips up a little." Then she winks, "But not so high you show *it* all off, if you know what I mean."

The men laugh at her innuendo. Jeremy calls out, "Hey, Cat, do you fling?"

"Do I fling?" I holler back, "I'm better than both my parents combined!"

Dad agrees, "That she is. My lassie came into this world flinging."

My mom grimaces, "Don't remind me." Another round of laughter is shared.

Josh shouts, "Go get your skirt on, Cat. I'm sick of dancing with these hairy apes!"

I don't have to be told twice. I dash out of the barn intent on getting my gear when I run smack into Ashley. "Where are you going?" she demands.

"To the house, to get my kilt. I'm going to show the brothers how we Scots dance."

"You want everything, don't you?" she snaps. "The house? All the men? It's like everyone is here for just your pleasure."

Uh-oh, crazy lady on the loose. I answer, "Ashley, I have no idea what's going on with you, but if you want to keep staying at my house you need to be reasonable. I have no problem if the network fires you. I have no problem telling them I don't want you here. It seems to me that you need me. So, if you want to stay, you'd better get your act together. Got it?" Then I add, "And no flushing tampons down the toilet!"

I'm not a rude person by nature, and I'm certainly not a confrontational one, but I've had enough of this chick's attitude. It feels good to speak my mind, and it feels even better to watch her face as the full impact of my words hits her.

Her expression morphs between looking like she's fantasizing about ripping out my hair and realizing the truth of what I say. I let her ruminate on her next actions, but I don't wait for her response. I simply walk away to get changed. When I see Nan, I tell her what I'm up to. She declares, "I'd better get dressed too! We need to even up the numbers."

My family spends the next two hours teaching the Renovation Brothers and their producer how to fling like a true Scot. Amid the sound of hammers, drills, and other sundry construction noises, we leap, jump, spin, and let it all hang out, releasing any pent-up stress we've been harboring.

If anyone is looking for the next big thing in workouts, the fling is the ticket. It should be taught in gyms across America. Not only would people get in shape, but they'd have the time of their lives doing it. Plus, you get a true idea of a person's nature when they fling, which makes it a great way to audition perspective dates.

That's when a brilliant idea hits me. Once this barn is up and running, I'm going to offer Scottish dance lessons on Monday nights. No one throws parties on Mondays, so the barn will be available. It'll be my public service to all the single people in town. We can call it the Wing and Fling and get Emily to barbecue a bunch of chicken wings. I'll have to make sure to invite Marcus, as well.

If I can set fire to the dating scene in Gelson, it'll feed right into my wedding business. I'm guessing once couples meet in my barn, it'll stand to reason they'll want to get married there.

Gay Camp and Wedding Dresses

Travis is sitting at the kitchen table still in his boy clothes when I finally come in from the barn. "What are you wearing?" I ask.

He looks confused. "Clothes?"

"I'd thought you'd have changed into Rhona after breakfast like you've been doing all week. I'm surprised to see you looking like Travis so late in the day." The guy in front of me looks like a handsome, upstanding citizen. He's even wearing an oxford cloth shirt, for heaven's sake.

"I'm trying to get Ashley to see me as a guy. Did you see the way she looked at me when I helped her up earlier? I'm pretty sure there was a spark."

I pull out a chair in front of him and a sit down. "Trust me, Trav, that girl is cuckoo for Cocoa Puffs. She's nuts!"

"Just because she freaked out when the toilets overflowed? That's a pretty standard reaction."

"She was rude to you!" I retaliate.

"She just doesn't understand me." He's being way too tolerant of the producer's snippy behavior, if you ask me.

"You think you can make her understand why you like to dress up in women's clothes?"

"I'm going to have to make some woman understand that if I'm ever going to date."

"That's a good point. But why her?"

He smiles. "She's gorgeous, for one. Also, she's kind of feisty. I like that."

"She's crazy," I mumble under my breath.

"Cat," my brother says, "she's perfect. Have you met our family? You don't grow up in the Masterton clan and hanker for sanity. That doesn't make any sense."

"You like her because she's nuts?"

He shrugs his shoulders. "Normal is boring. Who wants to be in a relationship with a dull person?" And right there I realize he's right. Ethan was my version of a boring person and that clearly didn't turn out well. Sam isn't off his rocker, but he grew up with my family, so he's comfortable around our colorful personalities.

"I may have yelled at Ashley this morning and threatened to send her packing if she doesn't shape up," I confess.

"Good! That ought to take some of the edge off her. I'll up my game, but be prepared, I'll be doing a lot of wooing in your presence. If she has to be on her best behavior in front of you, she's going to have to put up with me."

"Um, okay." I can honestly say that watching Travis try to gain Ashley's interest is not something I need to see. But if he needs to do it to get her out of his system, then so be it. I love my brother and want him to be happy. More than that, I want him to know I always have his back.

"How's Scottie doing?" I ask.

"His mom called the cops on him when he tried to take his

stuff out of her house. She told him he could have it back after he graduates from Gay Camp."

"They don't really call it Gay Camp, do they?"

He shakes his head. "It's called Adam and Eve Camp. They sent him in high school, but he failed. His mom is convinced he didn't want it enough."

"Of course he didn't. Why in the world would you want to be something you're not?"

"Some people think it's a choice," he answers.

I cringe. "Poor guy. What's he going to do?"

"He and I are going to break into his house and move his stuff out while his mom is at church on Sunday."

"You're going to rob her?" I'm borderline appalled, even though she totally deserves it.

"No, we're going to go in and remove Scottie's rightful belongings. We're not going to take anything of hers."

"You know this has 'prison cell' written all over it, don't you?

"You worry too much. We're going to be in and out within an hour. I promise, nothing can go wrong."

"Those are the famous last words of every bad plan in history, followed by 'hold my beer.'"

"You're a worry wart, Cat. I promise you, everything will be fine. Speaking of fine, I've been working on a couple sketches I'd like to get your opinion on. You cool with that?"

"Absolutely! Is it something for me?"

"Not unless you're getting married." He arches his eyebrow fishing for news about me and Sam.

"You're working on wedding dresses?"

"Yup. Wedding dresses are the most over-the-top designs out

there. You only wear them once, and it has to be enough to sear your image into people's memories for the rest of their lives. They're the ultimate design challenge."

I clap my hands together in excitement. "Show me, show me, show me!"

My brother is a puzzle. To see him now, he looks like a prepster enjoying a day off. Yesterday he looked like a bad-ass drag queen on his way to the Academy Awards. Two months ago, he looked like a derelict. He's a caterpillar turning into a butterfly. All he needs to do is stretch his wings and fly. Now that he's embraced who he is, I'm convinced nothing can stop him from succeeding in life.

I only wish he wasn't interested in pursuing Ashley, but I don't think I can stop him.

Forecasting More Showers

Sam calls, "I think we should go up to Chicago for the weekend. I need to get out of town for a couple days."

"What's going on?" I ask.

"I stopped by the dry cleaners to pick up my coats for work and they weren't there. Apparently, someone else paid for them and took them. And no one remembers what the person looked like."

"Who would want them?" I ask.

"That's just the thing. No one would want them. They're lab coats with my name embroidered on them." Then he asks, "What do you think? You game to get out of here?"

I could use a break, but I'm not ready to shack up with Sam. I'm still miffed about the whole lying about being at Betsy's thing. You might think I'm taking my anger too far, but you need to remember this was the guy who let me believe we were going away to college together, only to change his plans without telling me. Yes, I'm over it, but I'm still pretty sensitive when it comes to him lying to me.

Having said that, I really do need to get out of Dodge. Not to mention, I've been hankering for a spinach pie. I say, "Get a room with two beds,"—my meaning perfectly clear.

Sam stumbles over his words, "Um, well, okay then."

I veer away from the topic of our sleeping arrangements and ask, "Everything else going okay?"

"No. Today, when I got into my car to go to go to work, I discovered the front seat had been filled with snow. Then when I got to the hospital, I found my parking spot had been taped off with caution tape."

"Holy crap! Did you call the police?" I ask.

"Yeah, but they said it sounded like harmless pranks. They told me to keep my doors locked and to call back if something else happened. All I know is, I'm spooked."

Worried, I ask, "What if someone burns your house down with flaming bags of bread while you're gone?"

"My parents are going to keep an eye on the place for me." I miss Sam's parents. I make a mental note to spend some time with them when things settle down at the farm. For now, though, I'm glad they aren't trying to horn in on the spotlight like my family is.

With Travis and Scottie at my house, someone will be on hand for Nan. I don't want to leave her alone, although I'm sure she'd be fine. So, I say, "I'd love to get away from all the chaos. Even though the barn is the place getting renovated, the whole house feels like it's in transition."

"It is. You hardly have any furniture and what's left is so old and worn out, your parents don't even want it."

"I guess I should do something about that, but I really want to wait until everything is fixed up first."

"We can hit the River North neighborhood while we're in the

city and do some window shopping for furniture," he suggests.

"I'd love that! Where should we stay?"

"Let's stay at The Peninsula. It's in the same neighborhood."

"Fancy! I'm in. It's going to be nice to have a little peace and quiet."

He jokes, "That's why everyone goes to Chicago, for the serenity."

"They would if they lived at my house. It's been Grand Central Station here for the last couple of weeks. For a split second I was worried Nan and I might get a little lonely."

"Good luck with that. Once the guys finish the barn, they go to work on the house, right?"

"Actually, I talked to Tad this morning. He's gone ahead and hired a crew from Bloomington to start work on the house. They'll be here Monday."

"Where are you going to put everyone?"

"They're going to start in the kitchen, which will be a bit of a struggle, but it won't be too bad. Emily is going to set up lunch and dinner in the barn. We'll be eating a lot of cold cereal for breakfast."

"We better book you a massage this weekend to de-stress you enough to handle phase two of the onslaught."

Massage is my love language. I'd let a stranger on the street rub my feet if they looked like they were up to the task. "You're on! Maybe we should leave today."

"I wish I could. I'm on call tonight and I work from eight to four tomorrow. Why don't you pick me up at the hospital then? I'll bring my overnight bag with me."

"What are you going to do with your car? I wouldn't leave it at your house in case your stalker decides to move into it."

"My dad's going to keep it in his garage. He's going to put some portable heaters in it to try to dry it out before it starts getting moldy."

"Have you thought of anyone who might be behind your troubles?"

He doesn't say anything right away, which makes me think he may have an idea. But he answers, "I can't imagine what I've done that warrants this kind of vandalism."

I'm about to ask my question again when Nan runs in. She's opening kitchen drawers yelling, "I need a wrench! Hurry up and help me find a wrench!"

I abruptly hang up on Sam and open the junk drawer with the assorted tools my dad left in case of emergency. I ask, "Why do you need a wrench?"

"No time!" she yells. "Follow me." She runs up the stairs like Jack the Ripper is after her eighty-year-old self. So, not really fast, but there's definitely some urgency there. At the top of the landing, I see the cause of her hysteria. Water is once again coming out of the bathroom, but this time, it's airborne.

"What happened?"

"I turned on the shower to wash my hair and the shower head popped right off!"

I hurry in after her. "Why didn't you turn the water off?"

My grandmother looks startled as I reach around her to close the valve. "I know you're going to find this hard to believe, but the thought never even occurred to me."

I can see how in the excitement of the moment it didn't. I look around the bathroom, once again covered in water, and dread the cleanup. I tell Nan, "Why don't you use my shower downstairs while I wipe up the mess?"

She looks so relieved, I'm not surprised when she answers, "Thanks, lass. I'll see you later."

Boobs and Onions

Nan tells me to take my sexy underthings to Chicago. She says, "When you get to be my age, even your good underwear looks bad." She clucks her tongue. "You can't make a silk purse out of a sow's ear. You gotta make the most of gravity while it's on your side."

I'm not quite sure what the proper response is. I go with, "Do you miss wearing sexy underwear, Nan?"

"Honey, if my boobs weren't growing out of my belly button, I'd be all over it! At the beginning of a relationship, gals wear the trappings for their man, but a year in, they do it just because it makes them feel good about themselves."

She's got a point. I confess, "I don't have a lot of sexy underwear right now."

"Oh honey, you've got to go to that Agent Provocateur store on the computer. Woowee, there's some stuff to see!"

"How do you know about Agent Provocateur?"

"What do you think I do all day, lass?"

"I hadn't really thought about it before. Are you telling me you shop for underwear all day?"

"Don't be sassy. I peruse the world wide web and learn about our world." She winks at me and adds, "I know stuff, Cat."

I tremble at the thought. "Where exactly are you learning this stuff?"

"Well, first I go to the Google. Then I squirrel up the page until I see a little button that says, 'latest news' and I hit it. Then I squirrel down the page and you would not believe the amount of knowledge right there at my fingertips!"

"By squirrel down the page, do you mean scroll down the page?"

She looks unsure. "I don't know, is that what I mean?"

I nod my head. "I think so." Then I ask, "Do you have a preference for any particular news source?" I'm curious to see where she's getting her information.

"The Google is my news source, lass! It's all on the Google." She says this like Google is some mysterious crystal ball.

"Nan, Google is a search engine. It compiles data from the entire internet. It's not a news source in and of itself. What pages do you read most frequently?"

"Well, let's see. I like one called The Onion. You ever seen that one?"

I laugh out loud before I can stifle my response. "Nan, The Onion is a satire news page. It's a spoof on real news. In other words, it's all made up."

"No! Well, now that's disappointing. I quote that page all the time to the gals at bingo. No wonder they look at me funny." I'm guessing that's not the only reason they look at her funny, but I don't say so.

Then she changes the subject, "Will you bring me home a garlic and sausage pie from Eduardo's?"

"I thought you gave those up because of heartburn?"

"I'll be burping it up for a month, but it'll be worth it." She bats her eyes and pleads, "Pretty please? You know I nearly died when I went and burst my brain. I've got to enjoy the moments while I still have them."

It's true, her aneurysm could have easily killed her. We're all lucky she has this second chance. "Nan, if you want to burp sausage and garlic for a month, I'll hook you up."

She throws her arms around me. "You're my best gal, Cat. Thank you. You're going to need to stop and buy me a big beer, too."

"You don't drink beer."

"I do with pie." Then she instructs, "Make sure you get a sixteen ouncer and make sure it's not one of them pretentious microbrews. I want a Bud."

"Gotcha. Do you need me to get you anything special for the weekend?"

"Nah, Travis and Scottie will take care of me. We're already planning an outing for Sunday."

"Where are you going?"

"Oh, here and there. I'm going to make them drive me around like I'm Miss Daisy."

I can see it now, Travis in his sweater dress and pearls and Scottie in his plaid pants and beret, chauffeuring Nan around like she's the Queen of England. I kind of don't want to miss it, but the lure of getting out of town is much too strong to ignore. It's about time Sam and I focus on each other without all the distractions. I may not have totally forgiven him, but I do miss him. I want everything to get back to where it was before the Renovation Brothers came to town. He just has to quit lying to me.

Rude Much?

Jeremy calls out my name as I haul my suitcase out to the car, "Hey, Cat!" He runs over to join me. "Would you mind if I caught a ride into the city? Tad wants to tie up a couple things and doesn't plan on leaving until six. Josh is going to stay with him in case he needs one of us in front of the camera."

"Why are you in such a rush to get home?"

"Date. I know I said I don't have time, but my buddy has been wanting to set me up with his sister for months. I finally caved."

I tease, "Oh yeah, why'd you give in? Did you see her picture or something?"

He makes a very curvy feminine outline with his hands and waggles his eyebrows. "Like a brick house! Tall, brunette, and built like she was born to entertain the troops."

"Well, then, okay. Far be it from me to keep you from such a promising evening. Do you have your stuff?"

"Don't need it." He jumps in the car. "I want to be home by seven, so I have time to shower. Step on it!"

That's when it hits me. Sam has been avoiding the Renovation Brothers like they're a nest of cranial worms. He's not going to be happy I've just agreed for us to spend over two hours in the car with one of them. I try to think of a way out of it, but nothing comes to mind.

I reach into my purse for my phone to fire off a quick text of warning only to find it dead. How can that be? I just charged it. There's nothing to do but drive over there and hope for the best.

Sam is standing in front of the hospital when I pull up. He's got his overnight bag in hand and he's wearing a big smile—until he notices I'm not alone.

Jeremy jumps out of the front seat so Sam can ride shotgun. As he gets out, he sees Dr. Hawking and stops dead in his tracks. Then he looks at me and asks, "This is your guy?"

"Yup, Jeremy, this is Sam. Sam, this is Jeremy." I hurry up and add, "Jeremy needs a ride into the city and being that we're going there …" the obvious conclusion dangles in the air.

Sam's face goes from shocked, to annoyed, to uncertain at lightning speed. He finally sticks his hand out and unconvincingly says, "Nice to meet you."

Jeremy takes the offered appendage without great enthusiasm. "If you say so."

When we finally get situated in the car, the air is so thick you could cut it with a butter knife. I try to break the tension. "Jeremy, you should tell Sam about how well you're doing learning the fling."

After a couple moments of silence, he says, "I'm doing really good." That's it.

I try, "Sam, feel free to share your own flinging experiences." I'm grasping here, but my God, these two seem to have taken an instant dislike to each other.

Sam pulls out his phone. "I need to return a couple of emails."

I try, "Anyone want to listen to the radio?"

"I think I'll take a nap," Jeremy answers.

Okay, so no radio and virtually unresponsive passengers, now what?

I'll tell you what. Two hours and thirty-nine minutes of stone-cold silence. It's excruciating. Every time I try to make conversation with Sam, he cuts me off to check another email. Jeremy has been fake sleeping the whole way. How do I know he's faking it? Every now and again I catch him in the rearview mirror staring at the back of Sam's head like he's trying to bore holes through it.

These two guys hate each other. There's obviously something going on they're not sharing with me. As we enter the city I say, "Good luck with your date tonight, Jeremy." Then to Sam, I add, "He's got a hot date with a curvy brunette."

Jeremy responds, "Too bad she isn't a petite blonde." He leers at me like I'm an all-you-can-eat buffet with a world-class sneeze-guard and he's just been rescued after a month on a deserted island.

"I thought you liked them, tall, brunette, and bodacious," I answer.

"You're way more my type, Cat. But of course, you're taken." His tone drips heavy with disgust. What in the hell is going on? Jeremy hasn't flirted with me the entire time he's been in Gelson. Why fake interest for Sam's benefit?

Sam answers before I can. "That's right, she's taken. Don't forget it."

"Everyone's free-game until there's a ring on their finger. Am I right?"

Sam turns around so quickly, I'm worried he's gotten whiplash. "You are not right. Cat is mine, with or without a ring on her finger."

Jeremy shrugs. "If you say so."

How can two people hate each other so intensely unless they have a history together? The answer is, they can't. How exactly do these guys know each other? Clearly, now isn't the time to ask, but I'm definitely going to find out when Sam and I are alone. Obviously I've stumbled across yet another lie.

Elegant Confrontation

As soon as we pull up to the valet stand at the hotel, I jump out to get my suitcase out of the trunk. Sam hurries over to help me, but I wave him off. I'm mad and I want to make sure he knows it.

As we enter The Peninsula, he says, "I'm really looking forward to this weekend. How about you?"

I stop walking and stare at him. "Are you kidding me? Are you really going to act like that wasn't the most uncomfortable car ride in the history of humankind?"

He tries to look surprised. He's about as successful as the *Hindenburg's* last landing. "What do you mean? I was just tying up a few loose ends with some patient files, so we could enjoy our weekend."

"You were not. You were avoiding talking to Jeremy."

He sighs. "Well, the guy was totally rude. I mean, it's clear he has a thing for you."

"You were both rude and I want to know why. How do you know him?"

Sam flashes the international "what" gesture with both hands out in front of him, like he's trying to catch grapefruits falling from the sky. "I haven't been to your house since they've arrived."

"Do you know each other from before? Is that *why* you haven't been to my house? Is that *why* you didn't want me to apply to the show?"

"Cat, you're being paranoid. We were just male posturing, that's all. You know, two guys interested in the same woman. I just needed to make sure he knows you're mine, that's all."

"Jeremy isn't attracted to me. He's been extremely professional since I've met him. I would even go so far as to say we've become friends."

"You're not friends, Cat. Promise me you'll be on your guard and not let him worm his way into your life any more than he already has."

"Sam, he's renovating my barn. My house is next. He's clearly going to be involved in my life. At least for another month or so."

He exhales loudly. "Just be careful. Guys like him think they can have anything they want."

"He can't have me unless I want to be had, so relax. I suppose you'll want to come over to the house now and keep an eye on him. Well, you can forget it. You're no longer welcome at the farm while the Renovation Brothers are there. You got that?"

He nods his head and takes my hands. "I hear you and I'm sorry. I know I behaved poorly. The guy just rubs me the wrong way."

"You two barely laid eyes on each other before squaring off for a fight," I accuse. I'm not sold that Sam and Jeremy don't know each other, but I don't think I'm going to get any more information from my boyfriend. I'm going to have to work on the other butthead *when we get back to Gelson.*

When we finally resume our walk into the lobby of the hotel, I feel like I'm entering a grand tea room in London. The ceilings are impossibly high, a gorgeous crystal chandelier hangs from the center of the room, and gilded waterfall lighting accents the center columns. It's very *Downton Abby* and I love it. In fact, I'm pretty sure I could pitch a tent and live here. The idea has merit, especially during the remodel of my house.

When we check in, I discover Sam has spared no expense and booked a suite on the ninth floor, probably hoping the extravagance will make me change my mind about separate beds. Wrong. The trip up here has ruined his chances of that.

Our room is decorated in soothing cream tones, trimmed in navy. It's very elegant, and as much as I'd like to jump right into the king-sized bed, roll around in high thread-count sheets, and order room service, I run to see what the bathroom looks like. For a girl who grew up in the middle of corn fields and grain silos, I feel inordinately comfortable in regal settings. The sunken tub is to die for and I announce, "I'm going to take a bubble bath before dinner."

"Go ahead. Our reservation isn't until eight, so you have plenty of time."

I use the complimentary bottle of bubble bath. When the tub is full, I sink into it like a mermaid who's been sunbathing in the desert. The silky hot water feels heavenly—I turn on the jets to beat away the tension of the car ride up here which, as you know, was extensive.

The whirlpool turns off after twenty minutes, and I lie with my head against the wall enjoying the sound of silence. I feel a sense of tranquility overcome me. Then I hear Sam whisper/yell into his phone, "I don't care what you have planned for tonight. Meet me in the lobby of the Peninsula Hotel at ten. We need to talk."

I try to step out of the bath quietly, so he doesn't hear me coming, but by the time I put a robe on and get into the living room, I hear him say, "Thanks, Mom. I appreciate your looking out after the place."

Apparently, he's hung up on the call I'm interested in and has moved on to more mundane affairs. I do know one thing, Sam has set up a secret meeting in our hotel lobby, and I'm going to follow him and find out what's going on.

Feng Shui and Spleens

I slip on a red cocktail dress I bought a year ago and never wore because Ethan hated it. I now know it was the color he couldn't stand. Sam whistles under his breath. Once I'm in close enough proximity, he tries to pull me in for a kiss. "You look gorgeous," he croons in my ear.

I can't help but notice he looks pretty scrumptious himself. I don't want to notice as I'm still mad about his behavior with Jeremy, but there it is. He's wearing a black sports coat with a white shirt, unbuttoned at the collar. All you can see is his throat, but it ever-so-nicely hints at his muscular chest. "Thank you," I reply curtly, while stepping out of his embrace. "We'd better go, or we'll run the risk of missing our dinner reservation."

"Would that be so bad?" He smiles like he's entertaining more salacious thoughts.

Talk about optimistic. "Not gonna happen, buddy. I want to eat."

Sam puts his hand on my lower back and leads me out the door to the elevator. We ride in silence to the fifth floor, both of our minds obviously somewhere else. Mine is firmly nestled in anger, his is probably trying to figure out how to lessen my anger. Good luck to him.

Shanghai Terrace is charming. It has a 1930s supper club feel—I know this because I watch a lot of old *Thin Man* movies. There are tiny white orchids on the tables that look like petals floating in the air. It's like walking into another world.

The host leads us to a quiet corner right under a picture of a golden dragon. He pulls out a gilded chair for me. Sam sits across the table and immediately takes my hands in his. "I'm sorry again about the car ride up here. I acted like a child and I promise it won't happen again."

"Are you sure you don't have something you want to tell me about you and Jeremy?" I stare daggers through him like this is a CIA interrogation. Watch out, buddy, waterboarding might be next.

"There's nothing to tell. Jeremy and I obviously both have great taste in women, and I got jealous. Cat, I just found you again. Can you blame me for feeling protective of us?"

I don't blame him. I'm protective of us, too. But Jeremy doesn't have designs on me. I don't understand why he was flirting with me. He hasn't looked at me twice since the crew first started on my barn. He treats me like a sister. Enter Sam, and he changes his tune, like he's intent on making Sam angry.

When the waiter arrives, we order a bottle of Hakusuru saki and assorted dim sum to enjoy while we choose our entrees. The evening would be perfect if not for the dark cloud of suspicion hanging over my head.

Sam raises his water glass and toasts, "To us."

I join him, but when the sake arrives, I pour us each a shot, lift my cup, and say, "Bonzai!" before slamming back the warm rice wine, draining it all in one gulp. I feel like this night might require a bit of liquid courage.

Sam sips his drink and stares at me with a worried look on his face. I suppose a Japanese war cry may not have been the toast he was expecting, but it sure felt fitting.

I enjoy dinner in spite of my foul mood. The food is heavenly, and I feel a tiny pang of sadness that I've left the dining capital of the world to live in the middle of Illinois where the best Chinese food available is in the freezer aisle at the grocery store.

We clean our plates and even order the sesame balls filled with chocolate ganache and ginger cream for dessert. Because I'm not at all concerned about my belly popping out—read: no hanky-panky—I eat way more than my fair share.

Sam checks his phone, as he's been doing for the last hour; I'm sure his mind is on his impending meeting. He says, "Let me sign the check so we can head back to our room." He signals the waiter to complete his task.

As we're waiting for the elevator, he says, "Why don't you go on up? I forgot my toothbrush and want to see if the front desk has one."

I want to call foul on his ridiculous excuse. Instead I attempt to smile sweetly and agree. He hits the down button and his elevator arrives first. I call out, "Don't be long!"

"Believe me, I won't." Then the doors close.

I hit the down button right after so I can see what he's up to. I don't have long to wait. When the doors slide open into the lobby, I scurry out as fast as humanly possible and hide behind a large sculpted tree. I'm not sure it offers enough camouflage, but it's better than nothing. I want to locate Sam before I risk being seen.

When I spot him, he's walking toward a loveseat by the front entrance. He sits facing me. Crap. I can't move for fear of discovery. I crouch down a bit to hide my face behind a ball of leaves.

I'm so intently focused on the front door, I don't even notice the man who approaches me until he says, "Madam, may I be of some service?"

I look up to see a hotel worker staring at me with concern. "No, no, I'm good, thanks."

He doesn't seem to buy it. "I hope you don't mind me saying, but you don't look at all well."

And then like I'm channeling Sarah or something, I say, "My acupuncturist told me I need to stand like this every so often to cool my liver and help my energy lines open." I'm just making up random stuff on the fly.

"Why are you behind the plant?" he asks.

"Oh, this?" Think, Cat, think. Nothing is coming to me when I suddenly remember a crazy balanced living class Jazz and I took six years ago. We used to laugh at some of the ridiculous things they taught.

I end up saying, "The best feng shui is in the east corner of a room, next to greenery …" I look up and add, "under a mirror. Right now, I'm lined up for optimal energy flow and spiritual balance, which should really help the inflammation levels in my spleen."

He looks around as if searching for a butterfly net to capture me in before calling security. I stop paying attention though because the person Sam is meeting has just walked through the front door and sat down next to him. Holy crap! What in the hell is going on?

Hemophiliac Insanity

Jeremy's brother, Josh, walks into the lobby of the hotel. At first, I assume it's some bizarre coincidence, or random fluke. But then he turns around, sees Sam, and extends his hand in greeting.

I can't get close enough to eavesdrop without being spotted, so I stay in my contorted pose behind the potted plant and watch. There doesn't seem to be any animosity between them, even though they appear to be in serious discussion. Heads are nodding, hands are gesturing, a shoulder gets patted, all inside of five minutes. Then they stand up, embrace like bros, and part ways.

Before I know it, Sam is walking straight toward me. Luckily, the hotel worker is still nervously milling about my general vicinity—probably worried I'm going to steal the plant. I wave to get his attention and he comes over. "Could you please stand directly in front of me and maybe even put your arms around me?"

"Madam?" he gasps. He's acting like I just asked him to take off his pants and do the floss.

"My chi is dangerously close to bottoming out. I need to feed off your energy or I'm going to faint." Because it's not insane enough to sound like a parasitic alien straight out of *Dr. Who*, I add, "I'm a hemophiliac. If I start to bleed, I may not stop. I may die right here on the floor."

That gets his attention. If there's anything worse than hugging a crazy woman during your shift, it's trying to explain why you're standing over her dead body. His embrace is tentative at first, but my encouraging words of, "That's it. Yes, I feel my life force coming back. Just a little bit longer …" seem to do the trick. By the time Sam passes, I'm completely hidden in the lapels of Jonathan Clinger's jacket—I read his name tag while I'm hiding my face.

Once Sam is safely in the elevator, I push him away. "You're a dream. You just saved my life."

The poor guy looks like he wants to cry. "Anything for our guests, madam. Can I be of any further assistance?"

"Do you keep any extra toothbrushes behind the front desk?" I ask.

"Sadly, no. But our gift shop opens at eight. I'm sure they'll be able to help you at that time."

Just to toy with him, and because I'm still channeling Sarah, I say, "It's very important to brush your toenails at night. It helps to slough off any bad energy from the day." Then I semi-sprint to the elevator.

When I get to our room, Sam is already there. "Where were you?" he asks.

"Where was I?" I demand, "Where's your toothbrush?"

"They didn't have any, but luckily I found mine in the side-pocket of my bag."

I'm so beyond mad that Sam lied to me about not one, but both of the Renovation Brothers, I could spit. My curiosity is running on overdrive. I'm sure whatever he's hiding is the reason he didn't want me to do the show. My brain starts to spin one outlandish possibility after another, when he repeats, "Where were you?"

"I was, um, just trying to find a public restroom. They always have vending machines with Pamprin and tampons in them."

He looks disappointed. "Poor baby. Did it just, you know, start?"

"Yup." No fun for you, buddy—not that he could have possibly expected it.

Sam would have to be an idiot not to feel the arctic chill radiating from me. I decide to cut him the tiniest bit of slack while I figure out what he's up to. It'll be easier to catch him in additional falsehoods if he's not worried about anger oozing from my pores. So, once I slip into my jammies and wrap up in one of the complimentary robes, I ask, "Want to watch a movie?"

He joins me on the couch. "Sure." But instead of picking up the remote and finding one, he says, "I'd do anything for you, Cat. You know that, right?"

"So you say, but all I require is the truth, Sam. Are you sure you don't have anything you want to tell me?"

He looks like he's grappling with his response. He finally settles on, "I want to make sure all of your dreams come true. Even it means making you mad at me."

"Are you currently doing that?" This is obviously some kind of code. Too bad I didn't order a decoder ring from the back of a cereal box.

"I'll always do that," he answerers evasively. *Cryptic, and annoying.*

How does he think he's protecting me? I like both Jeremy and Josh. And even though Jeremy was horribly rude to Sam, I can't imagine feeling unsafe around him. So how can he be protecting me from them?

We sit side-by-side on the couch and rent *Love Actually*, because, OMG, the best romantic comedy ever. Am I right? You can't watch it and not believe that love always wins out. I could really use that kind of optimism at the moment.

Then I remember Emma Thompson's character. I still haven't forgiven Alan Rickman. He cheated on my girl and that kind of behavior does not wash in my book. Even his performance in *Sense and Sensibility* didn't make up for it. I'm not proud to say it, but the day he died, I thought, *That's the karmic wheel for you. You screw with Emma, and it's lights out.* No good can come from lying in a relationship, of this I'm certain. If only Sam understood that.

Flying Rocks and Jail Time

Over the next two days, Sam and I get a couple's massage, a couple's pedicure, we swim, eat, and explore the Magnificent Mile. I slightly lower my guard against him, because I really do need a vacation and I desperately need a break from all the stress. Also, courtesy of my nutty family, I've found it's best not to be a reactionary kind of gal.

We have a pretty good time, all things considered.

Over scones and coffee on Sunday morning, we discuss looking into a late check-out and hitting the pool one last time when I receive the following text:

Nan's in jail. I don't want to worry you or anything, I just thought you should know. Mom. My mom doesn't realize she doesn't need to sign texts.

I immediately reply: *What do you mean, Nan's in jail? What happened?!*

While the ellipses on my phone flash, indicating she's responding, I tell Sam. He replies, "Of course she is. That doesn't surprise me at all."

My phones beeps: *She got arrested. Threw a rock through Jenny Schweer's window. Travis and Scottie are with her. I'm off to bail them out. They've been charged with vandalism.*

Oh, no. Travis's plan to remove his friend's belongings from his family home clearly didn't go well. I'm not sure what they were thinking taking Nan with them. I know she was going to pretend to be Miss Daisy all weekend, but they shouldn't have included her in on their breaking and entering plans.

"So much for extending our weekend." I roll my eyes.

"Look on the bright side. At least she waited until the end of our stay to break the law. If that isn't a silver lining, I don't know what is."

"True dat. I guess we ought to head home now."

Sam signs for the check and we go back to our room to collect our belongings. He reaches out to hold my hands and says, "I had a great time this weekend. Thank you."

"Yeah, it was nice." He obviously senses I've been distant, but he probably assumes it's due to the car ride up with Jeremy. Little does he know, I know about both Renovation Brothers and every minute he doesn't level with me is another nail in our relationship coffin.

I let Sam drive home, so I can doze part of the way. Illinois in February is not the picturesque vista it is in warmer months. It's dark and gloomy and the once pristine snow is black from road dirt. Sarah jokes that it's a great big, cold bucket of suck. Graphic, but accurate.

I decide to send her a text.

Nan is in the slammer and tomorrow the crew from Bloomington shows up to demo the kitchen. Had a good weekend. How are you and Ethan?

She responds: *We're just about to sit down to eat a kombucha scoby. Yum!*

I feel bile rise in my throat. Scoby is an acronym for Symbiotic Culture of Bacteria and Yeast. It looks like a big disk of hard snot that forms on the top of kombucha or fermented tea. Sarah makes her own and it's pretty decent tasting. It's supposed to be one of the most beneficial health tonics around.

Why? So many whys? I ask.

Super good for you! It's a great source of protein, high in fiber, the good bacteria alone zaps your intestinal floral and fauna into bionic shape. I'll save some for you.

I release a full body shudder.

Taking a hard pass on that, but thanks for thinking about me.

Why's your grandmother in jail?

Threw a rock through Mrs. Schweer's window. Official charge is vandalism.

Sarah sends a string of cheerleader emojis. *When you think of it, it's kind of surprising she hasn't been incarcerated before now.*

Agreed. Are you coming over tomorrow?

Sounds like it's going to be a madhouse. Not sure I'd be any help. Keep me posted and I can alter my plans if you need me.

I sign off with a big thumb's up and put my phone back into my purse.

"Your house or the police station?" Sam asks when we drive into town.

"I guess my house. I can't imagine Nan is still in jail. She must be home cursing up a blue streak by now."

Yet, when we pull into the driveway, they are no other cars there. I run inside to check, but the house is empty. Sam asks, "Police station?"

I text my mom: *Where are you? Where's Nan?*

She responds: *Jenny Schweer is pressing charges. We're waiting for the judge to set bail. Should be home in a couple hours.*

Do you need me to come over? Please say no, please say no, please say no, I send out to the universe. I mean, what can *I* do to make the process go faster?

Nope. We got it covered. See you later.

I release my pent-up breath and announce, "We're off the hook. Want to help me pack up the kitchen?"

Sam and I spend the next half-hour boxing the last few remaining pots, pans, and dinner plates my parents left for me, when we hear a loud crash come from the living room. We run in to see a good-sized rock sitting on the floor in the middle of the living room. There's a piece of paper wrapped around it, secured by a rubber band. I open it up and read: "*Stay out of my family's business or you'll be sorry!*" It's signed Jennie Schweer. Who in the world signs a note that will tie them to a crime?

I look at Sam and burst out laughing. "I think we just got Nan's get out of jail free card." I call the police to let them know what happened and they assure me they'll send someone right over to take my report.

"Mrs. Schweer shot herself in the foot with this one," Sam says. It doesn't occur to either of us that this incident is anything but what it appears to be—payback, Old Testament style.

Before he leaves, Sam says, "Good night, Kitty Cat. I love you, and I promise everything is going to work out." Then he kisses my forehead and pulls me in for a hug.

I want to believe him, but first I need to know what he's been keeping from me and why.

Finally, Another Brother!

"Can you believe that crazy woman threw us in jail?" Nan yells.

"You threw a rock through her window. What do you think she should have done?"

My grandmother stands indignantly with her hands on her hips as she rails, "Listen to what I had to say, that's what she should have done. Plus, she played hooky on the Lord. If she was in church like she was supposed to be, I wouldn't have had to do it."

I interrupt, "You weren't at church, either."

"Yes, but I don't profess to being devout like she does. I'm a respectable enough person who has a relationship with her creator that can be maintained at home. Jenny makes sure to let the world know she's better than they are because she's at mass as often as a nun."

"Nan, you're missing my point. Why did you throw a rock through her window?"

"Because she told Scottie he was going to burn in hell for living a life of sin. I couldn't take it. I had to do something and there was a rock at my foot, almost like the good Lord put it there. So, I just picked it up and let it rip!" She nods her head for emphasis. "It felt good."

"I'm sure it did, but you do realize it wasn't the right thing to do, don't you?"

"How do you know? Maybe I shook her up enough to change her ways."

"No, Nan, all you did was make her mad enough to throw a rock through our window in retaliation. Does that sound like a woman who's suddenly going to come to her senses?"

My grandmother paces around like a caged grizzly bear. "What's wrong with people? It says right there in the good book, *Do unto others. Judge not. Let those without sin cast the first stone.*" Nan is shaking her fist like she's leading a revival meeting. "That judgmental harpy cast a stone right through our window!"

"Not until you cast one, first," I point out.

"She had it coming! There is no nicer boy on this planet than Scottie Schweer. What that poor thing did to deserve a mother like her, I'll never know."

"Are Scottie's things still at his mom's house?"

Nan throws her hands up in the air and shouts, "I didn't tell you! That horrible, wretched beast threw his belongings out her second story window right into the snow. She told her own son to take whatever he wanted and to get off her property and forget it was ever his home."

My heart sinks in my chest. "Oh, no." I've had other friends who've come out to their parents, but it's never been such a drama. Sure, some were surprised or upset. But only because they didn't want their child to be on the receiving end of discrimination. Not upset because they couldn't love them because of their sexuality.

I sit next to my grandmother quietly for several moments before asking, "Where is Scottie now?"

"Travis took him out for a beer. Actually, I think he may have taken him out for several. He was pretty shaken up when the coppers let us go." Then she suddenly shudders and announces, "I need to go wash off the stink of prison."

"The stink of prison?"

My grandmother looks appalled. "I was afraid they were gonna send me up the river. And as much as I don't care who sleeps with who, I was a little nervous about going to the big house with a bunch of them lesbians. You ever seen *Orange is the New Black*?"

I'm pretty sure the lesbians at the Ford County Correctional Facility would have taken one look at Nan and run for the hills, but I don't tell her that. Instead I say, "Yeah, that was a close call. Now that you're home you might want to consider staying on the right side of the law."

"Girl, you know it. I've been scared straight." Then she takes off to wash away the day.

I pick up my phone and text my brother: *How's Scottie?*

He writes back: *He wants me to take him to the courthouse tomorrow to change his name to Masterton.*

You should, it's a good name.

Travis replies: *It was tough today, Cat. We need to count our blessings that our family loves us the way we are.*

I used to think my family was strange and embarrassing. My dad with his kilts and dead animal friends, my mom with her crazy collections. But you know what? I'd take them any day of the week because they are the most loving, caring people I've ever known. Sure, they're weird, but they're good. They're loyal and true. You can't fake qualities like that.

I text my brother back: *Tell Scottie that as of today I have two brothers. Also, tell him, as our sibling, he has partial responsibility for Nan. It's only fair.*

Pancakes and Ponderations

I feel like I've been dragged across a hundred miles of rough pavement when I wake up this morning. My head hurts, my body hurts, and I could definitely use another three hours of sleep. But this is my last morning in my childhood kitchen and I want to go sit on the counter again before it's gutted.

I'm not the first one up. Travis is pouring a cup of coffee and mixing pancake batter when I walk in. "I thought this morning called for a special breakfast," he announces.

He's wearing a pink silk robe reminiscent of a nineteen forties movie star. He also has on false eyelashes and the bald cap he puts on before his wig. I say, "I see you're dressing up as Rhona today."

He nods. "I have to go into work. The cosmetic company has an investor meeting this afternoon. I have a presentation to make."

"What exactly do you do for them again?" I know he's told me, but I'm a little bit unclear about the details.

"I'm consulting on their new line of theatrical makeup. It's geared toward actors, models, anyone wearing a costume or trying to cover a tattoo or scar. I'm showcasing it on men in drag.

231

The thought being if it's strong enough to work on a five o'clock shadow, it'll cover up anything."

"And they pay you enough to support an apartment in Chicago?"

He laughs. "Most of my money still comes from advertisers on my YouTube channel, but don't worry, I'm doing just fine. I won't be moving in with you anytime soon."

"Yet you're here now, aren't you?" I tease.

"Yes, but I'm here to woo a wily woman. Apparently, that takes time."

My stomach lurches at the thought. "Did Ashley come back to the house last night?"

He shakes his head. "No. She said she'd be here this morning. I'm hoping to see her before I leave."

"Has she given you any encouragement?" I don't want to see Travis hurt and the TV producer seems to be about the most likely person I know to stomp on someone's feelings. I didn't see it at first, but she's totally the self-absorbed type.

"Not so much encouragement as less disgust than she exhibited in the beginning. That's a move in the right direction, don't you think?"

I joke, "I can hear the toast I'll give at your wedding. 'To Travis and Ashley! I knew they were a match the day the bride was no longer repulsed by my brother!'"

"I think that needs a bit of work," he says laughingly.

Scottie walks in and slumps down at the table. "I'm still drunk."

"You only had four beers," my brother says.

"Yeah, but I never have more than two."

"They were light."

"I still don't feel so good," he moans.

I fix him a cup of coffee and serve it with two aspirin. "I'm sorry about your mom. Yesterday must have been pretty awful."

He looks up miserably. "It was. It is. Life is hard enough, you know? I really didn't need this. I mean, why couldn't we have just carried on like we were, with me pretending to be what she wanted me to be, and her pretending not to see who I really am?"

"That's not a relationship. That's deception."

"Most relationships are built on deception, Cat. What do you think would happen if people were always honest with each other? People don't want the truth. They just want to hear what they want to hear and move on."

He's right. I've never appreciated the constant truth-telling I grew up with. "My family is brutally honest, no matter how much it hurts your feelings. In fact, they're one hundred percent against lying even if you beg them to."

"If I'd have told my mom who I was when I found out, I would have lost her a long time ago." A sob catches in his throat. "I love her, Cat. I just don't love her inability to accept me, but I love *her*."

I put my arms around him. "You get to the point in life when you have to put yourself first. Sometimes that means walking away from someone you love. For instance, I love Ethan, but I couldn't stay with him just to make him happy. I needed to figure out what made me happy."

He looks up at me. "Do you mind if I stay here for a while?"

"Not at all. My home is your home."

"I'm just not ready to walk away. I need to try to see her again before I go. I owe it to myself to try to finally connect with her."

My dad once told me that he believes we choose our parents. He thinks we have a big powwow in heaven before coming here and we sign up for the families we get. That makes sense when I think of my family. But as far as Scottie is concerned, I can't imagine him choosing Jenny. What in the world was he thinking?

Muscle Men and Liars

Travis leaves the house just as the crew of workers arrives from Bloomington. The new lot makes our small-town guys look like amateurs. They're wearing matching T-shirts, with their company logo on them, and their biceps look like they spend an hour a day bench-pressing cattle. They even wear whistles around their necks so they can get each other's attention in noisy situations. They're kind of intimidating.

Ashley is right behind them. She stops dead in her tracks when she sees Travis all dressed up as his feminine alter ego. My brother smiles brightly at her and greets, "Good morning, Ashley. I'm happy I got a chance to see you before I leave town."

The look on her face suggests she's trying to see my handsome brother underneath his false eyelashes and lipstick. "Where are you going?"

"Chicago." He doesn't say anything else and you can tell she wants to know more.

"Well, then. I'll see you whenever," she says.

"I'll be back for dinner tonight." She smiles slightly when she hears this before nodding her head and continuing inside.

Ashley helps out by instructing the workers where to begin.

Tad is still in charge, but he's out in the barn talking to the rest of the crew. When he comes into the house, he pulls me off to the side. "I'm not going to lie to you. It's about to get *meshugga* around here. The network wants us to be finished with everything in three weeks. That's a virtually unheard-of timeframe."

I nod as a jolt of excitement races through my body. I already feel like I'm living in chaos. But I'd rather push through and get to the light at the end of the tunnel as soon as possible, than drag it out longer. "What do you need from me?"

"I want you to pack the upstairs and move everyone to the basement. We're going to shoot footage of the guys gutting your kitchen and living room today, then tomorrow we're going to film them tearing apart the second floor."

"Ashley's staying here. Where do I put her?"

"Just throw her on the couch downstairs. The network will still pay you the same amount of money."

Nan and I can share a bed, but I wonder what I'm supposed to do with Travis and Scottie. They'll just have to haul their twin mattresses around the house and sleep wherever there's room. It's not like the crew is going to be working at night.

Jeremy comes in wearing a bright smile, as though he's forgotten the horrific car ride to Chicago. He hands me a pair of safety goggles and asks, "You ready to shoot the obligatory destruction scene?"

My eyebrows raise in question. He explains, "I'll give you a sledge hammer and then you, me, and Josh start tearing the place down. It gives viewers a sense of power."

I'm glad my parents aren't coming over until this afternoon.

I'm afraid the beginning of demolition will be more than they can handle. They're excited about the renos, but watching us rip everything apart might be a little brutal. "I'm ready." Then I ask, "Where is Josh, anyway?"

"He's in the barn. He'll be here in a few."

Once again, I wonder how the other Renovation Brother and Sam know each other. And why are they all keeping it a secret? Just thinking about the possibilities makes my head feel like it's going to explode. I conclude it's a more efficient use of my time to focus on what's happening here.

The morning passes with an otherworldly speed. I feel like Wonder Woman as I slam my hammer into cabinets and walls. By the time the brothers and I head to lunch in the barn, the entire first floor of the house looks like a tornado ripped through it. The crew is currently throwing the remnants of my childhood kitchen into the enormous dumpster that was delivered sometime this morning.

Emily is setting up two long folding tables with assorted sandwiches and salads when she spots me. "Wow, this is getting exciting! Tad told me to plan to feed lunch and dinner to thirty people every day until they're done."

"Thirty?" I ask.

"Fifteen construction workers, the television crew, and your family." Emily is pretty low-key, so I'm a bit surprised when she says, "Did you see those guys from Bloomington? Yum!"

"What about Marcus?" I ask. "Have you ever considered dating him?"

She jolts like I've just thrown a bucket of ice water at her. "I don't think he likes me."

"How can you say that?"

"I've seen him at Ten Pin several times, and he never looks my way. I bet someone like Ashley is more his type."

"How so?" I ask, full of curiosity.

"Well, you know, she's so stylish and everything. Actually, I've never seen Marcus flirt with local girls. He probably only dates women he meets in Champaign. A lot of Gelson hits the clubs there."

Both Marcus and Ashley have said that, which makes me more excited than ever to do something to give our singles an opportunity to meet right here in town. It might even bring some of the coveted Champaign/Urbana fish to our little pond.

I definitely get the feeling Emily would be interested in Marcus, if he were so inclined. Also, he seems a more reasonable connection than Josh, being that he's local. I'm guessing a little fling and some chicken wings might be a great ice-breaker for those two.

Bathing in the Dining Room

My parents tour the house before joining us for lunch in the barn. It turns out they aren't at all devastated by the state of the kitchen. As a matter of fact, Mags is positively thrilled. "Lord, I hated those cabinets! And the countertops were so stained I used to dream about pouring bleach on them and letting it sit for a week."

"I thought it would be hard for you to see everything go."

"Lass, it's a dream!" my dad exclaims.

Josh is standing nearby and obviously overhears. He asks, "Mags, Dougal, why don't you film the bathroom demolition with us tomorrow? You can hammer through the tile and help us remove the fixtures. It'll be liberating."

Mags declares, "I can't wait to rip it apart!" She looks more than a little bit maniacal.

This is the first time I've been around Josh since I witnessed his late-night meeting with Sam. Feeling like a spy, I smile and ask, "How was your weekend?"

"Dull, just like I like 'em," he answers flatly.

"Didn't go anywhere fancy?" *Like the Peninsula Hotel?* I stare at him intently as if my gaze alone could pick him up and move him across the room.

"Nope. Just hung out at my apartment all weekend. No, wait, scratch that. I went to the hardware store for a new hammer and stopped by the deli for some pimento loaf."

Liar, liar, pants on fire! Nobody under seventy eats pimento loaf. Of course, I can't say that. In fact, before I can say anything, Ashley calls from the doorway, "Josh, we need you in the house!"

He gives us a smile before jogging off. I say to my folks, "It's getting kind of exciting around here."

My mom gushes, "I bought you a housewarming gift yesterday. I can't wait to show you!" Her eyes are so glazed over with excitement that I can only assume it's a shortbread pan or a set of Ginsu knives.

"Thanks, Mom. But would you mind not giving it to me until I have a place to put it?"

"I couldn't, even if I wanted to. It won't be delivered for three more weeks."

Mysterious. Maybe she ordered me something from China, which is a cringeworthy thought. The last time she did that the item took six months to arrive and when it did it was the wrong color.

My dad asks, "Where are Travis and Scottie today?"

"Travis went into the Chicago and I think Scottie might be at city hall changing his name."

My mom shares her opinion, "Jenny Schweer and I went to high school together. She's always been a prissy girl. Always too good for everyone else, like she farts roses or something."

Farts roses. I have no words, so I change the subject. "You want to see the new countertops we picked out?"

Before anyone can answer, a loud crash comes from the

general direction of the house and someone yells, "Hurry up and turn off the main valve!!!"

I drop my paper plate and run. In the entryway, I see bodies darting around willy-nilly. There are men on the stairs and men sprinting through the living room. I search for the source of the ruckus and discover a bathtub right where my parents' dining room table used to be.

There's a hole in the ceiling with water pouring out of it like a waterfall. I call out to the first worker I see and ask, "What happened?"

"Looks like someone started to fill the tub and forgot about it. Must have been running for hours for this to happen."

I head downstairs to find Nan. She's sitting on the couch eating a bag of potato chips and reading a trashy romance like she's gone deaf and didn't hear the noise upstairs. "Nan, did you take a bath this morning?"

"Is that your way of telling me I stink? Don't be rude, girl."

"No, Nan. That's my way of asking you if you took a bath this morning."

She shakes her head. "Nope, took one yesterday. It's getting hard to climb in and out of the tub. I like to preserve my exertions and wash every other day."

"What about Travis and Scottie?"

"Couldn't say. Why are you suddenly so interested in everyone's ablutions?"

Instead of answering, I ask, "Didn't you hear that crash and all the excitement going on upstairs?"

"Lass, there's been commotion up there all day long. One little crash isn't going to upset me."

"Nan, the bathtub just fell through the second floor into the dining room. There's water everywhere."

"How exciting! Just let me finish my chapter and I'll come have a look-see. Clan McClintock just invaded the great hall of McCallister, and the chief has a serving lass pinned up against the wall. I think he's going to ravish her in front of everyone." Her eyes are bright with excitement.

"Stay where you are. It's crazy up there. I'll let you know when everything is cleaned up."

My grandmother goes back to her romance like she has no other worry in the world. I head up the stairs wondering what happened. Between all the mishaps at my house and pranks being pulled on Sam, I'm starting to think the two might somehow be connected. I hadn't thought so before because the upsets at my place could be plausible household disturbances. But now I'm not so sure. And then a thought hits out of the blue. Could the Renovation Brothers themselves be behind our troubles?

Barn Fiesta

Ashley is the first person I run into when I get back upstairs. She jabs a finger at me and growls, "Your house is a hazard. I've worked on more than ninety homes and none of them have been this big a nightmare."

It's hard, but I ignore her rudeness. "Did you take a bath this morning?"

"I took a shower at my apartment in the city." That's right. I forgot she didn't stay here last night. She's become an ever-present fixture, much like the stench of a startled skunk, I didn't even realize the air had cleared for a night.

"By the way, if you plan on still crashing here, you get the couch in the basement from now on. Tad's orders." It's pure joy to share her new arrangements with her.

She sticks her nose in the air. "I've procured other accommodations, so I'll have to pass on your less than gracious offer."

"Where in the world are you going to stay in Gelson, other than my house or Sarah's?" Don't get me wrong, I'm not going to miss her. I'm just curious.

"Airbnb had a couple places listed, I booked one of those." Before I can congratulate her on her brilliance—and let's face it, any idea that gets her out of here is brilliant—she storms away.

Cleaning up the flood derails the timeframe. It also upsets tomorrow's demolition as the floor needs to dry out and be stabilized before anyone can demolish more of the upstairs bathroom. Nonetheless, with an extra eight men on site, they have the mess cleaned up quickly and set to work prepping the rest of the downstairs.

I spend the afternoon sitting in the barn watching my dreams become a reality. The fireplace is nearly finished, and I visualize a large wooden plank for the mantle that will be used to display photos of the bride and groom. Of course, a holiday garland entwined with twinkling white lights and shiny red glass ornaments would be great at Christmas, or even simple candles, depending on the event. The moose head will likely hang from the stone wall above the mantle year-round. I definitely want a picture of it on the brochure I'm going to have made.

Tad joins me mid-afternoon and sits across the folding table. He declares, "Even though the scene looks like it's destined for crashville, you shouldn't wig. We've got it all in the hopper. At least you won't have Ashley jungled up in your business anymore."

I've been exposed to this odd man/child long enough now, my brain does an automatic translation: *Even though this reno looks like a complete mess, don't worry, it's all going to work out. At least Ashley's not staying here anymore.*

I smile, "I'm not worried. A bit frazzled maybe, but not worried."

"Coolio, Kitty Cat. Hey, I also wanted to talk to you about throwing a big shindig here for the final episode. I thought it would be the bomb to showcase the venue in full swing. How does that interview your brains?"

My mind immediately starts to fill with images. "Do you mean a wedding? I'm not sure I can find a couple in time and probably not one that will sign up before seeing a completed location."

"Nah, nothing so complicated. I was thinking along the lines of a big Scottish hoedown. You know, all the tassels and cronkites in skirts, throwing back a jug, and busting a righteous moby?"

"Tad, you're brilliant! That's exactly what we need to start booking the space. Can I invite as many people as I want?"

"Keep the list under a hundo. That way, the camera dudes can pick up the detail work. It'll make the barn look twice as big."

"We should invite all the workers and their significant others for sure. I mean, without them, this would have never happened."

"Nice. The bros and I will be there, as well, and I'm sure Ashley won't skip it. Just fill in around the edges and we're going to have ourselves one bitchin' fiesta, mama!"

"What date should I schedule the party for?"

"Make it April first. We should be cleared out by then and it'll give you time to pull it off."

Scottie walks in as Tad is about to leave. I grab him and pull him over. "Scottie, I don' think you've officially met Tad."

Tad's eyes pop open as he gives my new brother an appreciative look. Then he thrusts out his hand. "I'm super happy to meet you!"

Scottie smiles. "You, too. Cat here has been singing your praises. She says you're a creative genius."

Tad puffs up like a peacock. "Always nice to hear. Hey, if you want to Magoo the action firsthand, just let me know. I'd love to show you around."

Scottie shrugs his shoulders. "I've got nothing else going on right now, why not?"

The two take off leaning toward each other in a way that indicates definite mutual interest. I can't help but think my barn might already be bringing couples together and a little thrill shoots through me.

I grab the new sketchbook I brought along to design seating arrangements for the various kinds of events we'll host here. For our maiden voyage, working around the built-in bar at the back of the barn, I arrange the buffet tables first, then put the seating area in front of the fire, which leaves plenty of room for the dance floor. I can barely contain my excitement.

I grab my phone and call Sam, and it goes straight to voicemail. So, I text Sarah with the good news. She's so excited she texts back that she's coming right over. She's going to leave Ethan behind. I'm not sure that's a good idea being that she's never left him on his own yet, but what do I know?

Gypsy Mold

Sarah brings a spray bottle with her. It's a concoction she claims will eradicate mold spores before they can grow. "It's primarily tea tree, clove, rosemary and lemon balm oils." She shakes it up and declares, "It's a miracle worker!"

"What are you going to do with it, exactly?"

"Just spray it in the air for now. We don't need anyone breathing in pesky microbes." My friend has a long-standing distaste of anything mold related. It started in childhood when she accidentally took a bite of a sandwich with blue cheese in it. Ever since then, she's been on a one-woman campaign to rid the planet of mold.

"Sarah, I'm pretty sure it takes mold longer than a few hours to grow."

She nods in agreement. "True, but these oils work as an inhibitor as well, meaning they'll keep the spores from ever starting. Plus, they smell nice, so there's no downside."

At this point, I'd let a voodoo priestess come in and cast a charm if it would keep things on track. My parents lived in this house for thirty years and I cannot recall hearing of an exploding toilet, a dishwasher overflowing with suds, a shower head blowing off, or a bathtub in the dining room. Something very sketchy is going on here. Once again my mind drifts in the direction of the Renovation Brothers and their *possible* part in it.

Tad zeros in on us as we walk into the entryway and asks, "What's shakin' tassels? You up to something camera-worthy?"

My friend explains her plan and the producer's eyes light up with delight. "Groovy to the max! I'll get the guys over here and you can work your magic."

Within minutes, Jeremy, Josh, and the crew are standing next to us.

Camera focuses on the Reno Bros. with the bathtub in the dining room behind them.

Josh: With any flood, homeowners must be careful mold doesn't grow and spread. We cleaned up the initial debris from the overflow as soon as we discovered it. We immediately set up heaters and dehumidifiers to dry up the water and evaporate any residual moisture. While that will do the trick, Cat's friend, Sarah, thinks a little extra protection is in order.

Jeremy: Sarah has an additional way to fight off the dangers of mold. (Turns to Sarah) What have you got there?

Sarah: I made a solution of essential oils, which we're going to spray into the air to combat any spores that might grow.

Josh: Is there some kind of ceremony that goes along with this?

Sarah: Not that I know of.

Josh: Let's get Nan and see if she's got something.

Tad yells, "Cut! Someone get Cat's grandmother." Jeremy and Josh both assume the task.

Nan shows up a twenty minutes later dressed in a gypsy costume I remember her wearing some Halloween during my formative years. Her skirt is three tiers of brightly colored fabric. Her blouse is from the Bavarian barmaid collection, and she has a scarf tied around her head. There are tiny cymbals attached to her fingers. She looks like she's either going to put a curse on all of Romania or entertain them. To be honest, it could go either way with my grandmother. She's kind of random in her eccentricities.

She whispers to the brothers for several moments before joining the rest of us in the entry hall.

Camera focuses on the bros, the grandmother, and Sarah.

Sarah: So, Nan, how do we weave our magic together?

Nan: Just start spraying and I'll follow you, lass.

Sarah: (Looks at the camera and lifts the spray bottle into the air.) You don't want to soak the atmosphere, you just want to mist it. My tea tree oil concoction has an alcohol base. It will kill any germs.

Nan: (Starts a slow dance behind Sarah. She twirls around before snapping her fingers to play the cymbals. Then she claps her hands together.) Now, boys!

Jeremy and Josh: (Pick up grandmother under the arms and lift her high into the air. They begin to sing a song from the musical *Gypsy* with altered lyrics.) Where ever we go, she goes!

Nan: They follow me where I go! Through thick and through thin, with a bottle of gin …

Bros: We won't let mold win.

All together: We're gonna kick microbes together!!!

There are no words for how truly bizarre this episode is going to be. It's like the *Rocky Horror Picture Show* on steroids meets HHTV with a side of hallucinogenic drugs. You'd think I'd be immune to surprises from my family, but you'd be wrong.

Tads claps his hands in glee as he yells, "CUT! Perfect!" Then he looks at Nan and declares, "You're a star! Where have you been all my life?"

"Most likely right here in Gelson," she replies. "Why did it take you so long to find me?"

Jeremy sidles up to them and says, "Lucky for you I was in my college production of *Gypsy* and I made Josh learn all the songs with me."

The three of them walk off together, arm-in-arm, giggling like a bunch of school girls.

Sarah says, "Okay, now that the performance is over, I really do need to spray this around." She leaves me to pursue her task.

Ashley slithers up behind me and hisses, "I cannot express enough how much I dislike your family. You're all insane." She closes her eyes and takes a deep breath as though she's either trying to calm down, keep from hitting me, or both. "If these episodes don't ruin my career it'll be a miracle." Then she storms off in a huff.

The Meat Wars

Sarah screams, "He took the snowmobile into town and bought meat!"

That's the first thing I hear when I answer the phone. No greeting, no asking after my welfare, nothing. "Who is this?" I demand.

"You know perfectly well who it is."

"Who bought meat?"

"Ethan! The minute I left him home alone, he got on the snowmobile and drove it into town to buy meat."

"How do you know that?"

She shrieks, "There are packages from the deli crammed into my refrigerator!" I hear some rustling in the background. "Turkey! Roast Beef! Ham! My God, it's a murder scene!"

"Sarah, Ethan has been on your vegan kick for well over two weeks. His body should be pure by now, right?"

"Not anymore. You can't just go from vegan to carnivore overnight. If you're going to start polluting your body again, you must do it slowly. First you add some dairy, then an egg or two a week. You can't live a clean life and then just stop cold turkey. It's like speeding down the road at a hundred miles an hour and hitting a wall."

"That would be instant death."

"Exactly. Ethan has killed his new vibration. It's going to set him back a month."

"Is he sick?" I ask.

"Nothing that shows," she begrudgingly admits. "But I promise you, he's going to be constipated for a week and he's going to feel like a corpse tomorrow. I'm so disappointed I could cry."

"He must have really missed meat." It's the only thing I can think of to say. For Ethan to brave a snowmobile ride, which he considers nearly as dangerous as roller skating, he must have been desperate.

"I'm so mad at him, I'm ready to put him on a plane back to New York. If he doesn't want to take his healing seriously, I shouldn't even bother with him."

"Sar, you don't mean that. Wasn't your spirit guide the one who told you it's your duty to help those most in need?" I can't believe I'm quoting her spirit guide, but there you have it. It seems desperate times really do call for desperate measures.

"You know what they say, Cat. God helps those who help themselves. If Ethan isn't willing to help himself, why should I bother? There are plenty of other people out there who are ready to commit to good health, if given a little guidance."

"How much did he eat? The way you're carrying on, it sounds like he consumed an entire cow."

"He had two slices of turkey. But that's not the point. The point is he bought three pounds of the stuff. Three pounds!" she repeats for emphasis.

"I think you need to calm down. Maybe make yourself a cup

of lemon balm tea and sit in your mediation pyramid for a while."

"Some things are bigger than meditation, Cat!" she yells.

"Really?"

"Well, no, but this feels bigger."

"Where's Ethan now?"

"I told him to go for a walk. I couldn't bear to look at him."

I decide to champion my ex. "I bet he feels awful."

"Of course he does, with all those innocent animals inside him."

"That's not what I meant, and you know it. Plus, it was only two slices. I bet he feels bad for disappointing you. And that can't be good for his mental state." Then I tell her, "He wouldn't let me join him for lunch when I ran into him in town last week. He said you would think it was cheating because he was supposed to be there meeting new people."

"Really?" she sounds surprised.

"Really. He views you as his savior. I promise, if he went off the diet you set for him, he had a good reason."

"There is no reason for it. You either want help or you don't."

"What if going off makes him feel so bad, he commits to his health even more than before?"

My friend is quiet for several moments. "Maybe. But you know what this means don't you?"

I haven't a single idea, and I'm actually a bit afraid to hear the answer. With Sarah it could be anything. Maybe she has to throw Ethan out of an airplane without a parachute into a sea of vegan Jell-O to realign his chakras. Maybe she's going to starve him for three days to shock his system into rebooting. That's when it hits me. "The naked snow roll?"

"You got it! I'm gonna sweat him and roll him until he can't stand it anymore."

Poor Ethan. It isn't as though his life isn't hard enough. All he wanted was a sandwich. It probably brought him comfort. Now he has Sarah acting like he handed off secrets that won the war for the other side. The meat war.

The Truth Comes Out

I'm still put out with Sam for not leveling with me about what's going on between him and the Renovation Brothers. Tonight, I'm going to get answers. But when I arrive at his house, he asks, "How did filming go today?"

"Nan did a musical number from *Gypsy*, if that gives you any indication."

He asks, "Do you remember how she used to play Auntie Mame when we were kids? She'd put on that great big feather boa and pretend a Pixy Stix was a long cigarette?"

I laugh in spite of myself. "She'd parade down the stairs singing, 'We Need a Little Christmas.' How could I forget that?"

"It's not like it's the only weird thing she's ever done, you know. She used to do that back before she started calling people out in public. I can totally see how the memory slipped through the cracks."

We sit quietly for a moment before I say, "I want you to tell me about Josh and Jeremy."

"What do you mean? There's nothing to tell." His fingers start fidgeting like he's had a triple espresso followed by a gallon of Mountain Dew. He's obviously nervous.

"There's something going on. I know you think you're trying to protect me by keeping it a secret, but I demand to know the truth." I feel like Judge Judy. *Don't pee down my leg and tell me it's raining, boy. Speak up!*

Sam sighs. "Josh and I went to college together. We were roommates senior year."

"Why didn't you tell me that before?" I mean it's not like they were running meth for the Colombian drug cartel.

"Because if I went to college with Josh, I also went to college with Jeremy, and as you saw for yourself, Jeremy and I do not get along."

"And?" I prod.

"I thought it was best for your renovation if Jeremy didn't know I had anything to do with you."

"Why? What do you think he would have done?"

"I don't think he would have done anything. I just didn't want there to be a lot of tension at your house. I wanted him to come into town, do his job, and leave. No drama."

"Why don't you like each other?"

Sam hesitates, "I don't dislike him." Uncomfortably, he proceeds, "I started dating a girl senior year. She told me she was single, but it turned out she'd been with Jeremy for three months at the time. Josh told me his brother had been dating someone, but I didn't know her name. I didn't know it was the same girl until after we'd broken up."

"Why did you break up?" I want to know, and I don't want to know at the same time. Nobody ever likes talking about their exes, especially to their significant other, but this seems pertinent to our current situation.

"She and I moved in together and were a couple while I was in medical school."

"OMG, that was the girl you almost got engaged to!" Sam had confessed over Thanksgiving that he hadn't been pining away for me for fourteen years. In fact, he'd considered proposing to someone else.

He nods his head. "It was."

I exhale like I'm trying to fill a giant balloon. "I wish you'd told me this before I applied to the show!"

"Why, so you wouldn't have applied? Cat, you really wanted this. You told me how much it meant to you and how much it would mean for your business. I didn't want to keep you from your dream. And truthfully, at the time I didn't think there was a big chance they'd pick you. I was hoping it would go away with no need to dig up the past."

My fists and jaw clench in anger and I want to punch a wall, or Sam. "I don't think it was your place to keep something like this from me. I'm a big girl. I can handle the truth and should have been given the opportunity to make my own decision."

"But if you'd chosen not to do the show, I would have always felt guilty that you didn't get the renovation you wanted."

I interrupt, "So you took it upon yourself?"

"I'm sorry, Cat. I know now that I shouldn't have. But you have to believe I only wanted the best for you. I only *want* the best for you."

I ignore his plea and think about all the disasters that have been happening around my house. "Do you think Jeremy is the one causing all the chaos at the farm? Because I'm starting to think that."

"To what end? I mean, they're renovating anyway. Why bother creating trouble if they're just going to fix it?"

"To send you a message maybe?"

He shakes his head. "He didn't even know about me until you picked me up for the drive into Chicago, remember? Most of the trouble happened before then."

"So, he couldn't have been behind all the bad things that have been happening to you, either."

"Not unless he already knew about me, but you saw his reaction when he recognized me. He was really surprised."

"Did Josh know I was your girlfriend when this all started?" I ask.

He shakes his head. "I didn't tell him. Once I knew the brothers were going to take on your house, I decided to back off and let them do their thing. I knew you'd be mad at me for not being around more, but it seemed like the easiest way for you to get what you wanted with the least amount of fuss."

I interrupt, "Then they made my episode a two-part arc and changed the format so Jeremy and Josh would be around all the time, instead of just two days a week."

"Then there's that," he agrees.

I can see where he thought he might have gotten away with this.

"I wanted to tell you, Cat, but I didn't want to cause any trouble. You had a lot on your mind, and I figured it would be easier for you if I just stayed away."

I hate that Sam lied to me. He has a history of keeping things to himself, like making plans that don't include me. More secrets don't bode well for any latent trust issues I have. I understand he didn't want me to be mad at him, but I'm a big girl. That should have been my call, not his.

"Why is Jeremy still so mad at you?"

"He was really devastated by the breakup. I think it was his first real heartbreak. Not to mention it was a real ego-crusher. Apparently, he's hated me ever since he found out I was the one she left him for."

"Did you ever run into him while you were with this girl?"

"Yeah, but remember, I didn't know about their history while she and I were together, and Jeremy never tipped his hand. I didn't find out until we'd broken up, and by then, what could I have done about it?"

"I followed you to the lobby at The Peninsula. I know you met Josh there," I confess.

His eyes pop open. "I guess you spent the weekend having a lot of doubts about me."

"Let's call them concerns. I wanted to know the truth and I was mad you were keeping something from me."

"Cat, I'm so sorry. I didn't want to cause any trouble for you. I promise, if I could go back and do it differently, I would."

I believe him. Now that I finally know the truth, I can see that Sam was trying to do the right thing. Do I think he was also trying to protect himself? Hell, yeah, but I know he was mostly trying to protect me and help me get the renovation I wanted. I lean into him and rest my head on his shoulder. "All this could have been avoided if you'd just leveled with me from the start, you know?"

"I know. And I'm sorry. But Cat, there's something else I need to tell you."

"There's more?"

He nods his head. "Yeah, but I want to show you something first."

"Why drag it out? I want to know now."

"I'm going to tell you, but please, let me do this my way."

"Fine," I say. But I'm not happy about postponing the rest of his confession.

Scrapbooks & Delays

Sam stands up and stokes the fire. Then he walks to the bookshelf and pulls out a scrapbook. "My mom dropped this by the other day. It was in a box of stuff I'd left at home." He hands it to me and says, "I started this the week after we broke up."

I immediately flashback to that time. Sam upset my whole world. He broke up with me right as I thought our future together was about to take off. What could he possibly have put into a scrapbook as he was celebrating being free of me?

Like Superman trying to take a Kryptonite donut, I reach out to touch it, but it's nearly impossible. I've never felt so simultaneously drawn and repelled by anything in my life.

The front cover is the kind where you make your own design and shove it under a clear sleeve. It's titled, "My Life Until Now." There are questions marks surrounding it in varying shades of felt-tip marker. With a fortifying breath, I open it. The first page reads:

My name is Sam Hawking. I'm eighteen-years-old and I have just graduated from high school. I'll be going to Northwestern University in the fall and I've just done the hardest thing I will ever do. I broke up with the perfect girl. Her name is Cat and this is our story.

There's a picture of us underneath. We were seven, making mud pies in my front yard.

I pour over the pages like they're sacred text. The images are every memory that lives in my heart. We're little, we're laughing, we're eating a picnic lunch, we're playing tag. Scene after scene of an idyllic childhood. At the end of the first section is another message.

Cat was my playmate, my best friend, my confidante, and fellow mischief-maker. She was, and is, my heart.

The next part is from our adolescent years. We're awkward. There are braces, bad haircuts, questionable fashions, and let's face it, pimples. We weren't little kids anymore, but we weren't grownups. We'd barely started our transformation, and to tell you the truth, it's kind of painful to see. The comment after this series of photos reads:

Not everyone would stand by my side while I sported my wannabe boy band hairstyles. A true friend doesn't see those things. A true friend sees who you are inside.

I try to swallow down the emotion escalating inside me. Currently, it's climbing up my throat and about to choke the life out of me. I remember our time together; it's branded on my brain. The thought of Sam making this book for himself, after cutting off our connection, baffles my mind.

The third section is our "in love" phase. We were in high school and only had eyes for each other. We were happy in every picture: holding hands, laughing, enjoying school dances, sharing quiet moments when we thought we were alone. Clearly, we weren't. It was pre-cellphone days, so someone else took the picture. The message that follows reads:

The perfect girl loved me. I don't know what my future holds, but I'll always have the knowledge that the prettiest, funniest, happiest girl I've ever known, once thought I was wonderful.

Tears are streaming down my face but I don't try to wipe them away. This would probably be the proper time to say something, but the final pictures render me mute. They're of me during college. In the first, I'm strolling with friends across the quad. In another, I'm kissing a boy named Keith under a tree—that relationship lasted three dates. I'm home for Christmas and walking out of the barn—probably fresh from the loft after a thinking session. In all, there are fourteen snapshots of my college years.

All of them have a very editorial feel. I'm being distantly observed. I look up at Sam perplexed, but he gestures at the inscription.

Cat's okay without me. I'm not sure I'm doing as well. I've never known who I was without her. Even though it's painful to be apart, I've finally met me. I wonder what comes next.

I look up and ask, "You took these?"

He nods. "I had to know you were okay. I had to see you for myself." He takes my hands in his. "It was excruciating losing my best friend."

I don't know what to say. I've accepted our years apart. I met myself, too. I had adventures I never would have had with him in my life. I finally ask, "Why did you show this to me?"

"Because I need you to know how deep my feelings are for you. I need you to know that you've always been with me. We're entwined. Whatever happens from this point on, I need you to know how much I love you."

I lean in and kiss Sam for all I'm worth. Every ounce of emotion I've ever felt for him bubbles to the surface and nearly consumes me. When I finally pull back, I say, "I love you, Sam Hawking. I really, truly do." Then I tease, "It's kind of girly making a scrapbook though, isn't it?"

"Psh, I was full of angst and hormones. I'm surprised making a scrapbook is all I did." He squeezes my hands and says, "Now that you've seen the book, I'm ready to tell you the rest."

My stomach growls, wanting to be fed, but not until I hear what he has to say.

Just as he opens his mouth to finish telling me, his phone rings. He grabs it, saying, "I've got to take this, it's the hospital."

What? This is the worst possible timing! This is "watch out for that iceberg"-as-you're-colliding-with-it, timing. Why did he have to show me that scrapbook before finishing his story?

Sam begins to put his coat on. When he hangs up, he says, "They need me at the ER right away. A patient I released this morning is back with symptoms of cardiac arrest. I'm so sorry. I promise we'll talk soon."

Then he gives me a quick kiss before leading the way out his front door.

Just when I was starting to feel like everything was going to be all right. I miss the days when Sam and I weren't in a constant state of stress. I miss cuddling and kissing and not feeling like secrets lay between us. I miss having an empty house without problematic producers and dramatic family members trying to take over. More than anything, I miss feeling secure in my own life.

Inclusive Includes Drag Queens

I sleep like a drugged toddler. As soon as I close my eyes, I'm gone. I don't recall dreaming and I have no idea how nine hours elapsed when it feels like ten minutes. Nan is sawing logs beside me, so I sneak out of bed, trying not to disturb her.

I know Travis and Scottie are already up because their twin beds lay empty in the basement living area. I find them sitting at a card table in the destroyed kitchen sharing a box of cold sugary cereal. I pull up a chair to join them.

My brother is back to being in full-boy mode. I ask, "How'd the meeting go yesterday?"

"Fantastic! You know the designer, Lis Flannagan?"

"Yeah, I have at least four of her dresses."

"She was there."

"Why?" Scottie demands.

"She's designed a new line of clothes called *Inclusive*. She wants our makeup company to sponsor her shows."

"What does that mean?" I ask.

"It means we'll do the makeup for her runway shows in exchange for ad space and credit in the programs." He leans forward looking really pleased with himself. "I'll be in charge."

I clap my hands together in excitement. "How cool is that? What's the line all about?"

"Lis wanted to create a brand that's inclusive to everyone who wears women's clothing. The models will be comprised of high fashion models, plus-size models, everyday women, and wait for it … drag queens!"

"Get out of town!" Scottie yells, "What a great idea!"

My brother nods. "It's already getting tons of press." Then he tells me, "I'm going back to Chicago tomorrow to get to work on the initial concept. Looks like I won't be hanging around as much as I'd hoped."

"Good," I reply before I can stop myself.

"Not this again."

"You're too good for Ashley and I don't want you pining after her. Especially when I have to witness it."

Scottie says, "I agree. The woman's an ice cube." Then he adds, "I'll go home with you. I tried to see my mom yesterday, but she wouldn't even answer the door. I have to give it time."

"You're both leaving me?" Then I say, "Just put April first on your calendars. That's when we're having the big barn party to reveal the final renovations for the show."

"We'll be there with bells on," Travis says. "I mean, I can't miss my big television debut, can I?"

"What are you going to wear?" I ask.

"I think I'll put together one of my own designs."

"You should make all of our dresses! That way we can plug your talents to the whole country."

Scottie stands up and declares, "I told Nan I'd take her to the mall today. She's getting bored with the renovations now that there aren't as many opportunities for camera time."

"At least they're going balls to the wall to get the work done. They're putting in the cabinets and countertops today." I'm so very ready for countertops.

Scottie asks, "Anything you need me to pick up while we're out?"

"I need bath towels. Just get a couple sets. I'll get more once the bathrooms are done." I flashback to wiping up one of Ashley's toilet messes every time I dry myself after a shower. It's starting to wig me out.

"You got it. I'm going to go stir Nan's stumps and get her out of here. I promised her breakfast at the IHOP."

Travis and I sip on a second cup of coffee together and I tell him, "I'm really excited about your new gig. Your time has finally come, you know?"

"It's taken me long enough."

"Dad says everything happens in its own time. It's your turn, that's all." Then I tease, "Now, all we need to do is find you a good woman." I can't seem to stop myself.

"Let it go, Cat. I'll wind up with whomever I'm meant to be with. At this point, it's out of both of our hands."

Then, speak of the devil, who should walk through the kitchen door, but Ashley. Dear God, this woman is like a bad rash. She keeps showing up. It's not that she isn't expected, but she's thirty minutes early. And I cherish every single moment without her.

I look up at her and demand, "Why are you here before eight?"

She sneers at me, curled lip and all. I want to punch her. "I'm here to talk to your brother, not you." Then she smiles at him almost bashfully. Is that the word? Maybe the more accurate term would be flirtatiously, but I can't bear to allow myself to think she's actually flirting with him.

Travis jumps up and says, "I'm at your service, m'lady. What can I do for you?"

Ashley turns to me as bold as a fart in church and says, "Would you excuse us?"

I want to scream, "This is my house! Go excuse yourself!" But I don't. I merely walk away, hoping my brother isn't such a rube that he falls for her saccharine-sweet performance. The woman is poison.

I head downstairs where my catalogues are and start ordering dishware for my future events. It's all very exciting and I vacillate between two patterns before finally settling on the simplest. You can dress them up or down, so they'll be a perfect starter set. Once I'm booking parties, I'll add more.

While I'm busy shopping, the wall between the kitchen and dining room comes down. I can't believe what a difference it makes. The guys are going to put in a large island with a sitting area, and there will still be enough room for a dining table. Opening up the space allows us to add more cabinets and countertops, which will be beneficial to the caterers.

When I see my mom, she's near tears. "I love this so much! Why didn't we ever think to do something like this?"

I'm glad she didn't. I could just imagine my parents trying to do a DIY project like this. It would have taken months, if not years, to execute.

"How are you feeling about everything now, Mom? Is it easier to think of the old place changing now that you don't live here?"

"Oh honey, I know I was a little moody before we left. I think it had more to do with my saying goodbye to my past than anything you were planning on doing to the house." She smiles pleadingly. "Forgive me?"

"There's nothing to forgive. I can't imagine it was easy to move after being here for thirty years. The good news is that Nan and I still live here, so you can visit all the time."

"Absolutely," she agrees. "Plus, I get to watch you do things to the old place I never dreamed possible. And I don't have to pay the bill. Win-win all around."

Tad joins us and says, "Hola, tassels, it's going to be Ritzville in here, doncha think?"

I agree. "Jeremy told me they're installing the island cabinets tomorrow after moving the plumbing for the sink—countertops and fixtures by the end of the week. It's amazing to see everything coming together so quickly."

He asks, "Have you been upstairs?"

"I thought we had to wait a few days before you could start up there because of the flood."

"Had the inspector out this morning, and he gave us the green light. We're not filming the demolition though. Don't want to have that many peeps standing near an open hole in the floor. The guys are fixing it, and then it's full steam ahead."

He hands me a bunch of brochures. "I need you to pick out your fixtures. We're going to bring them in from Chicago, so they should all be in stock."

I smile at my mom. "What do you think, Mags? Want to help me?"

My mom is in near raptures at the thought of choosing new stuff for the house, even though she doesn't live here anymore. "It's like being a kid on Christmas morning. Let's do it!"

As we shop like a couple of lottery winners, I reflect on all the positive things happening in my life. I'm getting a fabulous renovation full on with free advertising for my new business. I'm spending a lot of quality time with my family, and I'm in love with a great guy—who may or may not still be on my poop list.

I manage to call Sam three times today in between all the chaos, but I don't hear from him until late. As soon as I pick up the phone I say, "I've been dying to know what else you wanted to tell me last night."

He says, "I need to tell you in person, Cat. Unfortunately, I work the next two nights and I'll be sleeping at the hospital. It's going to have to wait a couple of days."

"No fair!"

"I know. But please remember how much I love you. Once I tell you everything and you forgive me, then we're good to go. I promise."

"Forgive you?"

"A lie of omission, to do with how I know Jeremy and Josh. I really was going to tell you last night and I really am going to tell you soon. It just has to be face-to-face. Okay?"

Before I can say anything, he has to go. I hang up feeling bereft and more than a little worried. I can speculate all I want, but as I have no idea what he's going to tell me, I try to force it out of my mind to save my sanity. It doesn't work.

Girls' Night In

Friday night arrives before I know it. The crew packs up for their weekend in Chicago, the construction guys all head home, and it's just me and Nan. Sam unexpectedly works again tonight—his fourth in a row—so I promised my grandmother some quality girl time. According to her, we're going to bond. I don't know exactly what this means as I feel pretty bonded to her already, but she has plans.

When the house is finally clear of extra people, she comes up from the basement wearing a flannel nightgown and warm robe. She's got curlers in her hair and a silk scarf tied around her head to keep them secure.

"What are you wearing?" I ask.

She smiles radiantly. "This is my pajama party outfit. Every time I had a sleepover when I was a girl, we'd put our hair in rollers so we could style each other's hair the next day."

"We're going to do each other's hair?" I'm not opposed, but as we've never done this before, it's kind of weird.

"Don't be silly." She smacks my arm playfully. "I'm just setting the mood."

"For what exactly?"

"Our pajama party, of course!"

I feel like I'm a couple pages behind on the storyline. "Are we going to paint each other's nails and gossip about boys, too?"

She winks at me. "Always a possibility. But first we have to pop the popcorn."

"Nan, I have no idea where anything is. I think the pans are all out in a box in the barn."

She pulls a bag of microwave popcorn out of the pocket of her robe. "We don't need a pan for this!"

As my grandmother prepares snacks, there's a knock at the front door. I hear it open and my mom calls out, "I'm here!"

I look at Nan and she's got a grin on her face that's positively electric. "I invited some other gals over for our party."

"You did? Why didn't you tell me?"

"You've been working so hard, I wanted give you a little surprise."

God save me from surprises from my family, but this seems like it's going to be a nice one. "Who's all coming?"

"Just you, me, Mags, Sarah, and Emily. I invited another gal, but I'm pretty sure she won't show. It was just a spur of the moment thing."

My mom walks into the kitchen holding a Jell-O mold and a bottle of triple sec. "I'm so excited we're doing this!"

Before I can reply, there's another knock on the door. This time it's Sarah. She's all decked out in pjs covered in barnyard animals. She hands me a plate of hummus, naan bread, and a bottle of tequila. "Heya, chicks!" she greets.

Emily is close on her heels toting a can of frozen limeade and a bag of limes. She says, "I have more stuff in the car. I'll be right back."

The next person who walks into the kitchen isn't Emily returning. Hold onto your girdle, it's Dorcus Abernathy.

Nan greets, "Dorcus, you made it!" She relieves the minister's wife of the plastic bag she's carrying and offers to take her coat.

To say I'm shocked to see Nan's arch-enemy standing in my kitchen in her nightgown is a mammoth understatement. Emily comes back in with her snacks and my mom shouts out, "Let's get this party started!"

I haven't a clue what's in store for us tonight, but I confess to being excited to find out.

Margaritas & Confessions

Mrs. Abernathy corners me and says, "Thank you for including me. I didn't know what to think when your grandmother invited me, but I thought if we were going to bury the hatchet once and for all, this might be a nice new beginning for us."

What a sweet thought. I take Dorcus's coat and hang it in the closet. Then I look around at the destruction of the first floor and say, "I guess we should take this party downstairs where it's not so messy."

"Nonsense!" Nan declares. "Let's go out to the barn. The boys left us some space heaters. We can take some blankets with us and tell ghost stories."

Everyone agrees the barn is the place to go, so I grab a bunch of plaids we use as blankets and we make our way across the snow-covered lawn. I ask Sarah, "Aren't you afraid to leave Ethan?"

She shrugs her shoulders. "I told him if he eats any more meat, I'd drive him to the airport myself."

"How'd he take that?"

"He said the sandwich wasn't nearly as good as he remembered, and promised he was done eating animals." She adds, "At least until we're finished working together. He said he'd started feeling so separated from his identity that he had to do something that felt normal to him."

"Ethan has made more changes with you in a month than I thought he was capable of making in a lifetime. He seems kind of childlike."

"Exactly!" Sarah says. "The whole point of rebooting your cell memory is to bring your mind and body back to a childlike pureness."

"I think change is harder for Ethan than for most."

"For sure, but people are always capable of change. They spend so much time telling themselves they aren't, they no longer believe in their potential. In Ethan's case, he has to learn that he's capable."

"Does Ethan talk about his plans once he's through with your program?"

She shakes her head. "Not much. He did say he was going to have his mom pack up his apartment though."

"What?" I yell a bit louder than planned. "He's giving up his apartment?" I'm not emotionally tied to Ethan's place, but he is. It's the perfectly nondescript home under a thousand steps to the subway, he's always longed for.

"He says he can't imagine ever going back there and selling it will force him to embrace whatever comes next in his life."

I'm absolutely shocked. "Does that mean he's giving up his job, too?"

"Probably. Although he hasn't said as much. For now, he's still on paid medical leave, so I assume he'll stay here until that runs out."

I used to think the idea of Ethan staying in Gelson was the

worst possible outcome for me. I no longer feel that way. We seem to have firmly cemented our relationship in the friendship zone. If staying here will help him find his new groove, I'm all for it.

When we reach the barn, Mags turns on the overhead chandeliers which were installed just this morning. They're positively mesmerizing at night, casting shadows that dance around the walls like forest sprites. I feel like I'm in a fairy tale and I've just arrived at an enchanted ball. I look at my family and friends and see they're feeling something similar.

Then Nan says, "Jeremy laid out a fire for us. He says all we need to do is light a match." Then she cautions, "We can only use it until the wood burns out and can't add anymore, though. Something about seasoning the stone."

The ladies set the food on the table before pulling up chairs around the hearth. Sarah mixes a pitcher of margaritas while Emily strikes the match. Once we're all situated with plastic cups in hand, Nan raises her drink in a toast. "To family, friends, and new beginnings. May we cherish them all!"

Mrs. Abernathy pipes up with a, "Hear, hear!"

Sarah adds, "Damn straight!"

Mags throws her margarita back, and Emily says, "Thank you for including me."

Once we've all enjoyed out first drink, I declare, "What a fun way to christen the new barn!"

When we've finished our second cocktail, it's clear Dorcus is feeling no pain. She addresses Nan none to quietly, "Bridget, I want you to know something. Hugh never really wanted to marry me."

My grandmother looks shocked. "Then why did he ask you?"

"As you know, he and I were neighbors." Nan nods. "He heard me crying in my backyard one night and came over to find out what was wrong."

She takes a moment to collect herself, so Nan demands, "Well, what was wrong with you?"

The reverend's wife looks around assessing her audience before confessing, "I was pregnant."

"Damn!" Nan exclaims. "Tell me more."

Dorcus clears her throat. "Brian and I had, well, you know, gotten close. I found out about the baby the same day he announced he was going abroad for college." No one utters a word. We've been stunned into silence, so she continues, "I knew he didn't want to get married right after high school, and I didn't want him to think I'd trapped him. Hugh told me I was being silly and that he needed to know." She takes a fortifying gulp of her drink. "He proposed to me during lunch the next day."

Nan's face turns red in remembered outrage. "I was never so embarrassed in my whole life." Nan and Gramps had been dating and she thought they had "an understanding," so she was completely shocked by his betrayal.

Dorcus continues, "He didn't want to marry me. He just wanted Brian to see that I had options and that I probably wouldn't be around when he came back from Europe. His plan worked. After I turned Hugh down, Brian popped the question that same afternoon, albeit more privately."

Nan demands, "Why didn't Hugh ever tell me?"

"Because he didn't want to shame me and tell a secret he didn't think was his to share."

My grandmother spits out, "But you didn't have a baby for three years after getting married, girl. What happened to the baby?"

"I lost it two weeks after the wedding." She shakes her head. "I should have told you then, but I was so mad at you for being nasty to me at school. Then I was consumed by grief over losing the baby and worried Brian would think I'd trapped him. I was a mess. By the time I started feeling like myself again, it just felt like it was too late."

Nan looks like you could push her over with a feather. "I *was* pretty horrible."

"You were. But you had every reason to be and I'm sorry. I'm sorry I never told you the truth before now."

"I'm sorry for your loss, Dorcus," Nan says graciously.

The minister's wife takes my grandmother's hand and squeezes it. "Thank you, Bridget. That means a lot."

I think of all the wasted years of possible friendship between these two old gals and want to kick Gramps. I know the older generation has a strong sense of honor, but this seems a bit extreme.

As we share more camaraderie in the best barn ever built, a feeling of pure contentment washes over me. We've navigated around a lot of bumps to get to this point, but it looks like it's finally smooth sailing.

At least until I have an opportunity to talk to Sam.

Munchausen by Plumbing

We sleep in the basement, with Nan and Dorcus sharing my bed. Mom takes the couch and Emily and I crash on the twin mattresses recently vacated by Travis and Scottie. Sarah goes home at 2 a.m. because she's having second thoughts about leaving Ethan overnight. She doesn't want a repeat of "Meatgate" as she's started to refer to it.

The stove still isn't hooked up, so we put out a cold breakfast in the morning. Coffee is consumed in direct proportion to the amount of tequila imbibed last night. The party breaks up around eleven. No one's hair got styled, no nails were polished, but it was one of the best times I can recall having in recent memory.

When our friends are gone, Nan says, "Let's go into town. I want to pick out a book for our new book club." Nan, Dorcus, and Emily have decided to start a book club together. They're going to only read Scottish historical romances of the steamy variety. They're meeting every other Thursday night for dinner and some good old-fashioned trash talk.

"Sounds good, Nan. Just let me throw my clothes on and I'll be ready."

I run downstairs to get dressed and am about to grab my purse when I see something odd. There's a packet of papers sitting under the side table next to the couch. The title on the top page reads "How to Sabotage a House."

I pick it up and read the following:

If you want to sabotage the house you're renting, some favorite tricks are plugging the toilets, ruining the appliances, and causing a flood. Most landlords will never be able to prove any mischief created through plumbing issues. They're also the costliest to repair.

What the hell? All my issues have been conveniently listed. Two clogged toilets, a dishwasher that would have surely burned out if I hadn't caught the problem when I did, an exploding shower head, and a bathtub in the dining room.

I run upstairs and shake the paper at Nan. "Look what I found!"

She scans it before offering, "By all the saints, lass, we've got ourselves a mystery!"

"I'm a little nervous about going into town and leaving the farm unattended."

Nan says, "All the possible mischief makers have left for the weekend. I think we're safe.

She's probably right, but I still feel unsettled. On the way to the pharmacy, Nan and I try to figure out who could have been responsible. She decides, "I bet it was that snooty Ashley. I don't like that girl."

"Why would it be her? I mean, why would she make her own job any harder?"

My grandmother clucks her tongue. "Maybe she's addicted to attention. You know like them Munchausen people."

"Munchausen people? What are you talking about?"

"I read it on the Google. People make their kids sick on purpose 'cause they like to get attention from medical people. Maybe that's what Ashley does. She creates disasters so she can be the center of attention." Nan adds, "She was the one on the toilet both times, and she discovered the bathtub in the dining room. I bet she loosened the connection on the shower head and was planning on having it fly off during her shower. 'Course I foiled her plan by washing my hair at an unscheduled time."

The whole idea is kind of nuts and I'm not sure it makes sense, but I don't have any other suspects unless it's the Renovation Brothers. I'm going to have to keep a close eye on everyone when the crew comes back on Monday.

After we park the car and navigate the snow-covered sidewalks, we walk into the store so Nan can stock up on candy bars and tissues. I have no idea how she goes through so many tissues. I can't recall her ever having had a cold.

On our way to the book aisle, Mrs. Fleming calls out from behind the cash register, "I just put the new selection out this morning, Mrs. McTavish. I ordered some good ones!"

Mrs. Fleming and her husband own the pharmacy. She's been procuring books for Nan for years. When we hit the Highland romance section, there are three new titles; *Highland Whore*, *Heather and Lace*, and *Deflowering the Laird's Lass*.

I roll my eyes and stifle a giggle. The covers sport bare-chested men in kilts, along with young women wearing jewel-toned gowns that look like they're falling off. Inevitably, they appear to be standing in gale-force winds as their hair is always blowing about rather dramatically.

Nan scolds, "Girl, you don't know what you're missing. I swear, if relations were as good as they write about in these books, I'd be on the hunt for another man."

Words escape me. The thought of Nan married again is a frightening one, indeed. Not that I don't think she should find a nice gentleman caller, I just can't envision having a man move in with us, especially if my grandmother's thinking of trying to reenact any scenes from her books. Full. Body. Shiver.

After we pay for her purchases, we head over to Betsy's for some pie. Nan firmly believes daily consumption of pie is more important than taking vitamins. Who am I to argue?

As we cross the street, I look both ways and notice someone who looks remarkably like Ashley standing on the street corner. She's staring right at us. I have no idea why she's here on a Sunday. I thought she went back to Chicago on the weekends like the rest of the crew. Before I can call out to her, she does an about face, and scurries around the corner. My skin crawls at the sight of her and I simply cannot wait until she's out of my life. Which is going to be any day now.

Surprise, Surpsise!

Once we're inside the diner, I start to second guess whether I really saw Ashley. Maybe I just thought it was her because of Nan's concerns about her being the source of trouble at the house. I decide not to say anything, as I don't need my grandmother turning into a torch-wielding villager just yet.

As soon as we get settled in a booth, I hear the bell jingle over the door and I automatically look up to see who's come in. It's Sam. He catches my eye right before he looks down at his phone. He taps out a response to an incoming text before joining us.

"What are you doing here?" I ask. "I thought you were working this morning."

"No, thank God. I worked all night. I'm dead on my feet and desperately in need of a few hours of sleep, but more importantly I need food. Mind if I join you?"

Nan gushes, "Sit next to me!" As Sam scoots in beside her, she puts her hands around his arm to pull him closer. "We miss you around the house, lad. Where've you been?"

Sam puts his arm around Nan to give her a hug. "I've missed you, too. I've been super busy at work, but I promise things are finally going to lighten up. In fact, I predict you're going to get sick of having me around."

"As if I could ever get tired of seeing your handsome face!"

We order our food and make small talk about the weekend. Nan tells Sam about our sleepover. Then she asks, "What do you think about Cat's new underwear? Pretty snazzy, huh?" My grandmother surprised with me several items from Agent Provocateur. Most of which are way more daring than I've ever worn. Some of them are borderline kinky, which again has me questioning what goes on in her head.

Sam is familiar with Nan's lack of filter, but even so, her question seems to take him off guard. He answers, "I haven't had the opportunity to see it yet, but it's definitely something to look forward to."

I change the subject and say, "Put April first on your calendar. We're having a big party to show off the barn for the last episode of the show."

Sam chokes on his water, "Really? When did you find out about that?"

"Last week. I haven't had a chance to mention it yet."

Sam says, "I'm not sure you want me there. I mean, you know ..."

Nan's ears perk up. "What's going on? You two keeping a secret from me? I don't like it."

"I would never keep secrets from you, Nan," I reply. Before I can say anything else, the bell above the front door jingles again. It's Jeremy, of all people.

I automatically throw my hand in the air in greeting, before I realize what an awkward situation this might turn into. Sam turns around, sees the Renovation Brother and looks at me as if to ask, what now?

Jeremy joins us, scooting in next to me. "Hey Cat, Nan, what's up?" Then he looks at Sam and grunts, "Hawking."

"Jeremy," Sam responds.

"Fancy meeting you all here."

"I think it's more surprising seeing you here. I thought you were in Chicago until tomorrow," I say.

"I normally would have been, but I decided to drive down today. The rest of the crew is coming in later this afternoon. Looks like we might get a load of snow overnight and we didn't want to run the risk of falling behind schedule."

Maybe I really did see Ashley outside then. "Were you meeting anyone for lunch?"

Jeremy looks at Sam while answering, "Nope. I just remember you saying what great food they had here, so I thought I'd check it out."

"Did Josh drive down with you?" I ask.

"Nah, he was going to catch a ride with Tad. He had a couple things he wanted to do in the city today."

"Have you already dropped your stuff off at Sarah's?" I feel like as long as I keep up a barrage of small talk, I can keep any explosions at bay. I'll probably ask him about his hair products next.

"Nope. Thought I'd grab a bite first." Then he turns to Nan and says, "Did you know Sam and I went to college together?" *Oh, boy.*

My grandmother looks startled. "I did not! Did you know I went to Sam's college graduation? Were you in the same year?"

Jeremy nods his head. Nan adds, "That means I went to your graduation, as well. Now how 'bout that! That's what I call a small world. Have you boys been friends all this time?"

"Not so much," Sam answers at the same time Jeremy virtually yells, "No!"

Nan rubs her hands together, "Oh, I like intrigue. Sounds like there's a story here."

"No story, Nan," Sam says. "I was friends with Jeremy's brother, Josh. I didn't get a chance to know Jeremy very well."

Jeremy looks amused as he listens to Sam trying to spin a less-than-truthful version of their history, but he doesn't contradict him. Instead, he says, "Sam and I had a good mutual friend though. Didn't we, Sam?"

My boyfriend nods his head. "We did."

Jeremy grunts, but doesn't offer anything more. He appears to be reloading his verbal arsenal.

I decide I can't let this situation continue on its current track and say, "Well, just because you weren't friends in the past, doesn't mean you can't be friends now." I add, "I was just telling Sam about the barn party. He's very excited to come."

Jeremy cocks an eyebrow. "Really? I wouldn't have expected that." Then he chuckles to himself before adding, "To tell you the truth, Hawking, I'm starting to look forward to it, myself."

If looks could kill, Jeremy would be lying on the floor in a pool of his own blood. "I'll just bet you are, Jeremy," Sam says, looking green around the gills.

Speculation and More Speculation

Nan is all atwitter during the car ride home. "Those boys really don't like each other, do they?"

"Not so much, no."

"I think they're fighting over you, lass."

"Don't be ridiculous, Nan. Jeremy is nothing more than a friend. More importantly, he's the guy renovating my house, so let's not create any more drama than there already is, okay?"

"If you say so. I like him though. You think we should set him up with Sarah?"

"I think he and Sarah have spent enough time together that if they were attracted to each another, they'd have figured it out by now."

Nan doesn't like when I don't feed into her schemes. "Are you saying they don't like each other?"

"I'm saying it's none of our business whether they like each other or not, until they tell us something themselves." Personally, I don't think Sarah has taken a romantic shine to anyone recently. She's been so busy working and trying to save Ethan.

"Catriona Fiona Masterton, I'm an old lady and I need some excitement in my life! We've got to set someone up. The whole property is crawling with young single people, let's have ourselves some fun before it's too late."

"You mean before the renovation is over?" She nods at my question.

"Not going to happen, but …" I let the anticipation build for a moment. "I'm thinking of offering Highland fling lessons to single people in the area as a way of helping them find love. What do you think about that?"

Nan is nearly apoplectic. Her face is flushed with excitement and she starts waving her hand around excitedly. "Oh, sweet baby Jesus on a cross with a crutch and a party hat! That sounds wonderful! I'll give the lessons. No, wait, I'll be the matchmaker and assign partners. No wait, I can do both!"

"Why don't we work on a plan after the barn is up and running?"

"Okay, lass. But I'm going to start thinking about it now. What a fabulous idea!"

While I listen to my grandmother jabber away, my mind goes back to who might have sabotaged my house and who's responsible for Sam's troubles. There have been no recent incidents, but that doesn't mean they're done. And even if they are, I still want to know who's responsible.

I interrupt Nan's ramblings and ask, "Do you really think Ashley is behind the problems at my house?"

"I sure do. That gal is too big for her britches if you ask me."

"I don't think she's doing it for attention, though. There has to be another reason."

"Maybe she's jealous of you and all the good things you have. Maybe she wants to make your life harder."

I think back to when Ashley accused me of wanting everything for myself—the house remodel, a successful business, and all the men. Maybe she really is jealous, although that doesn't make a ton of sense as she's so successful herself.

I try to remember when the incidents started, and I think it was right after she was replaced by Tad. That's when it hits me, I bet it was Ashley! She must have decided to make Tad's job more difficult, so she'd look like the better producer. Maybe she wasn't after me, at all. More than anything I want to confront her, but I know I have to wait until the work is done. God knows, I don't want her ruining anything else.

When we get home, Nan excuses herself to take a nap. I head out to the barn to continue planning the big party. While the theme of the gathering is a Scottish hoedown, I've decided to keep the food more American. We're going to roast a pig over a spit in the fireplace and serve platters of root vegetables and salads. We'll have baskets of artisan bread and a load of delectable desserts. Beer, wine, and scotch will be available at the bar.

I walk every inch of the new barn and admire its beauty. I make a list of all the things I need to do before the day of the event. I'd have no worries throwing something like this together in New York City. I knew all my vendors there and could count on them to have everything I needed in stock. But here in Gelson, I have no such assurances. I'm so preoccupied I don't even realize someone's joined me until I hear a deep voice say, "We need to talk."

How Many Strikes
Before You're Out?

Sam looks more nervous than I've ever seen him.

"I thought you were going to go home and sleep after lunch. What are you doing here?" I approach to give him a welcoming hug.

Before I reach him, he answers, "The more I think about it, the more I'm convinced Jeremy's the one behind the pranks directed toward me."

"You didn't think he was responsible earlier. Why now?"

"Who else could it be? He must have found out about us before we drove him up to Chicago. In fact, that's probably the reason he wanted to drive with us. I bet he loved making me uncomfortable." Then he adds, "Cat, I need to tell you the rest."

A pit forms in my stomach big enough to swallow the Empire State Building. "I've been waiting."

Sam rubs his eyes like he's trying to gouge them out. Then he takes my hand and leads me toward my makeshift office table in front of the fire. He indicates I should sit down. Then he inhales loudly and drops a bomb. "Ashley is the woman I was seeing throughout medical school."

"Wait, what? Ashley? How? Why? Eeeew!" I've lost all ability to form a coherent sentence. Sam was in love with that snotty producer? I feel a wave of nausea roll over me. Actually, it's less of a wave and more of a tsunami ... being chased by a tornado.

"I thought the woman you were living with was in med school with you? Was Ashley in med school?"

"No, I said I lived with a woman while *I* was in med school."

"And that woman was Ashley?"

He nods.

"Why didn't you tell me?"

"I didn't tell you for the same reason I didn't tell you about Jeremy. In fact, the concerns I had about him paled in comparison to those I had about her. She obviously wasn't pleased when I broke up with her. She'd already started telling people I was planning to propose when it happened."

"But you hadn't proposed."

"No. I'd even started to warn her that I didn't think we were working out. The morning after I broke up with her, my tires were slashed. I chalked it up to vandals, but then my windshield was broken the following week. I was pretty sure it was Ashley."

Anger courses through me like food poisoning. "Sam, this is something I should have known from the start, regardless of the fact that you didn't want to get in the way of the renovation. I feel so betrayed right now, I don't know whether I want to wring your neck or walk away from you forever."

"Cat, no! If you could understand why I didn't tell you about Jeremy, you must understand why I didn't tell you about Ashley. She wasn't right in the head when we broke up."

"Nice. So you let a crazy woman oversee my renovation without warning me? Not to mention move in with me! That's not cool, Sam. Not cool at all."

"I haven't had any contact with her in over two years, so I just assumed she'd gotten on with her life and was doing okay. I knew she'd never do anything to you if she didn't associate you with me."

"Then why do you think Jeremy was responsible and not Ashley? It seems like she'd be the perfect suspect, considering she already has a past vandalizing your stuff."

"Because she doesn't know about us. If she did, Jeremy wouldn't be so excited about seeing the two of us together at your barn party."

"What if she didn't tell him she knew about us?" I counter.

"There's no way she could have found out."

I don't know what to believe, but I do know I'm madder than a wet hen in a snow storm. How could he have ever been involved with someone like her?

Sam takes my hands and stares deeply into my eyes. "Cat, I love you and I promise no more lies, ever. Even if I want to protect you from something. Please believe me."

I shake my head. "I need to absorb this, Sam. This is big. I didn't get back together with you easily. I had to think long and hard about whether or not I could trust your love after you lied to me in high school. I understand why you felt like you needed to go away to school unencumbered, but I don't understand how you let me believe we were going to go away together while making other plans for yourself."

"I was a stupid, stupid kid, that's how. I was so scared to tell you what I wanted that I made the break up a million times harder than it should have been. I was cruel and I'm so sorry for that. I would do anything to rewind history and not be such an idiotic ass."

"And now?" I ask.

"Now I just want you to have everything your heart desires. I wanted to protect you from my past, so your dreams could come true. Once you told me how much this renovation meant to you, I decided to do whatever I had to do to make that happen."

"I don't know, Sam. I want to believe you, but you'll have to admit your track record isn't the best with me."

"I know, Cat. I really do. And I'm sorry. Please give me one more chance to prove myself to you. Please."

I shake my head. "You're going to have to give me some time to think about this."

"Okay. But just know I'm here and I'll answer any questions you have. There's nothing else you don't know, I promise."

I don't respond. I just walk out of the barn and leave Sam behind. Questions buzz through my head like a hyperactive hive of bees. Can I really trust him? God knows I want to, but how many strikes do you give a person? Why did Jeremy ever agree to work with Ashley if she'd broken his heart? Does he still have feelings for her? Is he hoping to get back together with her?

All I know is that I have to keep my suspicions about Ashley and Jeremy at bay until this renovation is complete. I deserve my happy ending and I'm not going to let anyone get in the way of that, not even Sam.

Come to Jesus

I do my best to stay out of everyone's way. I don't want to accidentally come unhinged and start accusing them of wrongdoing ahead of schedule. I just keep my head down, and before I know it, it's time for the bling—wall painting, floor laying, changing out fixtures, and the like.

My mom can't stay quiet and has something to say about every detail. "I don't like the dark floors. You should go lighter. Wide planks, really?" I let her voice her opinions, but they don't sway me.

Tad walks in while she's complaining about the light fixtures and says, "Wait! I don't have any family squabbles on film yet. Let me get the cameraman." I've gotten used to nearly every aspect of my life being filmed, which is quite honestly creepy.

While the crew assembles, my phone pings. Another message from Sam. Of which there have been many.

Cat, I'm so sorry I didn't tell you everything upfront, but you have to understand why I didn't. When you said how important it was for you to do this show, my brain stalled. I wanted you to have everything without any of my drama getting in the way. Please believe me!

My finger hovers over the keyboard for a few seconds before I type back:

I think you were protecting yourself.

He replies:

I'm sure there's an element of that, but mostly I was protecting us. We'd just found each other again. We'd decided to move on and not talk about the past. Then my past collided with your present and I panicked. Then everything kept changing to keep the television crew there longer. I was wrong and I'm sorry.

I don't know, Sam. I need to think.

I didn't leave Ethan for Sam per se. In fact, Ethan is the one who broke up with me, I just didn't take him back when he came begging. But still, Sam was a big part of the reason I didn't go back. When you jump into a new relationship so quickly after ending another, there's always risk involved. Yet, Sam and I weren't new to one another. We've loved each other since we were children. We'd been in love throughout most of high school.

Can I treat our relationship like I would someone I'd just met? Yet, if this was someone I'd just met, there's little chance their past would have such an effect on me. My head feels dangerously full, like gray matter could start leaking out of my ears at any moment.

Somehow the rest of the day passes with my barely being aware of my surroundings. People come, people go, I pace the property lost in my own thoughts. I feel foggy and uncertain like I'm in a dream state. Sam pages me three more times, at two-hour intervals, until this one shows up right before I fall asleep.

Remember when Mr. Sheldon caught us passing notes in fifth grade and sent us to the hallway to think about our actions? Remember what we did?

Of course I do, and I laugh in spite of myself. Sam and I spent that half-hour filling our pockets with spit wads that we'd snuck into our teacher's desk drawer after he'd left for lunch. We thought we were so funny. It wasn't until we'd come to class the next morning and found our desks full of tennis balls that we knew we'd been found out. Match, set, point to Mr. Sheldon.

This is the depth to which Sam is entwined in my life. To have gone all these years not being a part of each other's worlds has been excruciating. To find each other again only to lose one another because of his past with Ashley seems absurd. Yet, I'm still mad.

I wake up the next morning to find seven new texts. Each one is a picture of me and Sam at a school dance together. I swipe through them slowly, absorbing each photo like it's a holy image. My scalp tingles at the memory of my youthful yearning. My hands chill in response to the emptiness I feel thinking of a life without Sam.

I don't answer any of his messages for the whole day, even though he's upped his game and sent more today than he did yesterday. They're filled with memories and dreams for our futures, apologies and promises that there will be no more secrets.

Once everyone sits down to dinner, I excuse myself and drive over to his house. I'm still not quite sure what I'm going to say to him, but when he opens the door and I see his disheveled hair and scruffy beard, I suddenly realize I've made him pay long enough.

Sam's living room is full of open photo albums—where he's obviously found pictures for the many messages he's been sending. There are dirty take-out containers strewn across the coffee table. The whole space is in disarray. I can only assume it's a mirror of what he's feeling inside.

"You're here." His voice is full of relief.

I turn to him. "I'm here."

He drops in front of me and wraps his arms around my legs. It's a submissive act, almost like he's worshipping at my feet. "Stand up," I say.

He does so as he takes my hands in his. His eyes plead with mine. "Please say you're back. Please say you forgive me."

I don't answer with words. Instead, I lean into him as though I've walked around the entire globe and I've finally come home. I gently touch my mouth to his until our breath merges as one. Then I let my lips say everything I feel without voicing a word. *I forgive you. I love you. I'm yours forever.*

Confrontation

Two days before the reveal, Nan and I are kicked out while the crew performs the final magic. My grandmother stays with Dorcus and I stay at Sam's. Yes, he gets to see my Agent Provocateur underwear and yes, Nan made some great selections.

The last several weeks have been excruciating, wonderful, nightmarish, and most definitely worth it. Sam and I are in a very good place. I realize how much we love each other, and I forgive his idiocy. As long as he doesn't make a habit out of it, we'll be good.

We're cuddled up on the couch enjoying a fire and some heated kisses when the phone rings. Sam answers. I can't hear the other side of the conversation, but he says, "Hey, what's up? Yeah, you're right. We were trying to figure out the best time for that, too. No, I definitely don't think we should wait until then. Wow, okay, I guess we can make it tonight." And finally, "If you're sure. Okay, bye."

I ask, "And that was?"

"Josh. He thinks we should clear the air with Ashley and Jeremy tonight and have our 'Come to Jesus' moment. He wants to figure out the logistics of the barn party and doesn't want any tension on camera."

I blow out a breath I didn't realize I'd been holding. "Where?"

"He thinks the best place would be at your house. He's hoping everyone will be more professional in their work space."

"But I'm not supposed to see the house until the big reveal."

"We're going to meet in the barn. You've already seen that."

The anticipation about how we're going to confront Ashley and Jeremy has been building. While I'm terrified how it's going to go down, I'm also relieved that it's finally going to be over.

"When are we meeting them?"

"Right now. Emily just served dinner, so everyone will be there for the next hour before heading back to Sarah's place."

We slowly get up and put our coats on. Sam says, "Try to remain calm. Don't let them pull you into any unnecessary drama."

I laugh. "You mean I'm not allowed to punch Ashley and call the cops on her?"

"Please, don't. Unless of course you'd like to see me do the same to Jeremy."

"Fine. I'm prepared to be a grown-up if you are."

I call Nan to let her know what's going on. There's really no need for her to be there other than to satisfy her curiosity. She'd be disappointed to miss a scene of this magnitude. When she doesn't answer, I leave a message telling her to meet us there as soon as possible.

"I feel like Mothra is flying around in my stomach."

"I know what you mean. I suppose we could avoid a scene entirely, if I didn't go to the party."

"No, you've got to be there! This means too much to me to

let a couple of bullies keep us from enjoying the night."

"I agree." He reaches over and takes my hand. His strength comforts me.

We reach the farm in ten minutes, but it feels like an hour, due to my building anxiety. From the driveway, we can see people milling around the barn. It's go time.

Oh No, She Didn't!

Tad is the first person to greet us. "Cat, you're here! Don't go into the house, k? Totes off limits until tomorrow when we film the reveal."

I smile. "Totes." Then I introduce, "Tad, this is my boyfriend Sam. Sam, this is Tad, the best producer at HHTV." Just a little dig at Ashley, even though she isn't nearby to hear it.

The guys shake hands and Tad declares, "Super dope to finally meet you, bro."

Josh catches our eye from across the barn and motions for us to come over to him. He's sitting at a table talking to Jeremy and Ashley, who both have their backs to us.

When we get there, I say, "Ashley, I'd like you to meet my boyfriend."

She turns around, sees Sam, and her whole body goes rigid. She looks from me to him and then around the barn before she tentatively holds out her hand. "Nice to meet you."

What? Why is she pretending she doesn't know him? I say, "I understand you and Sam have a history together."

She looks around again before whispering, "How did you find out?"

"How did I find out?" I point at Sam and then ask her, "How did *you* find out?"

She answers, "I saw a photo of the two of you on your mantel in the living room."

I'm a bit confused. "The only picture of us on the mantel was one when we were kids." Nan has managed to take the rest of them up to her room.

Ashley looks sad, and for a moment I actually feel sorry for her. "He had the same picture in a childhood photo album he had. I just didn't know who you were to him then."

Ouch. "Why didn't you say anything?"

"What should I have said? So, you're the bitch who stole my boyfriend?" Looks like the gloves are coming off.

Sam warns, "Ashley, that's not what happened, and you know it. Cat was living in New York when you and I broke up. We weren't even in touch."

She turns to him coldly. "We didn't break up. After five years together, you just walked out the door. We were supposed to get married and have a family. It was all settled."

He shakes his head. "It wasn't all settled. In those five years, you left me three times. Twice because you no longer wanted to be in a relationship with a doctor who had crazy hours, and once because you thought we might have gotten together too young and you wanted to explore your options. We'd only been back together for ten months when you started to tell people I was going to propose."

"Why didn't you?" she demands.

"Ash, we were more roommates than anything, and call me crazy, but you seemed more in love with the idea of getting married than you were with me."

Ashley says, "All of our friends were getting married."

"So, you thought we should too?" Sam asks incredulously.

She looks contrite. "We would have made it work."

"Is that all you wanted?" he asks. "To make it work? What about love?"

"I loved you," she says, but she's not selling it.

"Were you in love with me?"

Ashley doesn't answer, but the look on her face says it all. Instead she goes with, "I saw a future for us."

Jeremy, of all people, comes to Sam's defense. "I once saw a future with you, Ash, but you dumped me like a hot potato the minute Sam showed up."

Ashley looks wild-eyed for a minute. She finally says, "Jeremy, we were only dating for three months. It's not like we were emotionally invested in each other."

He replies, "Speak for yourself. You broke my heart."

"I don't believe you for a minute! You never acted like I'd hurt you."

Jeremy rolls his eyes. "A guy has to protect his dignity."

"Why did you agree to let me produce your show then?"

"I didn't! The network people hired you on their own. I sure as heck wasn't going to let our brief history get in the way of my career. If they thought you were a good fit, I was willing to try it."

Sam asks, "Have you been pining for her all this time?"

"What?" Jeremy asks. "Are you kidding? No!"

"Then why come after me?" Sam asks. "I mean, if you're not still carrying a torch for Ash, why all the anger?"

Jeremy looks totally confused. "What are you talking about?"

"Someone threw a burning bag of bagels at my door and vandalized my car before filling it with snow. Are you telling me you didn't do that?"

"Of course I didn't do that. Why would I?"

I turn to Ashley. "While we're on the topic of causing trouble, maybe you'd like to tell me why you were destroying things at my house."

Ashley takes a step back. "I didn't do anything to your house."

"The toilets, the bathtub, the soap in the dishwasher?"

Her eyes dart around the barn. I can't tell if she's looking for a person or if she's searching for the closest exit. "It wasn't me," she finally answers.

"Who was it then?" I demand. And just when I'm about to get the answers I'm after, Nan shows up.

She calls out, "Wait for me! Don't say anything else until I get over there." Leave it to my grandmother to make a grand entrance. As soon as she arrives, she demands, "What did I miss?"

"You missed Sam accusing Jeremy of vandalism, and you missed me confronting Ashley about all the chaos that's happened at our house," I explain.

Nan rubs her hands together in glee. "What did they say when you pointed the finger at them?"

"They said they didn't do it," Sam answers.

We're all standing around in a half-circle waiting for the other shoe to drop. Jeremy and Ashley are so tightly wound, I expect them to snap. Sam looks like he wants to wring someone's neck but doesn't know where to start. Nan seems to be the only one enjoying herself. We need that old detective Perry Mason to walk in and tie everything up for us.

My slightly insane-looking grandmother claps her hands together and declares, "They say they didn't do anything because they didn't!"

I'm beyond confused. "Nan, did you find something out?"

She laughs. "Nah, I've known who it was all along."

"Who?" Sam and I ask at the same moment.

Nan throws her hands in the air and declares, "It was me!"

Either my grandmother needs to be admitted to an insane asylum, STAT, or there's a lot more to this story.

Oh Yes, She Did

Nan explains, "I saw Ashley looking at the photos on the mantle the week after the renovation started. I realized by her reaction that she knew who you were. I should have hidden that one along with all the others, but I never thought she'd be able to recognize Sam when he was that young."

"Nan," I try to keep my voice calm. "I'm confused. What exactly happened?"

She looks at Sam and says, "Sam and I used to get together in the city."

Sam interrupts, a bell seemingly clanging over his head, "I introduced her to you once, in passing. How could you have possibly remembered her?"

Nan smiles brightly. "I remember everything! Sharp as a tack like that." Then she says, "Anyhoo, I saw a murderous gleam in this one's eyes," she points toward Ashley, "when she was looking at that picture. Then she dropped the frame on the floor. Not only did it break, but she stepped on it like she was trying to squash you both. That's when I knew she could be a problem. I decided to intervene before she could cause any trouble with your renovations."

I shake my head trying to understand what she's saying. "You acted out so she wouldn't? That doesn't make any sense."

Ashley pipes in, "Oh yes, it does! Every time one of those things happened, I found a note tucked under my pillow or in my purse, warning me to keep my mouth shut about my past with Sam or more trouble would follow."

Nan looks positively delirious in her excitement. "Saw that on *Law and Order*."

"So, you were scaring Ashley into keeping quiet," I recap.

She nods her head excitedly. "Yup." Then she looks at Ashley and says, "If you go to the cops, I'll deny it."

The producer rolls her eyes. "I'm sure you would, you horrible old woman."

I'm not sure what Nan thinks Ashley would have done had I found out about her and Sam earlier. "Nan, why didn't you just tell me about Ashley, so I could confront her and get it all out in the open?"

My grandmother looks perplexed. "What fun would that be?"

"I'm sorry, you did this all for fun?" I'm clearly not comprehending something here.

She answers, "I did it to keep Ashley from causing any trouble. I wanted to scare her into keeping her mouth shut and getting the work done. An added bonus was that she was motivated to get it done fast." She cryptically adds, "No one needs a ghost hanging around."

I have to know, so I demand, "Why did you do those things to Sam? That was horrible!" Even though I kind of condone her terrorizing Ashley.

"Honey, I had to! I had to make sure Sam stayed away from the house and didn't run into her." She points at Ashley.

"Don't you think he was smart enough to do that anyway?"

"You never know, lass. He might have decided she wasn't as crazy as she is and stopped by to clear the air. I couldn't have that happen until our house was fixed."

Sam asks, "Nan, how did you decide Ashley was crazy, when you're the one running around acting like a lunatic?" He looks genuinely concerned. I'm guessing he's worried her odd reasoning might be a side effect of her brain surgery. Of course, it might just be Nan, too. It's a hard one to call.

My grandmother answers, "She smashed the picture! I thought for sure that meant she was up to no good."

I'm still trying to put the pieces of this crazy puzzle together. "And I didn't notice the picture missing because you'd already taken most of them up to your room." Then I ask, "And you did that because you knew Ashley was the producer of the show before I applied?"

She answers, "I knew she used to be. I was hedging my bets in case she was the one who came."

I change the subject, "How exactly did you do those things to Sam when you're not even allowed to drive?"

"Dougal," she answers.

"My father?" I practically yell.

"Yup. I told him what was going on and he offered to help." Then she reaches into her purse and hands Sam an envelope. "Here you go, lad. That should be enough to cover any emotional damage and"—she winks—"the bagels are on the house."

Sam opens the envelope and finds an IOU that says: *Good for one free pizza of your choice to be shared with an old lady who loves you.*

Sam shakes his head. This isn't making any more sense to him than it is to me. "What message were you trying to send with the bagels?"

She waves her hand in response. "I told Dougal to light a bag of dog doo on fire and throw that, but he told me bagels were more civilized."

"And the caution tape?" I ask.

"I suggested spraying red paint in the outline of a body in the snow, but your dad said that was too scary. I thought the caution tape was pretty weak myself."

Sam says, "You're lucky I love you, old lady, because I'm the one in this scenario who could call the police. You really had me scared there for a while."

Nan finally looks the tiniest bit contrite.

Josh has remained silent while this whole scene has played out, but he's staring at my grandmother full of what looks like admiration. Finally, he starts laughing. "Is there anything we don't know about yet?"

Nan thinks for a moment before pointing her index finger straight up into the air and saying, "Yes, the rock through the front window. That was me, too!"

"Why'd you do that?" I demand. "Also, how did you do it? You were in jail."

"Dougal again. I figured if he threw a rock through our window, the cops would drop the charges against me, which is exactly what happened."

Sam shakes his head. "You're an evil genius, Nan. I'm a little afraid of you right now."

She looks up at him adoringly. "Lad, you've got nothing to

worry about in regards to me. In fact, you've got nothing to worry about as far as anyone's concerned. 'Cause I'm here to protect you." Nan, the enforcer. It's makes you tremble a little, doesn't it?

That Was Fun!

Nan has single-handedly released the tension in the air like a pin in an overly full balloon. Ashley keeps her head down and won't make direct eye contact with anyone. Jeremy looks contrite, like he knows he's been acting childish, and Nan is strutting around like she's recently been crowned Queen of the Universe.

Sam turns to Ashley and kindly says, "Ash, I'm sorry you're still hurt, but I've moved on. It's been over two years. You gave me an ultimatum and I made my choice."

"You were supposed to marry me!"

"I'd been telling you for months we weren't working. Then when I found out you started planning the wedding before I'd even proposed … it shouldn't have surprised you that I left." She doesn't look convinced.

Jeremy interrupts their conversation and offers Sam his hand. "I'm sorry I acted like such an idiot. I'm not pining for Ashley and I sure as heck haven't spent time being mad at you. Out of sight, out of mind as they say. But seeing you out of the blue kind of shook me up."

Sam shakes his hand back. "No worries, man. I get it. I'm still mad at my cousin for pouring milk on my Derek Jeter rookie card."

"I'm not a rookie card!" Ashley protests.

At the same time, Jeremy and Sam say, "You sure aren't." Leaving her to wonder at her own worth.

"You've got to be nicer to people, Ashley," I say. "When we first met, I really liked you. It wasn't until you were so rude to my brother that I changed my mind."

She looks sheepish. "I'd like to believe I'm normally a very nice person. This was an exceptional situation."

Jeremy tries to help. "We don't get any complaints about her at work."

Nan interrupts, "This is all well and good, but doesn't someone want to get me a drink?"

"I'd be delighted to, Nan. What are you having?" Josh asks.

"Glenfiddich for everyone!"

Josh leaves to find a bottle and Jeremy says, "I'm glad we've cleared the air. Sam, I truly am happy for you. Cat is a terrific girl."

Sam looks down at me lovingly. "She sure is."

"I agree!" Nan shouts.

Ashley doesn't look like she's on the same page as everyone else, but I can't really blame her. She's been tormented by Nan, blindsided by me and Sam, and removed as executive producer from her show. It's been a hard few weeks.

She excuses herself. "I'm just going to go into the house." No one tries to stop her.

A bit of compassion bubbles up inside of me. I know what it's like to have Sam leave and that's no easy thing. He left me at a time when a lot of high school romances break up, but he left her when she thought they were going to get married. I wonder what would have happened had she not given him an ultimatum and just let things run their course. Would they have wound up together?

I'm lost in my thoughts, when Nan claps her hands together and says, "That was fun!"

I give her a dirty look. "You have a lot to account for, you know that?"

She pulls me into a bone-crushing hug. "Sure thing, honey. Just let me get some food. Tell Josh to hang onto my drink. I'll be back in a jiff!"

My grandmother has a bounce in her step that is frightening. I thought she'd be a nice, quiet roommate and that we'd spend our free moments making memories. I had no idea she was such a wild card.

Jeremy accompanies Nan to the buffet, leaving me alone with Sam.

"Wow," he says. "I didn't see that coming."

I shake my head. "She's terrifying."

"She loves us."

"Yeah, she does. But thank God this renovation is over. Can you imagine what she might have done next?"

"No ma'am, I cannot. I think we should prepare ourselves for some changes in Nan. I'm hoping part of her poor decision making was a side effect of her surgery. People can struggle with appropriate responses post brain trauma."

"And you think that's why Nan made the choices she did?"

"I'm hoping," he answers. "Of course, there's a very real possibility this is just Nan."

He's right about that. My grandmother has never made the best choices. Just ask Dorcus.

We spend an hour sharing a meal with the crew who have transformed my house. It feels bittersweet. I've gotten used to having them around, but I'm also pretty darn excited to have them leave and let me get on with my new venture.

The Reveal

The next morning at nine, I'm standing in front of my house with my parents and Nan when Tad and Scottie arrive together. They walk over from Tad's car holding hands. First of all, I didn't know Scottie was back in town, and secondly, *what?!*

I nearly mow them down in my excitement to get to them. "What's going on here?"

Scottie's smile is so bright you'd think he was trying to signal the International Space Station. "I just had the best weekend of my life," he smugly tells me.

Tad seems pretty pleased, as well. He says, "Me too," before turning puppy dog eyes on my friend.

"Is this a new development?" I ask, full of curiosity.

"We've been pretty inseparable since you introduced us. We've spent a lot of time together getting to know each other," Scottie sweetly admits.

"We're boos," Tad adds.

"You're booze? What does that mean?"

"Not booze!" Scottie giggles. "Boos, B-O-O-S. You know, like I'm his boo and he's my boo?"

"Of course you are." This retro-chic hipster thing still catches

315

me off guard every now and again.

The fellas share a scorching hot look before Scottie says, "I'll meet you in the barn, boo."

Tad does a little jump in anticipation and his pompadour bounces accordingly. "Later, boo."

Well, if this isn't an exciting turn of events. Poor Scottie has been run through the wringer by his mother, but if that hadn't happened, he would have never stayed at my house. In which case, he would have missed meeting Tad. It looks like Mrs. Schweer has unknowingly given her son a nice parting gift. I still hope mother and son can rebuild their relationship someday, but if not, it makes me happy to know Scottie has someone to love.

The producer lines us all up and gives us our instructions. "Stay with the brothers and don't wander off. We want to get honest emotion when you see the house for the first time."

We happily agree, as he calls, "Places!"

Camera pans across the Masterton farm and stops on Catriona and her family.

Josh: So, Cat, are you excited to see the big reveal?

Cat: I really am!

Jeremy: It's been a long haul for sure, but we think you're going to love it.

Nan: Get on with it already. A lady could freeze her bits off waiting for you to open the door.

Josh opens the door and leads everyone into the foyer.

Josh: We knocked a wall down to create an open floor plan in your kitchen and dining room. This will give you a large space for the caterers to work while preparing food for your events.

Jeremy: (Walks to the kitchen) Follow me.

Cat: It's beautiful!

Mags: Oh my GOD, I've never seen anything like it! I could live here! Cat, I want to move back.

Dougal: Sorry, Mags, this place belongs to our little girl now. You've got a new house.

Mags: (To Jeremy) I want you to fix my kitchen next! Will you do that? Can you start tomorrow?

Josh: We'd love nothing more, Mags, but we've got to see what else we have on the books.

Mags: Did you hear that, Dougal? They're going to do us next!

The kitchen truly is stunning. The custom floor-to-ceiling cabinets are a sleek white with hidden drawer pulls. The counters are poured concrete except for the center island which is a rich contrasting black marble with white veining. There's a pot rack hanging above the island, with shiny copper pans suspended overhead. The huge farmhouse sink is big enough to bathe a German shepherd. And the floors are all wide-planked saddle oak that have been finished with a dark stain. Not only do they look great, but they'll disguise dirt dragged in between the kitchen and the barn.

I'm speechless. Nothing about this space resembles the childhood kitchen I grew up in. It's fresh and clean and full of so much possibility. Next, they reveal the updated bathrooms and new master bedroom. They didn't redo the basement as initially planned, as they added an extra space to the loft for the bridal parties to get ready.

My mom starts sobbing tears of joy or jealousy—I'm not sure which—when Tad calls, "Cut! You cats really know how to turn it on for the camera!"

We didn't turn on anything. What he saw was honest delight at a job well done.

By the time the reveal is over, I'm more overwhelmed than I've ever been in my life. The design team filled the house with gorgeous furniture and accents to set the stage. Being that I had no real furniture to start with, I'm pretty sure I'm going to buy most of it at the very generous wholesale discount that's being offered.

My house finally looks like a home. While everything in it is new, it still has the vibe of a very loved family dwelling. I'm a little concerned my mom will never leave, but as long as her collections are stored elsewhere, I don't mind. For now, anyway.

Jeremy approaches while I'm taking a quiet moment to absorb my beautiful new surroundings. "We're going to shoot the barn reveal the night of the party. That way it'll look its best for potential clients."

"Thank you, Jeremy. Thank you so much for all you guys have done here. I can't tell you what it means."

"It's an addictive job, you know? Everyone wants a fresh start at one time or another. We get to give them that in a visceral way. I feel like Santa Claus."

"You don't look like him," I joke.

He says, "I'm sorry about how I treated Sam."

"Don't worry about it, I understand." Curiosity wins out and I need to know, "But what's the deal with you and Ashley? You really don't feel anything for her?"

He shrugs. "I think she's a great producer. And now that she's on board with the changes we want to make on the show, she'll probably stick around."

"Yeah, yeah, yeah, but what about on a personal level?"

"That ship sailed long ago. It's hard to think about getting involved romantically with someone who dumped you." He seems to catch himself as he remembers that's exactly what I did.

"Jeremy, you can't always take everything at face value, and you can't live in the past. Sam and I needed to find out who we were without each other before we could commit ourselves to each other as adults. As hard as it was to be apart, it was for the best. Maybe it's the same for you and Ashley."

"I don't think so, but I do know one thing. I have been avoiding committing to a partner, and I think I'm ready to find what you and Sam have rediscovered in each other. You guys make being in love look very enticing."

"Thank you. It's been a journey, but it's been well worth the wait." The bumps in our path have made me realize Sam and I are completely committed to each other. His heart was in the right place and that's what makes it possible to forgive him.

What the Future Holds

As I peek into the barn the night of the dance, I am overcome by how rich my life is. Despite having a remarkably odd and often terrifying family—of course, I cite Nan and my parents—they're so full of love and goodness, it more than makes up for their shortcomings.

Across the room, Sam is standing next to my brother, who's elegantly attired in a Masterton plaid ballgown with a crisp white sash draped across his shoulder. Sam puts his arm around Travis and pulls him close to his side. He pats him on the back giving him encouragement, support, approval, or maybe a combination of all three. I'm not sure what it is, but it causes a warmth of happiness to radiate through my extremities. Sam is not only important to my life, but my family's as well.

I have more friends in Gelson than I could have ever expected after being gone for so long. Happily, I can include Ethan in that group. He and I have come a long way and will hopefully remain in each other's lives.

Jeremy startles me out of my thoughts when he comes up behind me and asks, "You ready?"

"I sure am." In fact, I'm readier than I've ever been about anything. "Let's do this thing."

Camera begins to pan around the Masterton barn.

Josh: Well, Cat, this is it. The night of the big barn reveal. How do you feel?

Cat: Excited, blessed, a little anxious …

Josh: Anxious, why?

Cat: Because I'm embarking on an adventure that will help launch couples into their new lives together. I want to make sure I do justice to their love and commitment to each other.

Jeremy: Oh, I don't think there's any doubt you will. Let's go in and show our viewers what a Masterton Country Barn Party looks like.

As I step through the open doors, my dad, looking every bit the Scottish chieftain, whistles to get everyone's attention. He lifts his glass high in the air and toasts, "To my daughter, Cat! May the rain only fall to water your crops. May the sun always shine within your heart and may there always be a wee dram for times of trouble."

A rousing cheer goes up as the Celtic band we hired from Chicago begins playing. Thanks to Nan and her new Highland Romance Readers Club, the crowd is swathed in assorted plaids. My grandmother, Dorcus, and Emily bought bolts of fabric from the three fabric stores within a twenty-mile radius. They handed out lengths to the guests as they arrived. According to Nan, "Now everyone attending the party can represent for Scotland."

The crowd is on the dance floor and my family begins to lead them in a Highland reel. The dance is awkward for most, but it's so full of joy and celebration that everyone enthusiastically kicks up their heels and lets loose. My world spins in a frenzy as I hop and leap to the sounds of my childhood. There are few moments in life that are so perfect you can't imagine improving upon them. This is one of those times for me.

When the song ends, Sam drops to one knee in front of me. The room becomes silent and the camera crew turn their cameras on us, recording *the moment*. Sam clears his throat of emotion before he says, "Cat." Then he bows his head and pauses again, as though steeling his courage. He nervously asks, "Remember when you saw me having lunch at Betsy's and I told you I was meeting with a drug rep?"

Unable to speak, I nod.

With more certainty he continues, "I was meeting a jewelry designer. I commissioned this." He pulls out a black velvet box from his jacket pocket and opens it up. Inside, a platinum scrolled band of Aberdeen knots with three diamonds, sparkles brightly. It positively bowls me over. He starts, "The knots represent how deeply entwined we are in each other's lives. They show our journey, which has not been without its troubles, but they also show the strength of our bond. A rope with knots is always stronger than one without. The diamonds are our past, present, and future. Catriona Masterton, would you do me the great honor of becoming my wife?"

A jolt of pure love shoots through me like an electrical shock. I stare deeply into Sam's eyes for several moments. I see everything there—love, hope, and possibility. I see my future. The ring is more than a symbol of our love, it's a promise. "Yes, Sam. I'll marry you."

He whoops as he rises, picks me up, and twirls me around as the band plays "Flower of Scotland." The room spins in slow-motion like this is a fabulous romcom movie. My parents joyfully lead the crowd in yet another Highland fling. As the world swirls around me, I see Tad and Scottie dancing their hearts out and Nan looking more pleased than I've ever seen. Even Ethan and Sarah have joined in.

Once I'm on my feet, I grab Sam's hand and drag him toward the coat closet that is hidden in the shadows. I want to give him a little preview of exactly how excited I am to become his wife. The road to our engagement has been full of stumbling blocks and I want to let him know more joyful times have arrived.

As we walk into the closet, I'm about to throw myself into Sam's arms, but then I see we're not the only ones who were looking for a private space. Travis and Ashley are there, engaged in a rather heated liplock. The sight is so shocking I can't seem to absorb it. It's isn't until Sam pulls my arm that I realize we should find another location for our rendezvous. My brother and my fiancé's ex are so preoccupied with one another, they're not even aware they have company.

I can't say I'm thrilled about stumbling upon them, but Travis's romantic entanglements aren't my decision. If Ashley and my brother are meant to be, so be it. I'm going to very happily focus on planning my wedding while they do whatever they do. But just so you know, I'm not planning their wedding, should it come to that.

As I drag Sam off in search of another secret spot, a rush of pure contentment permeates my being. I realize life is what you make of it. There's no formula for happiness. Sometimes the road can seem dark and scary. Sometimes it's full of heartbreak and loss. But as long as you believe it's going to work out, as long as you can see the words "and they lived happily ever after" finish your story, who cares how you get there?

Life is about love and acceptance, tolerance and forgiveness. It's about the weird and wonderful people who share your journey. I know I have weird and wonderful in store for me and I can't wait for what comes next.

I would be SO grateful if you'd leave a review on Amazon and/or Goodreads!

Thank you, lovely reader. I appreciate you!!

If you haven't read the first book in the series, *Relatively Normal* yet, its available online.

Check out **The Reinvention of Mimi Finnegan**—winner of the silver medal at the International Readers Favorite Awards, finalist at the RONE Awards, and honorable mention at the London Book Festival!

Chapter 1

"A BUNION?" I shriek.

"It would appear so," answers Dr. Foster, the podiatrist referred by my HMO.

"Aren't bunions something that old people get?"

"Yes," he replies. "That's normally the case, but not always. Bunions grow after years of walking incorrectly, or in some instances, not wearing the proper shoes."

Still perplexed, I ask, "What am I doing with one then? I'm only thirty-four."

He says that by the atypical location of my bunion, he can deduce that I have the tendency to walk on the outsides of my feet. He explains that while some people walk on the insides of their feet, giving them a knock-kneed appearance, others, like myself, rotate their feet outward, causing a waddle, if you will. I have a look of horror on my face when he says the word "waddle." I have never been accused of such a disgusting thing in my life. But before I can form a coherent response, he continues, "The extra ... weight (and I'm sure he pauses to emphasize the word) that the outside of the foot is forced to endure by walking that way eventually causes it to grow an extra padding to help support the … load." Am I wrong or does he pause again when he says that word?

Playing dumb, I ask, "And I'm getting one so young, why?"

Clearing his throat, Dr. Foster answers, "Well, a lot of it has to do with genetics and the structure of your foot." Then adds, "And a lot of it has to do with the extra weight (pause and meaningful look) you're placing on it."

I am so aghast by this whole conversation that I finally confess, "I have just lost forty pounds." Which is a total lie by the way. In actuality I have just gained two. But I simply can't bear the humiliation of him calling me fat, or what I perceive as him calling me fat.

The doctor smiles and declares my previous poundage did not help the inflammation at all and announces it may have contributed to my bunion. He checks his chart and declares, "I see you're a hundred and seventy pounds. At one hundred and fifty, you should be feeling a lot better."

"But I'm five-eleven," I explain.

"Yes?"

"I'm big boned!"

He looks at me closely and says, "Actually, you're not." Picking up my wrist, he concludes, "I would say medium, which means one hundred and fifty pounds would be ideal." Of course the photo of the emaciated woman on his desk should have tipped me off as to what this guy considers ideal. She is wearing a swimsuit with no boobs or butt to fill it out and painfully sharp collar bones. She bears a striking resemblance to a death camp survivor.

All I can think is that I haven't been one-hundred-and fifty-pounds since high school. There is simply no way I can lose twenty pounds. I want to tell him he has no idea how much I deprive myself to weigh one seventy. In order to actually lose weight, I'd only be able to ingest rice cakes and Metamucil. But I don't say this because he'd think I'm weak and unmotivated and he'd be right, too. Plus, I just bragged that I lost a record forty pounds, so he already assumes I am capable of losing weight, which of course would be the truth if it weren't such an out-and-out lie.

The doctor writes a prescription for a special shoe insert that will help tip my foot into the correct walking position and then leaves, giving me privacy to cover my naked, misshapen appendage. As I put my sock back on, I decide I am not going to go on a diet. I'm happy or happyish with the way I look and that's all there is to it. When I leave the room, Dr. Foster tells me to come back in two months so he can recheck my bunion. In my head I respond, "Yeah right, buddy. Take a good look, this is the last time you're ever going to see me or my growth." I plan on wearing my shoe insert and never again speaking of my hideous deformity.

The true cruelty of this whole bunion fiasco is that I'm the one in my family with pretty feet. I have three sisters and we are all a year apart. Tell me that doesn't make for a crazy upbringing. At any rate, the year we were all in high school at the same time, my sisters and I were sitting on my bed having a nice familial chat, which was a rare occurrence as I'm sure you know girls that age are abominable as a whole. But put them under the same roof fighting over bathroom time, make-up, and let's not forget the all-important telephone. It was an ungodly ordeal to say the least.

My sisters, to my undying disgust, are all gorgeous and talented. Renée, the oldest one of the group is the unparalleled beauty of the family. Lest you think I'm exaggerating and she's not really all that and a bag of chips, let me ask if the name Renée Finnegan means anything to you. Yes, that's right, "The" Renée Finnegan, the gorgeous Midwestern girl that won the coveted Cover Girl contract when she was only seventeen, fresh out of high school. Try surviving two whole years at Pipsy High with people asking, "You're Renée's sister? Really?" The tone of incredulity was more than I could bear.

Next is Ginger. She's the brain. But please, before you picture an unfortunate looking nerd with braces and braids, I should tell you that she is only marginally less gorgeous than Renée. She was also the recipient of a Rhodes scholarship, which funded her degree in the history of renaissance art, which she acquired at Oxford. Yes, Oxford, not the shoes, not the cloth, but the actual university in England.

The youngest of our quartet is Muffy, born Margaret Fay, but abbreviated to Muffy when at the tender age of two she couldn't pronounce Margaret Fay and began referring to herself as one might a forty-two-year-old socialite. Muffy is the jock. She plays tennis and even enjoyed a run on the pro-circuit before a knee injury forced her to retire. She did, however, play Wimbledon three years in a row and, while she never actually won, the experience allows her to start sentences with, "Yes, well, when I played Wimbledon …" And make pronouncements like, "There's nothing like the courts at Wimbledon in the fall." Muffy is now the tennis pro at The Langley Country Club. Her husband Tom is the men's tennis pro, insuring they are the tannest, most fit couple on the entire planet. Their perfection is enough to make you barf.

I am the third child in my family, christened Miriam May Finnegan which against my express consent got shortened to Mimi. For years I demanded, "It's Miriam, call me Miriam!" No one listened, as is the way in my family.

While sitting on my white quilted bedspread from JCPenney, my sisters, in a moment of domestic harmony, decided we were all quite extraordinary. Renée was deemed the beautiful one, Ginger, the smart one, and Muffy, the athletic one. With those proclamations made, they appeared to be ready to switch topics when I demanded to know, "What am I?"

It's not that my sisters didn't love me. I don't think they thought I was troll-like or stupid, it's just compared to them, I didn't have any quality that outshone any one of theirs. So, after much thoughtful consideration and examination, like a prized heifer at the state fair Renée announced, "You have the prettiest feet." Ginger and Muffy readily agreed.

Listen, I know you're thinking "prettiest feet" isn't something I should brag about. But in my family, I would have been thrilled to have the prettiest anything, and I am. They could have just as easily said I had the most blackheads, or the worst split ends. But they didn't, they awarded me prettiest feet and I was proud of it. Until now. Now I have a bunion.

As I sit in front of my car in front of the Chesterton Medical Center, I become undone by the horror of having lost my identity in my family. "Who will I be now?" I wonder. Oh wait, I know, I'll be the spinster, or the one without naturally blonde hair, my true color hovering somewhere between bacon grease and baby poop. Hey, wait, I know, I'll be the one who needs to lose twenty pounds!

I turn on the ignition in my Honda and hop on the freeway heading for the Mercer Street exit. Yet somehow, I miss my turnoff and I've hit Randolph before I know it. With a will of its own, my car takes the exit and drives itself to the Burger City a half mile down the road. I demand, "What did you do that for? This is no way to lose twenty pounds." Not that I had agreed to do any such thing. But I wasn't looking to gain weight either.

Typically, my car doesn't answer back, a fact for which I am eternally grateful. It simply makes its wishes known by transporting me to destinations of its choosing: Burger City, The Yummy Freeze, Dairy Queen, Pizza Hut. I've actually thought about trading it in, in hopes of upgrading to a car that likes to go to the gym and health food stores. But, no, this is my car and as a faithful person by nature, I realize I should do what it's telling me.

As the window automatically lowers and the car accelerates to the take-out speaker, I hear the disembodied voice of a teenager say, "Welcome to Burger City. What can I get you today?"

Someone, who is surely not me, answers, "I'd like a double cheeseburger with grilled onions, two orders of fries and a root beer, large."

He asks, "Will that be all?"

Still not sure who's doing the answering, I hear someone who sounds remarkably like me say, "I'd like an extra bun, too."

"What do you mean an extra bun?" He squeaks. "You mean with no burger on it or anything?"

"That's right." He informs me that he'll have to charge me

for a whole other burger even though I just want the bun. I tell him that's no problem and agree to pay the dollar seventy-five for it. I'm not sure what causes me to order the extra bread, but I think it boils down to my need for carbohydrates. I have either been on The South Beach Diet or Atkins for the better part of two years and I've become desperate for empty calorie, high glycemic index white bread.

You may be wondering how I could have been high protein dieting for two years and still need to lose twenty pounds. The truth is that I cheat, a lot. For two weeks I jump start the diet with the serious deprivation they encourage and then by week three when you're allowed to start slowly adding carbs back into your life, I become the wildebeest of cheaters. They suggest you start with an apple or a quarter of a baked sweet potato. I start with an apple pie and three orders of french fries. I have been losing and gaining the same thirteen pounds for the last twenty-four months.

As soon as my food arrives, I pull over on a side street and inhale the heavenly aroma of danger. The fries call to me, the double cheeseburger begs to be devoured in two bites, but the bun screams loudest, "I have no redeeming nutritional value at all!" So I start with it. And it's pure pleasure. Soft and white, clean and bright . . . it looks at me and sings, "You look happy to meet me." But wait, this isn't Edelweiss, this is a hamburger bun.

After the bun, I eat a bag of fries, then the burger, then the other bag of fries, all the while slurping down my non-diet root beer. My tummy is cheering me on, "You go, girl! That's right, keep it coming … mmm hmm … faster … more." From the floor boards I hear a small squeak, "Stop, you're killing me!" It's my bunion. I decide its voice isn't nearly as powerful as my stomach's. While I'm masticating away, I start to think about the word bunion. It's kind of like bun and onion. B-U-N-I-O-N. That's when I notice I've just eaten a bun and a burger with onion. I start to feel nauseated. If you squish the words together, I've just eaten a bunion. Oh, no. I think that this may have possibly put me off Burger City forever.

I have a long history of going off my food for various and sundry reasons. For instance in high school, Robby Blinken had the worst case of acne I'd ever seen. It was so bad that his whole face looked like an open, inflamed sore. I felt really sorry for him too because he was shy and awkward to begin with. Having bad skin did nothing for his popularity. Then one day, Mike Pinker shouts across algebra to Robby, "Hey, pizza face, that's lots of pepperoni you've got!"

I cringed in disgust, looked over at poor Robby whose face turned an even brighter shade of red due to the public humiliation and bam, I was off pizza for a whole year. And pizza was one of my favorite foods too. It's just that every time I looked at it or smelled it, I thought about Robby's complexion and there was no going back.

Then there was the time I went off onions in college. A girl in my dorm was blind in one eye and there was this white kind of film covering her iris. Whenever I talked to her, I couldn't help but stare right into the blind eye. I was drawn to it by a strange magnetic pull. Then one day it hits me, Ellen's pupil looks like a small piece of onion. I went off onions for three years.

Now at thirty-four, years since I've had a food repulsion, I realize that after my first bun in months I may have gone off them. The onions aren't such a loss as I already have a history there, but buns? I love buns!

Around the second bag of fries, I unbutton my jeans to let my stomach pop out of its confines. Sitting in my red Honda with my belly hanging out, sick at the thought that I just ate a bunion, I do what any reasonable person would do. I drive to the strip mall where the Weight Watchers sign flashes encouraging subliminal cheers to the masses. "Be thin, we'll help! We love you! You can do it, you can do it …"

So, like the little engine that could, I squeeze into a compact spot and walk through the front door before I can come out of my trance. Twelve dollars later, I've received an information package and a weigh-in book. Marge, my group leader, takes me in the back to weigh me. "One seventy-two," she declares. I want to tell her I was just one seventy at the doctor's office but then I remember the bunion I just ate. Marge continues, "You know, you're right inside the acceptable weight for your height. Are you sure you want to lose twenty pounds?"

I'm sure. After all, I'm single with a bunion. It feels like it's time for some drastic measures. As I have shown up in between meeting times, Marge gives me the basics of the Weight Watchers program and encourages me to come to at least one meeting a week. She also suggests I get weighed at the same time every week as the weight of the human body can vacillate up to six pounds during a twenty-four-hour period. "Consistency of weigh-in times," she claims, "is the answer." I briefly wonder if Doctor Foster would have told me to lose weight if I was only one hundred and sixty-four pounds.

Chapter 2

I'm allowed to eat twenty-nine points a day. I keep telling myself this as I sit at my desk and wait for lunch. With my handy little points app, I discover that my forage to Burger City the other day was worth thirty-two points. Thank goodness I ate that bunion. That'll be one less temptation for me while I attempt to lose this weight.

Three days ago, after my trip to WWI (Weight Watchers, first attempt, not to be confused with the World War) I stopped by Rite Aid to pick up my shoe insert. I've been wearing it since and am having serious equilibrium issues. I can only wear it with loafers or tennis shoes as it's a foot-shaped silicone wedge and won't fit into heels. The whole contraption pushes me towards my proper posture, but I swear it's dislocating my center of gravity at the same time. I have never been considered graceful but now I'm downright klutzy, as demonstrated by the five large bruises covering my legs. I seem to tip as easily as a sleeping cow and have not been landing in the softest of places either.

Eleven fifty-eight, eleven fifty-nine, come on noon. I want to eat. I had a bowl, and by that, I mean one cup (which is really only half of a bowl), of raisin bran and half a cup of skim milk for breakfast. At ten, I gobbled up an apple and an ounce of part-skim mozzarella cheese. For lunch I'm having a turkey sandwich on the softest white bread on the planet. It's low-cal but has enough fiber to jumpstart a dead person's bowels, ergo giving it the Weight Watcher's seal of approval. I'm also having a salad with fat-free raspberry vinaigrette. When I packed my lunch this morning, I registered how beautiful the food looked, all orange and green and red. It really was a feast for the eyes even though the portions would leave a Lilliputian begging for more.

I'm trying to do what Marge told me and that is to appreciate my food on all levels. Enjoy the beauty of it, the smell of it and last but not least, the taste, which I am supposed to do while chewing the ever-loving crap out of it before swallowing. This way it will take me longer to eat and I will start to fill up before overdoing it. It's all a load of hooey if you ask me. I'm so hungry by feeding time that I've inhaled my meal before I know it. Yesterday I was crawling around the base of my desk when my co-worker Elaine asked me what I was looking for.

"My lunch," I answered, "I think I dropped it."

Elaine looked slightly alarmed and declared, "Mimi, you just ate your lunch."

"Really?" I asked, more than a little surprised by this knowledge.

Elaine confirmed it was so, but that didn't stop me from picking up and eating a stray peanut I found on the floor from my South Beach days. Tick, tick, tick, NOON! Time to strap on the old feed bag.

I scurry into the break room and fill a glass with cold water. I know I'm blending diet tips here, but South Beach recommends a glass of Metamucil before each meal to help fill you up. It works beautifully too, except that with all the fiber I get on Weight Watchers, I find I need to be close to a bathroom at all times. As I munch on my salad, my boss, Jonathan Becker, walks into the break room.

Jonathan embodies all that is right with the world. He is thirty-eight, smart, funny, remarkably good looking and talented. He is also married to my sister Ginger. How, you wonder, did that happen when I should have had first dibs on him? I haven't a clue, really. It must have been fate. I mean heaven knows I didn't introduce them. I am not in the habit of trying to help my perfect sisters show me up even more by introducing them to perfect men. That is not my way.

Ginger met Jonathan completely independently of me as she was showing a tour group through the Museum of Contemporary Art. She is the director of the museum, but still enjoys educating the masses by pitching in with docent duties every once in a while. At any rate, Jonathan's parents were in town and he was taking them to the requisite tourist spots when they stumbled into the museum. In front of one particularly abstract painting, Felicity Becker declared, "I suppose the medium here is human feces?"

Ginger smiled and explained how the artist was trying to express the sepia tonality of his native Cuba; the tobacco and human waste were representative of a culture that repressed its own and refused to let it rise above menial servitude. I think she may have quoted Descartes and then conjugated several verbs in Latin for effect. Whatever she did, it was like a mating dance to Jonathan because he asked her out that afternoon and thereafter until they became man and wife a short year later.

When they first started dating, Ginger carried on and on about how smart and funny her boyfriend Jonathan was. Then the day came when she brought him to brunch to meet the family. I had just regained the thirteen pounds I lost on Phase I of South Beach and was not looking forward to meeting the Ken to my sister's Barbie. I remember pulling on my brown skirt with the elastic waist thinking, "Who am I trying to impress anyway? It's not like this guy is coming to see me."

When I drove up to my parents' house, I saw that Muffy and Tom were already there as well as Renée and her husband, Laurent, along with their two kids, Finn and Camille. I walked in and made all the appropriate rounds of kisses and hugs. But the truth was my heart just wasn't in it. Once Ginger introduced her new boyfriend, it would just be me, Mimi Finnegan, spinster.

Ginger and Jonathan walked in the front door as I was filling the water glasses on the dining room table. I heard them before I saw them. Ginger announced, "Hello everyone, we're here!" The whole family tore off towards the entry like a stampeding herd of cattle at the sound of her voice. Everyone that is, but me. I wanted to enjoy the last few moments of not being the only sister without a significant other. So I poured water and concentrated on breathing deeply.

They all came into the dining room moments later and I plastered a smile on my face, prepared to be all that is gracious to Ginger's new beau. When I first saw Jonathan, I was confused and mistakenly thought maybe my Jonathan from work had somehow shown up to be my date so I wouldn't be the family pariah. Then he saw me, and I knew that wasn't the case. His face morphed somewhere between total and utter shock and open-mouthed bass. "Miriam, is that you?" Because before Jonathan learned my family nickname, I went by my real name at work. Now they all call me Mimi, too.

"Jonathan?" I squeaked.

He strode over and slapped me on the shoulder in a very platonic way and said, "Well, I'll be. I didn't know you and Ginger were sisters!"

I countered, "And I had no idea you two were dating." It occurred to me Ginger should have known Jonathan and I work for the same PR firm. You would think that when he revealed that he worked at Parliament, Ginger would have remembered that I work there, too. But the truth is, while brilliant, Ginger has never been wired for details. For instance, she knows the square root of one million, six hundred forty-two thousand and eight, but she can barely remember her own birthday. She's kind of like Rain Man that way.

The brunch was unbearable and lasted about twelve days. I must have gained three pounds, as the meal became show and tell for the Finnegan family (as I didn't have that much to show or tell, I ate). Jonathan had never met us as a whole, so we owed it to him to trot out the whole dog and pony show. With circus music running through my head I could see myself as the ringmaster. "If I could have your attention in the center ring, I'd like to introduce you to Renée! Yes, that's Renée "supermodel turned designer" Finnegan and her high-profile fashion photographer husband, Laurent Bouvier. But please, before you leave center ring, notice their perfect and charming offspring, Finn, who was recently featured in the Gap Kids ad, and little

Camille, the Ivory Soap baby!"

I drank so many mimosas that day I was forced to stay over at my parents' house and sleep it off. In my drunken haze, I swear I heard my mother say, "Now if only Mimi could find someone to love her." There was laughter and then my dead Grandma Sissy started reciting dirty limericks.

Available now!

About the Author

Whitney Dineen is an award-winning author of romantic comedies, non-fiction humor, and middle reader fiction. She lives in the beautiful Pacific Northwest with her husband and two daughters. When not weaving stories, Whitney can be found gardening, wrangling free-range chickens, or eating french fries. Not always in that order. She loves to hear from her fans and can be reached through her website at https://whitneydineen.com/.

Join me!

Mailing List Sign Up
whitneydineen.com/newsletter/

BookBub
www.bookbub.com/authors/whitney-dineen

Facebook
www.facebook.com/Whitney-Dineen-11687019412/

Twitter
twitter.com/WhitneyDineen

Email
WhitneyDineenAuthor@gmail.com

Goodreads

www.goodreads.com/author/show/8145525.Whitney_Dineen

Blog

whitneydineen.com/blog/

Please write a review on Amazon, Goodreads, or BookBub. Reviews are the best way you can support a story you love!

Other books by Whitney Dineen:

Romantic Comedies
Relatively Normal
Relatively Sane
She Sins at Midnight
The Reinvention of Mimi Finnegan
Mimi Plus Two
Kindred Spirits
Going Up?

Non-Fiction Humor
Motherhood, Martyrdom & Costco Runs

Middle Reader
Wilhelmina and the Willamette Wig Factory
Who the Heck is Harvey Stingle?

Children's Books
The Friendship Bench